CONTENTS

INTRODUCTION

Margot Bennett was one of the finest British crime writers of the 1950s, and *The Widow of Bath*, first published in 1952, is one of her most impressive books. The mystery puzzle is intricate, the characterization strong, the setting evocative, and the prose elegant and witty. For a modern reader, there is an additional bonus in that Bennett offers a vivid picture of a long-vanished world.

There's even a pleasing period flavour to the dust jacket blurb of the original first edition, which proclaimed: 'The intensity of the psychological conflict is as vital to the story as the peculiarities of the murder. In this purely British thriller the characters are drawn with a French precision and the story moves at the pace which has until now been almost an American monopoly.' Bold claims, but they are justified: this is a book to be savoured.

The protagonist is Hugh Everton, a young man who has adjusted his life to respectability after serving a short prison sentence in connection with an incident which almost cost him his life. While working in a junior role for the British Embassy in Paris, he was duped by a man called Freddy Ronson and betrayed by a beautiful woman called Lucy. While visiting a hotel in the course of his work for a travel agency, he encounters Lucy again.

Lucy's circle includes a man called Atkinson, supposedly a retired colonel, whose 'well-bred voice made the smallest talk sound like culture', but who bears a disturbing resemblance to Ronson. There is also Gerald Cady, whose 'manner suggested that he was looking for a safe place to hide.' Lucy is married to a retired judge called Bath ('an obsolete battleship who believed that his guns could still roar'), who believes 'that it is the duty of every citizen to expose and so help to destroy evil'. The judge's only passionate need is for a legally clear conscience.

Lucy invites Everton, Atkinson, and Cady back for drinks, only for the judge to die in mysterious circumstances. Lucy duly becomes 'The Widow of Bath'—but the question for Hugh is whether she was responsible for the judge's demise, and if so, how she managed it. Matters are complicated by the fact that Hugh still finds Lucy almost impossible to resist, even though he remains emotionally drawn towards the judge's niece, Jan.

Quite apart from the tantalizing puzzles that Bennett poses, there is a compelling picture of a country struggling to come to terms with the return of peace after years of conflict and confusion. As Inspector Porthouse tells Everton, 'You expect a bit of flotsam... after a war. You even let some of it drift in, without too many questions.' The characters who yearn for a better life include Zoe, who works in a hat shop and is desperate to escape her drab existence in the seedy south coast town.

The resort is marvellously evoked: 'A small, safe harbour brought a few sailing enthusiasts to the town; these were welcomed, as they tended to put the rents up and keep the rates at a comfortable level... everyone was able to congratulate everyone else...that the place was unspoilt... although not for long, for behind this respectable English dream the small mean houses grew like thistles in an abandoned field.'

The wit and satire match anything to be found in the books of that great exponent of stylish crime writing, Raymond Chandler. There's a wonderfully sardonic riff on the idea of 'dark tourism' as Everton considers a crime scene: 'When the full account reached the newspapers, the sightseers would arrive. If the murder was never solved, the National Trust might take over. Murderer's corner... The thought of the silent figure on the floor, the floating form in the bath, would draw the crowds more certainly than the quill in the empty ink well, the knowledge that forgotten poetry had been composed in the room that had looked on the lake before the garage was built. This way to the room where he cut her up. Threepence extra admits to the kitchen where the poison was mixed. Why not be photographed with a gun at your head, in the chair he sat in while he bled to death?'

The Widow of Bath was the fourth novel written by Margot Bennett (1912–80), whose career I discussed in some detail in the introduction to the British Library edition of *The Man Who Didn't Fly* (which was first published in 1955). Her early life was eventful. Born in Scotland, she went to school in Australia, and had jobs in a shop, an advertising agency, a hospital, on a magazine, a New Zealand sheep farm, a radio station; and tallying cargo on a copra boat in New Guinea. Her first two mysteries, featuring John Davies, were widely praised, and she followed them with a mainstream novel, based on a treasure hunt in rural Cornwall, *The Golden Pebble*. She told the publishers of *The Widow of Bath* that she liked 'opera, swimming, and late nights'. She also found time to get married and have four children.

In his history of the genre, *Bloody Murder*, Julian Symons heaped praise on Bennett's writing: 'Turn to almost any page in her books and you will find an unexpected and right turn of phrase. These talents are put at the service of a skill in plot construction that is never mechanical, although it is sometimes too intricate. She uses as mere incidents tricks that would serve other writers as material for a plot.' Of *The Widow of Bath*, he said: 'There are a dozen clever deceptions in the book, twice as many as most writers would have given us.'

To produce novels that combine such rich texture with high levels of entertainment demands confidence and energy as well as literary gifts, and Margot Bennett's zest for fiction faded all too soon; she moved away from crime writing while still in her forties. She concentrated on writing for television, and in 1959 she scripted a six-episode version of *The Widow of Bath*, starring Guy Rolfe, Barbara Murray, and John Justin. A youthful Peter Sallis played Cady, and there were also roles for Andrew Cruickshank and Fay Compton. The producer was Gerard Glaister and the music was written by Ron Grainer. Given the array of talent assembled, it is regrettable that the series appears to have been wiped, and no known recordings exist. For a long time, Margot Bennett's crime writing career also fell into oblivion, but I'm confident that readers of *The Widow of Bath* will agree that her novels not only deserve to be remembered, they also continue to give a great deal of pleasure.

MARTIN EDWARDS
www.martinedwardsbooks.com

THE WIDOW OF BATH

'I'VE EATEN THIS MEAL SO OFTEN,' THE YOUNG MAN SAID TO the waiter. 'I know its face, but I forget its name. What is this soup called?'

The waiter picked up the menu and held it against his nose. He shut his left eye, narrowed the right. Then, triumphant, forgiving, he put the card down and turned to Everton.

'It is named Oxtail Soup, sir,' he said in a voice thicker and stronger than the soup.

'Thank you. Has it poisoned many?'

The waiter allowed himself a flattened smile, and prepared to drift away.

'Wait a minute. Have you broken your glasses?'

'I do not wear glasses,' the waiter said angrily. He snatched the plate of soup from the table and marched out of the dining room.

The young man who had eaten so many meals alone in so many hotels took a notebook from his pocket and wrote: "food bad, service vile, waiter probably on the run from Viennese police. Good view of the sea obscured by yellow curtains." He turned his head to look at the windows and saw, for the first time, that the table behind him was occupied. He picked up the notebook again and pressing hard on the pen, wrote: "company odious."

With his hand on the notebook he sat and considered himself. His face was hot and dry, his knees were quivering, his head felt iron-hatted. "It might be influenza," he told himself, trying to be amused.

He picked up the pen and wrote: "'The reasonable man feels no passion. No passion of any kind." He changed "feels no passion" to "is swayed by no passion." Then he crossed out the whole statement.

'Your veal-and-ham pie,' said an ugly voice at his elbow. The short-sighted waiter was back again.

'Thanks. But wait a minute. Didn't I order chicken?' Everton asked, trying to feel his way back to the normal world.

'The chicken is—finished.'

'You should learn to say "off." That's what they say in England.'

'I have waited in England a long time.' The waiter walked away, angry once again.

Everton tried to be interested in him, but his mind was rushing between high banks; there was no overflow to spare for the waiter.

He ate his veal-and-ham pie without tasting it; this was easy enough, as it had no taste. He tried a little to assimilate the conversation of the people behind him, but only the trivial words came through. The table seemed to have its silent areas; there were five people, but only three voices. He saw that his own unpleasant waiter, walking softly like a mouse aware of a trap, was circling the other table. He was serving chicken. Was this intolerable? How agreeable it would have been to have stayed for ever in the world whose idea of the unendurable was poor service. Luxury is wasted on the permanently luxurious. "Waste no luxury" should be his creed, he thought, still trying to hold the situation down and paint a new face on it. The important thing was to be a reasonable man. Would he be recognized by the back of his head? he asked himself, afraid. He put down his knife and fork, pushed his plate away, scowled a negation at the approaching waiter, and with his quick, light, frightened step, walked out of the dining room towards the bar.

The bar was small, neat, cold. It had high, red stools, low grey chairs, small red tables. It was a place for assignations and whispers, rather than for merry alcoholism. The barman was warm, untidy, soft, nervous. He had brown, fluttering eyes and the elements of a moustache. He spoke real English with an artificial accent.

'Are you a Ruritanian?' Everton asked lightly, from the surface of his mind.

'Italian, sir,' said the barman, polishing the glass he held, with the enthusiasm of the craftsman.

Everton sat on a stool by the bar and ordered whisky. He drank it with the slow, meditative, wine-tasting air of the man who knows he is going to drink too much before the end of the evening.

He was on his third drink when the girl came in; the silvery fur coat swinging over her arm, her gloves held in one hand, her whole appearance a cautious announcement of her intention not to stay.

He looked at her sideways and said flatly, 'Well, Jan. Going to have a drink?'

'Whisky, please. Hugh, what are you doing here?'

'Drinking,' he said.

'I didn't mean that. What are you doing here, in this place?'

'Drinking,' he repeated. 'I'm eating and drinking my way along the coast. Degourmetizing myself. If that were still needed,' he added.

'Do you have a job, or... or—I mean, are you all right, Hugh? Since... it's so long since I've seen you. Are you all right about—about money, and so on?'

'Offering to lend me money. And so soon? I see we can never meet as equals. You are trying to drive me down to the level of economic man. You're determined to scourge me with money. It must be wonderful,' he said, looking into his glass, 'to be rich and have no conscience. Your money is wasted if you are rich and guilty. Do you still potter around with an easel?'

'I teach art in a local school. The private side of the paint-box is closed, the attic abandoned, life tidied up.' She smiled at him briefly.

'And I've been swept out with the rubbish?'

'Yes, Hugh,' she said, smiling steadily this time. 'You have.'

'You have that merry-eyed steel-lipped look,' he said. 'The kind that all nice girls wear when they're trying to make sure the past shan't interfere with the present.' He lifted his glass, but not so far as his lips. 'If I've been swept out with the rubbish why do you follow me in here?'

He put the glass down again and looked at her. She was a pretty girl with her dark, almost neat, head, spoilt, as usual, by a wisp of hair loose at the back. She had a small nose, a short upper lip, wide-spaced teeth. She had been restless, energetic, melancholy, gay, erratic, and often too earnest.

'I wonder what you are now?' he said aloud.

They sat and looked at each other, thinking of the shared past, but they were like painters of different schools working on the same scene, and their separate pictures were almost unrelated.

'I think I'm curious,' she said, 'to know if I've been pushed back into the mist or if I'm still in your mind.'

He shook his head. 'You're trying to draw emotion out without paying any in,' he said. 'So the question is returned to drawer. How is your dear uncle?'

She looked cautious and abstracted. 'He's here to-night with Lucy. You met her, didn't you?' She looked at him flatly. 'He's an old man, now.'

'An old, cold man,' Hugh said. 'He always was, from what I heard. Pure ice from the diaphragm up. Has Lucy's temperature dropped much?'

Jan's face grew pinker. He had always thought that she blushed too easily, but to make her blush by talking of other women was a game that was out-of-date.

'I don't see much of them,' she said, 'even though I live with them.'

'Is that better than the abandoned attic?'

'It's different, I have to stick around because—oh, because there's something wrong!'

'What sort of wrong? Desperately wrong, or just an extra hat in the hall?' Jan had always been a great moralizer, he remembered with a morose irritation. He had to remind himself that he was not interested. Not interested in Jan, not interested in extra hats, not interested in the past.

At that point the door opened and the past, the frightening past, came in.

'Here they are,' Jan said hurriedly. 'I must go. We live not far away, if you're going to be around for a day or two.'

She slid off her stool, and the blonde woman who had come in with three men behind her moved forward swiftly.

'Off already, Jan? Are you going to introduce us to your friend?'

'Yes, I must go now,' Jan said easily. 'And I think you know him already.' She picked up her gloves. 'Well, good-night, all.' Wearing her poise a little too ostentatiously, she left the bar.

Everton looked at his glass as though it were a microscope and something of importance to science might move under it.

Lucy, who didn't like the social stage to be too crowded, waited until Jan had left before she cried, 'Why, it's Hugh!'

He stood up. 'Hello, Lucy.' He looked at the hand she held out. It was large, soft-skinned, pink, but strong enough to stand up to the weight of the rings she wore.

'Diamonds and rubies,' he said staring. 'You'll be knocked down one night, Lucy. For one reason or another.'

'Not by anyone here, I hope,' she said, lightly withdrawing her hand.

The melancholy barman laughed so loudly that even Everton looked at him in surprise.

'Odd sort of staff here,' said the long-faced man who had come in with Lucy. 'Get us all some brandy,' he added mildly to the barman.

'Have you nothing to say except that I may be knocked down?' Lucy asked Hugh.

He looked at her. Golden hair, white skin, jewels round her neck, dark frock that held the light.

'Only that you still glitter,' he said. 'Bad for moths.'

'The light doesn't mean to hurt the moths,' the long-faced man said. He had neat, grey hair, a neat, grey moustache, a tidy bearing, stiff, upright, clipped, stern, a gallant air. Perhaps he had been a horse in the Charge of the Light Brigade. 'My name's Atkinson. Is he a mystery man, Lucy, or will you introduce us?'

'Major Atkinson, no doubt,' Everton said. 'But I thought we knew each other. I could be mistaken. It's always happening to me. Perhaps you have a brother with ginger hair. A brother called Freddy Ronson.'

'My name is Atkinson. The rank is Colonel. Retired,' the other man said quietly, eyes darting to see if there was a joke in ambush. Everton continued to stare at him.

'It's a pity Ronson didn't show me his birthmarks,' he said. 'Funny, though. We knew each other well enough.'

'Don't talk nonsense, Hugh,' Lucy said. 'This is my husband, this is Gerald Cady.'

Everton glanced at the plump, cold Cady with neither alarm nor interest, then turned towards Gregory Bath, the husband of Lucy.

Bath's body seemed the wrong shape for his mind. The years had thrown a blanket of flesh over his face and dropped a pillow on his stomach. His eyes, trying to struggle from the pit, were frozen, masked, and a little bulbous behind his glasses, as though he were doing logarithms in his head. He looked as ancient in experience as a lonely monster in a side-show, but he was only a retired judge. "Judge not" thought Everton, who was slightly confused by fear, "Judge not, for no one will take the trouble to judge you."

The judge, in his high, cold voice, was asking Everton if they had met before. Everton replied that they might have met but somehow they never did. The judge, practised in sensing guilt, evasiveness, or even embarrassment, turned his head slowly towards Lucy, but she was already engaged in an easy conversation with Atkinson and seemed to have lost interest in Everton.

'Is it long since you have seen my wife?' Bath persisted. Perhaps he sensed the possibility of there being a case to come before the court.

'I suppose it's two or three years now,' Everton said. 'We last met at some kind of dinner.'

'I remember,' Lucy said, turning round. 'I think you were being rather disagreeable, weren't you, Hugh?'

'I thought, on the other hand, that I was almost ridiculously agreeable,' Everton replied. 'But perhaps I am giving too much weight to the circumstances.' He realized that the conversation was becoming double-edged. One of the edges would cut him soon. He turned to the judge, almost hopefully.

'Do you like this hotel?'

'The staff is peculiarly foreign and too often unreliable,' the judge said, looking remotely at the melancholy barman. 'I come here frequently, but the waiters seem always to be strangers. Perhaps I should say that I come here frequently because the waiters seem always to be strangers. I am sure I haven't seen that man before. Perhaps he was something left over at the end of a United Nations conference. What country do you come from?' he said suddenly to the melancholy barman.

'Italy, sir.'

'And from what part of Italy?'

The barman looked around for help. He could almost be seen struggling along the peninsula. 'Genoa,' he said, in modest hope.

Everton sympathized with him. The judge's manner would have made any man doubt the efficacy of lonely truth. Evidence would be demanded.

'It is some years since I have been to Italy,' the judge began, in his false, agreeable, legal tone, 'but I remember Genoa well. What part of Genoa did you live in?'

Everton turned towards Lucy with a sweeping gesture that upset his glass. 'Careless of me,' he said in surprise. 'Wipe it up, will you?' he said to the barman. 'And get me another.'

The barman moved quickly. The judge, with his features immobile, watched the pool of liquid being swabbed from the bar. He did not speak. Everton felt he was waiting for the answer to a question that had not been asked.

'Don't have another here, Hugh,' Lucy said, and Everton felt that if the judge had been an active man he would have nodded.

'Come home and have a drink with us,' Lucy went on. 'Why don't you all come back?' she said, evidently struck by a new idea. 'Unless you want to go to bed, Gregory,' she added to her husband.

'It's not my custom to go to bed at half-past eight in the evening,' he said with apparent tenderness. Everton, realizing that a few minutes would be spent in keeping down the undercurrents of matrimony, allowed himself a moment's speculation on the depths of the matrimonial river, then turned slowly towards Atkinson.

'Do you see much of Lucy and her husband?' he asked, and waited eagerly to hear the quality of the other's voice.

'I suppose we're friends, in a way,' Atkinson replied in his reserved, confident voice. The accent was that of the correctly educated Englishman. Ronson had probably spoken correctly enough. Was the same music, played by different performers, still the same? Atkinson spoke like an Englishman who went about with a dog at his heels. If Freddy Ronson ever had a dog at his heels it would be a police dog.

'He's retired, hasn't he?' Everton said, nodding towards Bath. 'Has she?'

'I don't think she ever worked,' Atkinson replied.

'I meant did she like living in a quiet seaside town?' Everton explained. He intended his tone to be bland.

'Perhaps I don't know her well enough to explain her likes and dislikes,' Atkinson said, stiff, withdrawn, the gentleman confronted with the cad.

'Freddy would certainly have known,' Everton mumbled, and was glad he had stopped drinking. Remarks like that were uncivilized and possibly dangerous. He withdrew again into thought. One man may have the same complexion, length of nose, and shape of face, as another, and yet seem very clearly a different man. A snapshot of Ronson might have seemed like a snapshot of Atkinson, but Ronson's face had been brutal, sly, and secretive, while Atkinson's was melancholy, cautious, and conventional. Ronson had talked with all his face, he had been violent in his gestures; Atkinson was mean with his expressions and kept his hands in his pockets. The suspicious circumstance was that two men so different should ever be confused. Even if Atkinson was not Ronson, it was still possible that Ronson had been Atkinson. A man could be an actor; an actor might wish to disguise himself from the police.

'Let's get our coats,' Lucy was saying. 'We must be home by nine. And I'll drive you, Hugh. You don't mind, do you, Gregory? I'm longing to hear what he's been doing since I saw him last.'

'It's nice of you to be so interested,' Everton said when they were in the car. 'Doesn't your husband mind? I thought he was sensitive.'

'Don't be bitter, Hugh,' she said, her eyes on the road ahead. 'I didn't behave well, but would it have been any better for you if I'd ruined myself for the sake of making a romantic gesture?' She changed gears smoothly. 'Surely it was enough that one of us should suffer. And you wouldn't have made your gesture if you hadn't wanted to. You were only living up to your own idea of yourself. Rather a delightful idea too.'

Everton was silent.

'Well?' she said.

'I was examining that speech to see if the words Thank you were included in it,' he said. 'I find you haven't changed. I have. I'm suspicious, frightened, and not at all romantic now. But I'm still curious. It's curiosity that has put me in this car beside you. You knew a man called Ronson, didn't you?'

'I did and so did you. But I never cared for him. He was—well, undesirable. I haven't seen him for years. Hugh, you're not drunk, are you? This business about Atkinson. Why, he even sounds different. Ronson was—coarse. I dropped him very quickly.'

'I didn't drop him quickly enough,' Everton said slowly. 'And as a result…' He hesitated, 'I've turned into a reasonable man.'

She stopped the car and looked at him. The pallor of night was on her face, but her hair still held its brilliance.

'What would a reasonable man do now?' she asked softly.

'You're luminous,' he said, looking at her hair. 'The burnt reasonable man dreads the fire.'

'He wouldn't even warm his lips—just once?'

He kissed her, happy in his awareness that he was choosing trouble.

'It's just a form of saying Thank you,' she said. 'Words mean nothing between us, Hugh.'

'I think it's better that they retain their function and mean something.' He smiled at her without tenderness. 'So let me use one or two and ask what you mean to do with me. Or what you're trying to make me do?'

She still had the trick of appearing not to listen. 'Will you do something for me, Hugh?' she asked.

'Naturally I'm willing to pay for every favour,' he said cheerfully. 'I'm so glad to find I'm not—excommunicated.'

'All I want you to do is just stay around to-night. Don't say you have to leave early, or anything like that.'

'Am I allowed to ask why, or would that sound too hopeful?'

'Just because I'm nervous. I want company.'

'Isn't your husband company? I thought that was why people married. And the dubious Atkinson? And Jack Cade, or whatever he's called?'

'Cady. They're both company. But I'm nervous. I can't explain. I'm rather sensitive to atmosphere. Gregory has so many enemies. And—even I might have enemies. Be my friend, Hugh.'

'What are you worried about? Quarrels, exposures, private detectives, ultimatums? Blows with blunt instruments? Or Atkinsons turning into Ronsons and being coarse?'

'I haven't anything in mind. I just think things are sinister. You don't know this quiet seaside town—and we're not even in the town.' She started the car again.

'I'll stay late,' he said. 'So long as I'm not being asked just as a husband-sitter. But tell me one thing—or, rather, a series of things. Are you as luxurious, greedy, mercenary, unscrupulous, selfish, faithless, ambitious, and lax as ever?'

'I'm a civilized woman,' she said, 'and here we are.'

2

THE HOUSE THAT LAY BEFORE THEM IN THE MOONLIGHT WAS unlike both the sea-boxes and the bijou castles that builders have scattered round our shores. It had a flimsy, colonial look; tall, narrow, rakish, with painted shutters, wrought-iron balconies, and, on the ground floor, french windows opening on to verandahs roofed against the flighty English sun. It was a Folly, a merino millionaire's folly; perhaps there were some carved sheep on the lawn. The judge had lived in the Colonies. Had the house tugged at his heart-strings, or whatever judges fastened their hearts with? But retired professional men like to live by the sea, even when the sea means an inland suburb of Bournemouth.

This was not Bournemouth. The house stared down across the bald cliff into the dark depths. "The impersonal sea, the purifying sea," Everton thought, staring down at the shadowy boat in the bay. "The whispering, roaring, muttering, silent sea. The active, uneventful sea."

'Did you come here to contemplate eternity?' he asked Lucy.

'We've had to let our town house,' she said. 'We're hard up, you know.' She lifted a hand to her shining hair.

'Just lay that hand on a pawn-broker's counter and he'll carry you past this month's overdraft,' Everton said. 'Or did you cut those rings out of old beer-bottle tops? And is that your yacht down in the bay?'

'Nothing to do with me. I'm frightened of boats,' Lucy said.

Everton continued to stare. 'It's very quiet here. Now, in the moonlight, it's almost secret. Or are there some hermits in that wood? You'd hate a really contemplative hermit, wouldn't you, Lucy? You always liked to drag people into the drama. You still do. Or why am I here to-night?' He laid his hand on hers. 'Do you want an audience for some big scene?'

Her hand was cold.

'You always talked too much, Hugh. And you suppose and wonder so many things that you stumble into drama that doesn't exist. And a hermit would never survive the woods. Through the day there are so many cars looking for a place where there are no other cars that the hermit would probably start a sixpenny car park. Don't you think we'd better go in,' she said, and he realized that she was talking rapidly in an effort to drag the situation down to an appearance of the social norm. 'The nearest we have to a hermit,' she went on quickly, 'is the old woman who's our neighbour. She writes poetry, not to be printed, just to read, and she does breathing exercises on the cliff in tune with nature. She's mad.'

They went into the house, Lucy still talking automatically. Everton saw nothing in the house to suggest poverty. The judge, with his gross, intellectual face, looked opulent. Atkinson, whose well-bred voice made the smallest talk sound like culture, was discussing carburettors with Cady, while the judge prowled up and down, shouting for Baxter.

Baxter, Lucy explained to Everton, was not a butler, but an Old English sheepdog, highly valued by her husband. He had been missing since morning. She had walked all day looking for him, and the judge had sat at home, waiting for him to be produced.

Was he a good watchdog, Everton asked. He was told shortly by the judge that Baxter was no sort of watchdog at all.

'He was a well-bred dog. He'd keep quiet even if you stepped on his tail,' the judge added.

'I hope that one day I'll live up to Baxter,' Everton said. 'Was he good with sheep?'

The judge paused in his anxious perambulations.

'It's possible that he's never set eyes on a sheep in his life,' he said.

'He's just a lap dog,' Cady said, beaming nervously. 'Sixty pounds of lap dog.'

This remark offended the judge, who repeated in an unfriendly voice that Baxter was a well-bred dog. 'I always knew what he was doing when he was in my house, and that's more than some people can say of their guests, hey?' If these words had been delivered from a judicial eminence to a tense court, seeking relief from the suspense of a murder trial, they would have been greeted with gales of laughter, Everton thought, and was amazed to find that in this private house there was also a gale of laughter.

Bath, like most judges, mellowed under the influence of his own wit. Drinks were produced, and Everton, sheltering behind the conversation of the others, was free to wonder what had brought them together.

Cady was a youngish man, probably still in his twenties. His face seemed round and vacant, his manner suggested that he was looking for a safe place to hide. He had an immature, a slightly bullied air. Everton looked at his hands, but although they were freckled, there was no ink on them. Surely he and ex-justice Bath had nothing in common? If he was a friend of Lucy's her taste had coarsened. She had never had taste, only greed. If Cady admired her, she probably thought him admirable.

He looked at her with his melancholy, reflective gaze. She was showing so much tender affection to her husband that Everton wondered for a moment if she liked him, but he dismissed as impracticable the idea that any woman could like the judge. As a husband he would be too inclined to keep his wife either in the witness box or in the dock. If Lucy was tender, it was because she wanted to hide or to gain something.

A servant brought coffee. There was nothing sinister about the servant, but he was a man, which suggested money in the house.

Atkinson, cup in hand, moved over to Everton.

'It's always better to have coffee privately,' he said. 'The stuff they serve in that hotel is abominable.'

'I didn't stop for coffee,' Everton said. 'I was frightened. By the food,' he added.

'Dreadful service, too,' Atkinson murmured, looking grave. 'Are you staying long?'

'Just a day or two,' Everton said. 'I move around.'

'Restless?' Atkinson asked, with his meaningless social smile. 'Have you been abroad recently?'

'Why do you ask? Have I a faraway look?'

'I thought travelling might be your line of business.'

'I know just enough about business to keep out of it,' Everton said. 'I live in a non-commercial world all of my own. If anyone offered me a hundred pounds for nothing, I'd sooner not sell.'

'If they offered you a thousand pounds for nothing?'

'Then I think we'd have moved away from nothing. It would have an ambiguous name, like next-to-nothing.' He appeared to hesitate. 'A thousand pounds, of course, might destroy my immunity. It would be a bad bargain. I paid a lot for immunity.'

Atkinson's hand went to his pocket. He drew out a pen and began to play with it. His fingers, that should have been long and slender if they were to match his manner and his voice, were short and thick, with a thin fuzz of reddish fair hair on the back of each. 'You must tell me where to buy immunity,' he said gravely. 'It sounds useful.'

'You should ask your brother Freddy,' Everton said, driving himself to look away from the fingers. He felt overcome by nausea and fear. He looked round for a way of escape from the engulfing room, but Lucy was calling to him. She wanted him to be sociable, she said, and to play bridge. But before they began would Atkinson mind fetching her cigarette case from the car?

"That gambit was probably used in the Ark," Everton thought, struggling back to self-control. "In a moment she'll find she left it somewhere else and go out to tell him. I suppose she must make what chance she can to explain me."

When Lucy, with expressions of remorse, discovered her cigarettes in her handbag and hurried out to retrieve Atkinson, the judge's well-padded face remained unruffled, but, without movement, he gave the impression of leaning forward slightly. Everton and Cady, too, waited in silence. The others were talking affably when they returned. There was no reason for suspicion: nothing had happened, but the emotional atmosphere had changed, as it changes in the concert hall when the strings give way to the brass.

Everton refused to play in the first rubber. He watched the other four settle down at the bridge table. The time was ten-thirty. In another hour he would go away. "And I hope I mean it" he added to himself. He watched Lucy and the smile she had for every man at the table, a smile that must be a lie for someone. "Lucy means trouble," Everton thought, "I don't want trouble: it follows that I don't want Lucy." Logically, the conclusion seemed sound, but it might be advisable not to depend entirely on logic. It would be safer to run.

The first rubber ended quickly.

'The cards were against you, Gregory,' Lucy said. 'But perhaps it's time they were. You've always been so lucky.'

'I have never been particularly lucky,' the judge answered. 'Except in being able to develop a slight skill in pursuing the course of another man's thoughts.'

'And the other woman's thoughts?' Cady asked, grinning.

Atkinson frowned. 'Do you mean telepathy?' he asked with courteous interest.

'I mean that as a functionary of the criminal court I have had a long experience of the effect of greed, hatred, and fear,' the judge boomed. 'These are corrosive passions, and I have learnt to recognize the corroded.'

'But surely you don't meet them very often at the bridge table,' Lucy said, with a very plausible laugh. Everton saw that the others sat as still as himself.

'You are always willing to credit people with too much honesty, my dear,' the judge said to her quietly. 'Even when you write references for servants, to choose a trifling example.' Lucy looked involuntarily at Atkinson, and then turned quickly back to her husband. 'You must train yourself,' he said, 'to accept the fact that others do not always behave as you would wish. And now,' he continued in a different voice, turning to Everton, 'I hope you'll take my place at the table.'

Everton waited. He felt there was more to be said.

'Or perhaps you would like me to show you the house,' Bath went on, in a voice that was excessively cold. 'There's a view of the sea that I find entrancing when I am not able to sleep. I find there is always something happening at sea,' he said to the others.

Atkinson put his glass carefully down on the table.

'We'd better get on with the game, hadn't we?' he said to Lucy.

'You wouldn't like to see the view?' Bath repeated to Everton.

'Please, Gregory, we want him to play,' Lucy said without raising her head. 'And I know you'd like to go to bed.'

'I'm sorry if it's going to hold up the game. But I think I would rather like to see the view. I may never be here again,' Everton said. 'I shall probably be leaving the hotel to-morrow. And someone who has been in exile,' he smiled at Lucy, 'doesn't like to miss anything.'

'I'll take you to the library,' the judge said as they left the room. 'And there you can look down on the bay and out to sea so far as the moonlight will allow. I'm a slow walker, Everton. My health is not good. I have lived too robustly, and my heart is in the condition that follows such a life. This is the library. We will turn out the light so that we may look at the sea.' He laid his hand on Everton's arm and guided him slowly to the window. 'My physical condition is poorer than it appears,' he said. 'Does that open up a delicious prospect for you, Everton? Or do you mean to leave to-morrow and not return?' He took his hand from Everton's arm. 'We will turn out the light,' he repeated.

'I mean to leave to-morrow,' Everton said, turning away towards the bookshelves.

'You need not look at the shelves to see if I prefer Sartre to Dumas,' Bath said. 'My taste, as you will see at once, is legal. I am happy enough to be surrounded by an account of every kind of villainy known to man and to reflect on the wisdom or occasional stupidity of the judgment.'

Everton took his eyes from the books and switched off the light. He stood still for a moment, and then said again, 'I mean to leave to-morrow. Have we finished with the sea?'

'No. You must be aware there is something wrong in this place. How aware are you? You said Atkinson resembled someone you knew? Whom?'

Everton sighed. 'I think he's a man called Freddy Ronson. But if he is, he hasn't only dyed his hair and grown a moustache. He's changed his voice. Ronson's tone was nearly the same but—but there's a difference in production. This man's voice is clearer, vowels softer, doesn't move his lips so much, his whole face is much more contained, less emotional.'

'Not an impossible change. Who was Ronson?'

'He was a man who helped me into trouble,' Everton said shortly. 'It wouldn't interest you.'

The judge waited, wheezing slightly. 'I can't make you speak, Everton,' he said. 'I have a feeling that you have been in—shall we say in difficulties? Every man keeps his own accounts. The accounts may be ludicrous. The criminal may subscribe to charity, the coward make a faltering effort at heroism, the seducer spare a woman for her youth. The accounts may be pitifully inexact, but the effort to keep them is made by nearly every man. You are not corroded, Everton. You are not even hardened. I think you are a foolish young man, whom it pleases for the moment to wear an air of tragic bravado.'

'Thank you,' Everton said. 'What am I to do then? Support an orphanage, or spare someone's aunt? I don't think I like these legal histrionics,' he added savagely.

'What you are to do in the first place is to pay the debt you owe me. And you may begin by telling me what you know of Atkinson— or Ronson.'

Everton looked in the moon-darkness at the judge's face, despising it fold by fold of flesh. This foolish old man had spent a lifetime as a self-indulgent autocrat. He had been invested with the power of office; the office had been taken from him; he imagined in his villainous vanity that authority still clung to him. He was an obsolete battleship, who believed that his guns could still roar. He should stay in the garden and potter about with carnations. But instead he had to marry the wrong wife and mix with the wrong people and talk about greed and corrosion at the bridge table.

The judge still waited, and Everton, intent on proving that he could not be dominated, that the battleship was sinking, stared into the small, cold eyes. Staring, he found there was nothing behind them. The eyes were vacant and hopeless, the fleshy face drooped in despair. The words of command were habit, there was no belief in them. The judge did not expect to be obeyed. He knew that his guns were obsolete. Everton's hatred slowly trickled away, and he was left empty.

'Ronson,' he said unhappily. 'He was a dangerous man; I thought it was clever to know him. I was in a—an emotional cross-current at the time. I was fond of a woman. I was spending too much. She needed money badly—for some purpose. I seemed to be friendly with Ronson. He asked me if I'd be a kind of courier. I was—well, that doesn't matter. But I had a subordinate position at the Embassy in Paris. I had a car with C.D. plates. The job he offered was driving someone to a quiet spot on the frontier. I refused. Said I'd expose him. Very noble. I woke up in a sort of casual ward, but I shouldn't have wakened up at all. I wasn't meant to. One of those crazy fishermen who never catch anything in the Seine caught me. The biggest moment in his life, it seems, when he felt something on his line. He handed me over for dead, and someone got the water out. That's all,' Everton ended flatly.

'And didn't you denounce this man?'

'Even if I'd been able to prove anything I wouldn't have had the time,' Everton said. He looked doubtfully at the judge.

He had already talked too much, but he felt cooler and happier.

'The time. And what about the inclination. When you did have—the time—did you attempt to expose this man?'

'I never saw him again. I'd been in a lot of trouble. I felt like keeping away from more. I'd left Paris. When I saw him—thought I saw him—to-night, I was worried,' Everton said, sweating. 'And what about it. You don't know what it feels like to be up against someone who wants to murder you and nearly does.' Everton felt his voice rising up the scale and he tried to pull it down again. 'I don't want revenge. I want to be left alone.'

'But you came here to-night.'

Everton did not answer.

'When did you meet my wife?'

'Oh, years ago. I think your niece introduced us.'

'If I could trust you, Everton,' the judge said quietly, '—but I can't. Not because of anything you've told me. But because you knocked your drink over in the bar to-night. And now we have admired the sea long enough. You are a frightened man. You are also rash. I advise you to be careful. And I also advise you that it is the duty of every citizen to expose and so help to destroy evil.'

'But have you done so?' Everton asked smoothly.

The judge turned away from him and walking slowly towards the door, switched on the light. They left the legal books behind. As they went into the hall Everton half imagined that he heard a step on the stairs, hesitant, soft, flurried. Perhaps the manservant was cat-footed.

Bath hesitated, and looked up the stairs. He steadied himself against the door, then, speaking in a low voice, he said to Everton, 'Good-night. Will you make my excuses to the others. I must go up now,' he said in a weary voice.

Everton stayed in the hall and watched him mount the stairs with his lumbering, resolute step, then he turned back to the other room.

Atkinson looked up when he came in and asked pleasantly if the sea had been up to standard. Cady was playing patience, and Lucy studying her finger nails, or, perhaps, her rings.

The time was eleven five, and for people who wanted so much to play bridge, Everton thought, they played very badly. Cady, his eyes wandering from Lucy's to Atkinson's face, was clearly just able to remember that bridge was being played. Lucy smoked without stopping, and twice played a card of the wrong suit, Atkinson studied his cards for five minutes before making a bid. "They're waiting for the train to start," Everton decided, when Atkinson looked quickly at and away from his watch for the third time running.

When the cards were dealt again Everton left his on the table. 'Are you sure you're enjoying this game,' he said. 'Or are we all a little tired? Or waiting for something?'

Cady was the only one who answered. 'I'm not waiting for anything,' he said, with his wide, pointless smile. 'I was thinking.'

'And what were you thinking?' Lucy asked savagely.

'I was thinking I'd lived around here for a long time,' he said. 'And perhaps it was time I changed. What about Devon. Now, I'd rather like to go to Devon.' He looked at the clock. The time was eleven thirty-one.

Lucy had not listened to the answer. She picked up her cards, then, when the noise of the shot came through, she stiffened, and dropped the hand.

'It must be Gregory, shooting at rabbits,' she said.

From the garden there came the noise of a dog howling.

'And that must be Baxter, retrieving the rabbit,' said Everton.

'Pick up your cards, Hugh,' she said through her teeth. Everton saw she was fighting to hold back some emotion. He thought the expression on her face was one of pure amazement. She started to her feet and then sank down again with a sigh.

'I think—I think I'd better go and see,' she said in a whisper. 'Will you all wait here. Please, please, wait here.'

She ran out of the room, and the men sat and stared at each other.

3

L UCY HAD BEEN OUT OF THE ROOM FOR TWO OR THREE MINUTES before anyone spoke. Then Atkinson, who had been shuffling the cards thoughtfully, dropped them on the table.

'Perhaps I'd better go and see if there's anything wrong,' he said.

'Perhaps we should all go,' Everton said without conviction.

Cady had been quiet as a badger waiting in his sett for a dog to pass. Now he kept his head down, but he moved his eyes sideways towards Everton.

'Lucy said wait here,' he murmured. His face was solemn, he looked unnatural without his grin, as though he had suddenly lost his teeth.

'Perhaps we should wait,' Everton said. 'We might interrupt a great reconciliation scene. He's shooting at rabbits, she said. She may be in the garden, driving them towards his window, or perhaps their hands are meeting over the furry little body. If it's a habit of his to shoot at rabbits with a revolver, you have nothing to worry about.'

Cady's silence collapsed. 'What do you mean, reconciliation? They had nothing to be reconciled about. They were a happy married couple.'

'You've moved into the past tense fairly smoothly,' Everton said. 'I don't know if they have any reason for disagreement. I shouldn't have thought of Lucy as having a vocation for the ray of sunlight career. A man's declining years could be very adequately brightened by a much dimmer wife.'

'Do you know what I would call you?' Cady said. 'I would call you verbose.'

'That's a literary word for a public school type to use,' Everton said in a half-heartedly offensive voice. He was listening for a groan, a scream, hurried footsteps. He thought he heard them all, but his imagination was grinding out the requisite background. Had there been a note of reality in the footsteps? He looked at Atkinson, and he believed he saw a man whose mind was racing. Atkinson was certainly listening with almost desperate attention, while his hands with their reddish stubble mechanically stacked the cards. Then, very faintly, they heard the sound of a step on the stairs. Atkinson put the cards down and waited. There was no other sound.

Atkinson stood up. 'I'm going to see what's happened,' he said. 'Wait here.'

Everton nodded after him. 'That's two of us gone,' he said. 'Is it your turn next, or mine? Neither, perhaps. It seems we have an important waiting function to perform.' He found that his irritation with Cady was intense and unreasonable. He was passing on the disgust he felt for his own inadequacy. He knew he should have gone upstairs. He knew he should have gone up at once. But he was alone, and he was too near the sea, the impersonal, dangerous, obliterating sea. Atkinson would have the sea on his side: the sea was always on the side of the murderer. The reasonable man would leave Atkinson's affairs alone.

'Stop whistling,' he said sharply to Cady.

Cady stopped whistling and said without resignation, 'Why did you have to be here to-night?'

'Now, that's quite a question,' Everton said softly. From the beginning the party had not been merry. In this opulent house they had sat with their heads in the thunder clouds. It was the kind of party you tried to keep to yourself, not at all an occasion to share with chance-met friends. Whatever it was that had persuaded Lucy to ask him to her house that night, it was certainly not the conviction that he would enjoy himself or that the others would like his company. She had seen him, she had pounced, she had dragged him off to the lair. If she had wanted him as an emotional experiment, another, a slacker, night, would have been more suitable. She might have hoped he would protect her. Surely not from Atkinson. And she might have wanted an independent witness. A shot was heard. We were all together. Four of us. One almost a stranger. No one at the bridge table could have fired that shot. The end of this would be that if he was not to oppose Atkinson, he must support him. "I'm an orange or a lemon," he thought miserably.

'I don't think I want to play with such big boys,' he said aloud to Cady.

The servant materialized beside them.

'I beg your pardon, gentlemen, I thought I heard—a shot.'

'We have been told that your employer is shooting rabbits,' Everton said briskly, 'and we're waiting to see the game-bag.'

'Thank you, sir,' the man said, and went out.

'Do you think he ties his eyebrows to his teeth at night, to keep them from rising?' Everton asked.

'You're a great talker, aren't you,' Cady said. 'Verbose.'

'I'm a thinker, too,' Everton said. 'What do you suppose has happened to that dog?'

'I don't know,' Cady said. 'I don't know anything about anything.'

'That's the line,' Everton said approvingly. 'You, too, can stop when the traffic lights are red.'

Cady grunted. 'It's about time those lights changed or we'll have to go upstairs and find something out.'

Everton was still disinclined to rise. He was trying to think of a way to prolong the conversation, to postpone the trouble for even sixty seconds more, when he heard laboured footsteps in the hall. He sat still, while his sixty seconds dwindled away. He was clutching at the last of them when Atkinson, sober-faced, came in, half dragging, half carrying Lucy.

'She fainted,' he said. 'Her husband's been shot.'

He guided her to a chair and she sat swaying and groaning.

'Give her a drink,' Cady said, in what Everton thought a very calm voice. Everton, his hand trembling, poured some whisky in a glass and tried to make her drink. Lucy's teeth snapped shut and she pushed him away.

Everton straightened himself and said to Atkinson with a sudden, staccato nervousness, 'I think I'll go upstairs and have a look at the body. I'm nearly experienced with corpses.'

'We ought to look at the body,' Cady agreed, a strange grin spreading over his face and up to his pale eyes.

'Then you'd better not touch it, nor anything in the room,' Atkinson said sharply. 'The police will be called.'

Everton and Cady went into the hall together, and up the stairs. There were four doors on the landing, only one was open, and Cady, standing slightly in front of Everton, peered in. It was a large room. The french windows on the right stood open, and the little balcony was empty. The room looked as though someone had been searching for the plans of the latest bomb. The door of an empty wardrobe stood open, the clothes it had held had been tossed around the room. The drawers had been dragged from the desk in the corner, and papers fluttered in the breeze from the open windows. The bed had been hastily unmade, chairs were overturned, a lamp upset.

'Perhaps one lot of secret police met another lot and they had a fight,' Everton said foolishly, trying to keep his eyes from the figure in the middle of the floor. He didn't like blood, but, looking down at last, he saw there was very little blood.

The judge was lying with his knees bent, half on his back, half on his side. His right forearm covered his eyes, as though there were something he had not wished to see. His left arm lay by his side, the fingers inert and empty. Walking softly across the room, Everton looked down on the drained face, and, beneath the protecting arm, saw the edge of the bloody hole on the forehead.

He heard a soft, fluffy breathing behind him. He turned and looked at Cady, whose pale, plump face was illuminated.

'I say,' Cady said, 'they've done him in. He's dead.' He bent down over the dead man. He might have been smelling the blood. Then he straightened. 'It's years since I've seen one,' he said. 'Funny there's not much blood. Now he's for the darkness and corruption.'

'Now he's for the glaring light and the autopsy,' Everton said. 'And that will do for me, unless you think we should look for clues and have the solution with three carbon copies for the police when they come.'

He turned to leave the room, but Cady did not move. The silly, excited grin seemed fixed on his face.

Everton caught him by the arm and shook him.

'Come downstairs,' he said.

Cady looked at him blankly, and the grin faded away. 'We'll go down,' he said tonelessly, and followed Everton, dragging his feet like a reluctant schoolboy.

In the hall they found Atkinson playing with the telephone. 'Damned thing's out of order,' he said. 'Now what?'

Lucy seemed to have revived. 'You'll have to take your car,' she said, 'and fetch the police.'

'Anything wrong with that?' Atkinson asked, appealing to the others.

'Nothing,' Everton said, although afterwards he wondered why he hadn't suggested that Atkinson take his car to the nearest telephone. The police station would be in the town, five miles away. 'Nothing,' he repeated. 'But do you mind if I come with you?'

'I think you'd better stay,' Atkinson said easily, but Everton caught the insult in his tone. Atkinson had smelt out his craven desire to run away.

'Don't leave me alone,' Lucy wailed, and Everton abandoned the harder course.

'Don't bother to invite me, I'm staying,' Cady said abruptly. He sat down at the card table. Lucy swayed towards the sofa. Everton stood scowling by the fire. Atkinson left the room without speaking again.

Lucy began to talk feverishly. Had she loved her husband enough? No. She hadn't. Had she made him happy? No. If she had insisted that he stayed at the bridge table, if she had gone upstairs with him, if she'd warned him more of the enemies a judge must have, would it have been different? Yes. Was it her fault? Yes. If she had been another sort of woman, a woman who liked staying at home every evening, would the man, the murderer, have been able to creep into the house and lie in wait? No. If they had dined at home the house would have been securely locked up. What did Everton think? What did Cady think? Everton, still staring into the fire, said nothing. Cady, who had left the table and was wandering round the room, was also silent. In the tiny pause they heard the sound of a car.

'Oh, God, I need friends, I need help,' Lucy cried. 'Say something, one of you.'

'I don't know what kind of friends you need, what kind of help,' Everton said in despair. 'Why am I here? Why did you bring me here?' He moved over to the sofa and stared down at her. She began to cry. Cady quickly turned his back and moved over to the window.

'Don't cry, Lucy, please don't cry,' Everton said. He felt that time had anchored him in this night for ever.

Lucy's sobs became louder and louder. She held her hands over her ears, arched her back, and began to scream.

'If you go on like this I'll have to hit you,' Everton said. Lucy fell back on the sofa and banged the floor with her feet. 'It's what a masterful man would do,' Everton said loudly. 'What about you, Cady?'

Cady, still looking out of the window, did not turn round.

'Think of something cheerful,' Everton shouted to Lucy. 'Think of the clothes you'll be able to wear at the murder trial. The Press photographers, the all-night queue gaping as you sweep past in your simple widow's weeds from Paris.'

Lucy's screams stopped. 'You beast, you brute, I've always hated you. How dare you speak to me like that?'

'Well, it's better than getting a jug of cold water and pouring it over your face,' Everton said. 'Take my remarks as a kind of verbal anti-hysteria slap, containing no malice.'

The servant appeared in the doorway. 'I beg your pardon, sir. I thought Madam was having hysterics.'

'Madam has stopped now,' Everton said. 'And you were right with your other guess, too. You heard a shot, and it killed your master. Now find me a flashlight, will you? I want to go and look for that dog.'

'Oh, Hugh, it's dangerous out there in the dark!' Lucy cried.

'Why is it dangerous for me and not for Atkinson?'

She took a small compact and a wispy handkerchief from her handbag, and dried her eyes ostentatiously. When she had finished Everton sat down beside her and took the handkerchief from her hand.

'It's dry,' he said. 'I mean, it feels dry. How absorbent lace is, after all that's been said against it. You wept gallons, the casual observer would have thought. You mustn't be so sure that every observer is casual.'

She looked at him as though she would like to use her claws. He held the handkerchief up and sniffed appreciatively.

'I can see it would make you feel better to hold this over your face. It's almost like breathing diamonds.'

She took the handkerchief from him, and they waited, looking at each other, until the servant came back with a bicycle lamp.

Everton let himself out of the front door, and walked forward a few steps. His feet made a grinding noise, but when he stopped the only sound was the gentle surge of the sea. The shadowy yacht still lay motionless down in the bay, and he watched it for a moment, expecting the dark sails to unfold and hang slack in the nearly still air. But there was nothing, not even the rattle of a chain or the splash of a buoy. Everton sighed, and walked slowly on, remembering again to whistle softly for the dog.

A light shone from a room on the first floor, and Everton, looking up at the balcony, decided morosely that he was standing outside the judge's room. He stood there in silence, looking at but not thinking of the ladder that leant against the wall next the balcony. His mind was on the fact of death, and as he stood, vulnerable in his sadness, lethargy lapped over his mind until the will to act had been submerged. He waited without movement for several minutes, until there crept into his numbed consciousness the knowledge that something behind him also waited. There was no noise, the silence was a positive thing. He fought for the will to move again, and then turned round suddenly and leapt at the outline of the figure on the lawn. His hand clutched a garment: a woman's voice cried, 'Let go, oh, let me go!' Amazement slackened his grasp, and the figure slipped away.

He stood, alert and trembling. The woman had vanished into the bushes. It was not his business to follow her. He was already, he remembered evasively, looking for a dog.

He whistled again, and thought he heard an answering whine. He turned on the torch, and moved it until the light fell on what might have been a bundle of old sacks. He walked towards the bundle.

'Here,' he said. 'What are you called? Here, Baxter.'

The bundle quivered and whined. Everton walked over and touched the dog gently. It snarled. 'That's the spirit, Baxter,' he said approvingly. 'You haven't met me before and I might be an enemy. The world is full of them. But I am not an enemy. I am the kind of man whose pockets would be full of bones if he hadn't changed his coat. I am glad to see that you find my conversation reassuring. It has a depressing effect on most people.' He talked on gently, running his hands over the dog as he spoke. 'You feel as though you've lived a very soft life, Baxter, but I think you have paid for it all in the last twelve hours. Ah.' His hand was passing down one of the hind legs when the dog yelped and snapped at him again. 'So it's broken. Well, it must be a great strain, carrying all that weight on three legs.'

He stopped to think. The dog must be carried in, but it could scarcely be tucked under one arm, like a Pekinese. Two hands would be needed to lift it, and it would probably bite his ears off. He bent over it and clasped his hands together round the chest and stood up. Fully extended, the dog was only a few inches shorter than himself. He had to keep the broken hind leg off the ground, and after a few steps his mouth was full of wool, too full to curse the fact that a car was roaring up the drive. That would be the police.

He shuffled on, and just as he reached the front door the car stopped, and four men joined him on the doorstep. His face was full of sheepdog, and he could not even give them an explanatory smile. When the servant opened the door he slid the dog gently down on to the thick carpet.

'His leg is broken,' he said. 'I think we need a vet. as well as a doctor, a photographer, a policeman, and a legal adviser.'

'I will telephone Mr. McCutcheon in the town,' the servant said. 'He has always attended when Baxter has indigestion or worms.'

Everton took a handkerchief from his pocket and wiped the dog hairs from his mouth. 'I'll take you into Mrs. Bath,' he said to the police party when he had finished. He noticed that they were looking at him with a kind of crafty distaste, and he was about to remind them that they were supposed to be impassive, but his synthetic instinct for caution helped him to keep back the words. It was easier to talk your way into trouble than out of it again.

When Lucy saw them she cried, 'The police!' and collapsed on the sofa once more in a brief semi-swoon. 'I'm sorry,' she said, recovering quickly. 'I must pull myself together and try to help.' She dabbed her astonishing eyes with the lace handkerchief. 'But I'm sorry,' she said, running her eyes like a love-ray over all the newcomers. 'I'm sorry, but I can't go into that room again.'

'It's upstairs on the right,' Everton said helpfully.

'You stay by the door, Jay, we'll go up,' one of the men said to the uniformed constable.

'Splendid,' Everton said. 'It's safe to lock the door now. The murderer has gone.' He was rewarded by a combined look of hostility from everyone; then the three men left the room.

'How do you mean the murderer has gone?' Lucy snapped.

'Well, how do you mean? Is he still here?' Everton asked with an air of real interest. 'I think I hear Atkinson's car in the drive now.'

Atkinson came in, gave Lucy the look of silent sympathy that one political prisoner might extend to another, and then, looking bereaved, sat down by the card table. He picked up the cards and began to shuffle them. It seemed to be his form of occupational therapy.

'What will they do?' Lucy asked tonelessly.

'Take photographs, and measurements, and fingerprints and so on,' Atkinson said, with an appearance of calm. 'Then they'll ask us all if we shot him and if we didn't, do we know who did?'

'And do we?' Everton asked.

Atkinson gave him a look of noble forbearance, like a horse who endures the barking of a dog.

'Public questioner number one is on his way,' Everton said.

The plain clothes man strolled into the room, looking more hostile than before.

'Which of you has been in the bedroom where the man, your husband,' he nodded to Lucy, 'was shot?'

Lucy brought out her handkerchief again. 'I found him,' she said in a quavering voice. 'Then I think I fainted.'

The look of hostility remained.

'We were playing bridge,' Atkinson corroborated. 'Four of us. We heard a shot. Mrs. Bath went up. When she didn't reappear I followed. I found her in a fainting condition, brought her down, went to fetch you. The other two—Cady, Everton, then went up to see for themselves.' He looked blandly at Everton. 'That is, I did not leave the house until the others came back downstairs.'

'And what did you see upstairs?' The plain clothes man asked Cady.

Cady looked hopeful.

'He was lying on his back, more or less,' he muttered. 'One arm over his face. A hole in his head, as far as you could see. And the room turned inside out.'

The man turned to the others and they nodded confirmation.

'If you can think of anything else, think of it now,' he said in a tired voice. 'Because the body isn't there any more.'

*

Half-an-hour's patient questioning hadn't, Everton thought, produced very many facts. All the rooms on the ground floor had windows or doors leading to the encircling verandah. The murderer could have chosen any one of five entrances or exits. If he had been an agile man, he could also have climbed up to any of the first floor balconies. It was the reverse of the sealed room murder.

'But the balconies are terribly shaky,' Lucy had said doubtfully. 'We're having them mended. If he had climbed up to one it would have been just as likely to come away in his hand. Unless he was a very small man.'

The inspector at this point had sent the constable up to investigate. He had come down with the report that the balcony in the judge's room was very shaky indeed, although some of the others weren't so bad. A small man might have come in there, but he wouldn't have cared to carry a dead body out that way. 'Must have come down the stairs,' he said.

Inspector Leigh expressed surprise that they had all sat around playing bridge while a man was shot and carried out of the house, and when Everton said gently that they had stopped playing after the murder and observed a long, uneasy silence, he was asked sharply how he had known a murder had been committed. He had no explanation to offer, although he knew that from the moment he heard the shot the reason for it had been clear. He was asked what they had done after the shot, and he said that they had sat around, talking and crying, and that he himself had gone out to find the dog that had howled just after the shot.

Leigh then took Atkinson into another room. They were to be questioned one by one.

'If he does it alphabetically, this is going to be tiresome,' Everton said. 'Atkinson, Bath, Cady, Everton. The rest of you will be settling down to your innocent slumbers by the time he gets to me.' He sat still with his head in his hands. In the end he would be questioned, and what was he to say? That he thought Atkinson was a man called Ronson who had thrown him in a river, years ago? Or was he to step very carefully, and put all his energies into being as ignorant of the matter as a St. Bernard dog of the binomial theorem? He closed his eyes, and let his headache bump his thoughts around. When he opened them, Jan was standing beside him.

'Hugh!' she said. 'Hugh! Oh, why are you here? Why did you have to come here to-night? Oh, what a fool, what an outrageous, abominable fool you are to get mixed up in this.'

'Ssh!' he said. 'Even my ears have walls. I refuse to listen to you.'

Jan put her hand to her head and stared at him, but he kept his eyes sullenly on the ground. She had every right and every reason to think him a fool, but a note of affectionate despair would have made her seem more lovable. She had always shown a tendency to reform others by direct accusation. A woman like Lucy, who was very happy to be with any man who combined a dramatic instinct with an admiration for herself, a woman who found the road to ruin immensely interesting, had her counter charms to set against Jan's wholesome, healthy attitude. The man who married Jan would have a well-run home, a cosy little wife, and not a moment to let his baser instincts out for a run round the yard. But look what had happened to the man who had married Lucy. The white hands clinging to the coat lapel would be preferable. Jan would never allow her husband to apply for a bullet in the head.

'Why did he marry Lucy, anyway?' he said aloud. 'She's the kind of woman who gets diamond necklaces in her Christmas stocking, not little bits of paper saying she's married.'

'Damn you! you're always talking of Lucy,' Jan said. 'I call you a fool, and at once you begin to talk of Lucy. And when I knew you before you used to keep me up till three in the morning, telling me you could never care for a woman like Lucy. Now when my uncle's been murdered because of Lucy you still talk about her and expect me to join in the delicious game of analysing her character.'

'And don't you want to?' Everton asked. 'You sound to me as though nothing in this world could stop you analysing her character.'

'Lucy brought you here to-night, didn't she?' Jan asked in an exhausted voice. 'And I suppose you must know why.'

'I've torn my mind up in strips and thrown it out of my ears, wondering why,' Everton said.

'Because she's absolutely certain,' Jan said contemptuously, 'that you'd tell any lie and commit most crimes just for the sake of hearing her purr.'

'Not true,' Everton said, shutting his eyes. 'I don't intend to tell any lies, and I don't need to tell any lies.'

'Perhaps you don't have to lie,' Jan said, 'but I'm sure you're already taking care not to ask yourself obvious questions.'

'Such as?'

She looked at him and shook her head. 'If you can't think of them for yourself you won't try to find the answers anyway,' she said, and turned away, looking as dejected as a child that finds its Christmas stocking empty.

He stood up and put his arm lightly round her shoulders.

'I do love you, Jan,' he said. 'I'll ask all the questions and find all the answers and be a six-column hero in the newspapers. And I'm truly not a slave. The trouble about Lucy is she thinks I am a slave and I've always been too lazy to break my paper chain and walk away. And now Hawk-face is at the door. He wants to ask if I've been killing many judges recently.'

4

INSPECTOR LEIGH WAS A SHADOWY, YAWNING FIGURE, WHO, SEEN through Everton's exhausted eyes, seemed to swell and diminish as he leant across the desk. The two men looked at each other silently for a moment, both struggling for perception. Leigh was a flabby, loose man, with a truculence that suggested he was not the perfect bureaucrat. The truculence now seemed to be directed against Everton, but there was nothing the Inspector could hold against him except the dog.

'How is the dog?' Everton asked. 'Did the vet. come?'

'The dog,' Leigh said dreamily. 'Oh, yes. The vet. came. The dog's hind leg is broken and it has various abrasions.' He paused. 'I haven't had much time so far to think of the dog, but now I've thought about it I'd like to ask you if you see anything peculiar in what I suppose amateurs would call the case of the dog?'

'He did bark in the night,' Everton said with a faint smile. 'At least he howled. But that was after the shot.'

'Perhaps this was one of the shots that wasn't a shot, like the books,' Leigh said, yawning again. 'I mean, perhaps the shot was a fake and then the dog howled and then his master was killed?'

'I see what you mean,' Everton said. 'The judge went upstairs, fired a shot at the dog that broke its leg. It howled. That frightened a cat, placed in a pre-arranged spot. The cat bolted, setting off a photo-electric cell that released a trigger that fired a shot, silenced, that killed the judge. I like these scientific murders.'

'Clever, aren't you?' the Inspector said, waking up.

'It was you who suggested the shot was a fake,' Everton said wearily. 'There was only one shot, the dog howled after it.'

'And then?'

Everton hesitated. 'He was killed by a shot, so far as I could see.'

'Close range?'

'I don't know,' Everton said. 'It's not my subject.'

'Big hole, large hole, powder burns?'

Everton shuddered and closed his eyes. 'There was no gun in sight. His arm was over his eyes. There was a hole. Not big. It was his right arm over his eyes. There was blood—not a lot. I didn't look any more.'

'Now tell me what else you know,' Leigh invited. 'I mean about the dog.'

'I'm told he wasn't a watchdog,' Everton said, happy to be released from contemplation of death.

'Told by whom?' Leigh asked quickly.

'By the judge himself, earlier this evening.'

'I'll check on that,' Leigh said, and Everton was suddenly enraged.

'I'm not telling you lies,' he shouted. 'There's no reason why I should. Check as much as you like. Bath said the dog wasn't a watchdog, and the others heard him.'

'If he wasn't a watchdog, why did he have to be got out of the way?' Leigh asked.

'If he had been a watchdog,' Everton said, 'I suppose the murderer would have killed him. Not stolen him for the day, beaten him up, and let him go.'

'There will be an explanation for that,' Leigh said. 'There's an explanation for everything, in the end, and it's usually the obvious one. I see you haven't had practice in thinking about the obvious. Anything else about the dog?'

'No.'

'Nothing at all?' Leigh asked, in rather exaggerated surprise.

'I think there is something,' Everton said slowly. 'It's been worrying me, only I haven't actually thought of it. Wait. The servant said… Yes, I know. The servant said he would phone for the vet. You say the vet. has been. So the phone worked. Did it?'

Leigh nodded.

'When the body was discovered the phone was out of order,' Everton said. 'They mended it quickly, didn't they?'

The Inspector had been listening to Everton without looking at his face. He was a man who very often kept his eyes on his own hands, particularly when he was listening. This often gave him the appearance of nearly exhausted patience. When his eyes flickered up quickly and slid away again they seemed angry.

Now he sighed and said: 'Odd that you should notice about the telephone.' He let his glance slide up to Everton's face and off again. 'It wasn't out of order,' he said. 'It's one of these extension phones where the extension can be switched off. The phone was on in the library and switched off in the hall. No one thought of it at the time. Not even you. That's all.'

'Not even me,' Everton agreed. 'It was the first time in my life I'd been in the house. There were others who lived in the house or were constant visitors. It's the first time I'd met any of them, except Mrs. Bath.'

Leigh picked over this statement like a parrot looking for food among the nutshells, then he shifted his sly glance quickly up and down again, and Everton realized that he was committed to his lie. It was too late now to begin the long story about Atkinson's resemblance to Ronson. It would be better to stick to the lie: to correct it would make him seem dishonest.

'Mrs. Bath is an old friend?' the Inspector murmured.

'We used to belong to the same set,' Everton said with an appearance of great candour.

'And what set was that?'

Everton's mind moved slowly back into the past. What kind of people had he known and mixed with? People who had money, but never quite enough. What had they talked of, at those innumerable parties? Mostly of money, because they knew they had special rights in the oyster and limousine field. They had talked of how to pick up easy money, how to live tax free, how to avoid the currency regulations and the cold winter and the shortage of heat, light, passports, petrol, real Scotch, or whatever was, at the moment, hard to obtain. They had talked of where to place bribes and how to triumph over the Customs. They were the inheritors of death duties, the self-appointed new élite, the people above the trifling irritating laws. No one could mix with them without developing proprietorial instincts towards all money. The life they led had its risks, and their hectic appreciation of these exhausted them spiritually. Their emotions were casual; intellectually they were as bare as a beech tree in December. Lucy, with her taste for drama, her passionate conceit, her feline energy, and her reckless curiosity, had blazed among them like a fire in a dead wood. She had been married then, but the judge had appeared curiously non-existent—and how, indeed, could he have accompanied her into these shallows of depravity?

'What set?' Everton repeated. 'Oh, just people who believed in having a good time. I suppose I was only on the edge of it. I had to knock off occasionally and do some work.'

The Inspector took his eyes from his own hands and studied Everton's. He said nothing: silence was one of his weapons.

Everton's fingers were tightening on the arm of his chair. He tried to order the stiffness out of them.

'As you were about to ask,' he said lightly, 'in the Foreign Office. I worked in the Foreign Office. That is, I was moved to—to the Embassy in Paris. I was a kind of menial.'

'And now?'

'I'm another kind of menial.'

'Have a cigarette,' the Inspector said. 'Take your time. I'm bound to ask what you do now.'

Everton took a cigarette and the Inspector watched him with gentle interest while he tried three times to strike a match. When the cigarette was lit Everton was so absorbed in the work of smoking it that for a minute or two he was able to be as silent as the Inspector. Then he sighed, and said:

'I work for a travel agency. I'm employed to go round and report on the amenities of various hotels.' He waited, hopeful of being interrupted by a question. None came and he plunged on wildly. 'You might call me President of the Bad Food Club. You know, I find where the curry soup is deepest and the mince has the biggest lumps of gristle. And cod—I keep a sharp eye out for cod, cold fried eggs, and yesterday's potatoes. I'm training myself to be the opposite of a gourmet.'

'Now, that's what I'd call quite a change from being in the Foreign Office. Do you like it better?'

'No,' Everton said, and waited.

'If you could just give me the details of when and how you worked for the Foreign Office, so that we can make our routine check,' the Inspector began, but Everton interrupted him.

'Let's get it over,' he said. 'I resigned from the Embassy because I didn't want to be there when I was arrested. I-I took the opportunity to borrow someone else's cheque-book. It happened to be a bank where I didn't have an account, but I put my name to a cheque for three hundred pounds and managed to cash it with a man I knew. He ran one of those night clubs—you know, the sort of place where farmers spend their pork-and-veal money. I thought I was raising some cash in a day or two, before the cheque came back. Then of course I could have told him some story about the wrong cheque-book. But it didn't turn out that way. I might have done something, but shortly afterwards I fell into the Seine and there was a warrant out for me before I'd finished waking up in hospital. I was unable to restore the money and in any case I had no defence to offer. I spent a few months in a French jail thinking it all over.' He had been speaking in a high, dry, controlled voice, and now he sat perfectly still.

'It might have been worse,' the Inspector said soothingly. 'Giving away high-class scientific secrets or something of the sort. Fraud. Only three hundred pounds and then you try to drown yourself in the river. That's what you said, wasn't it? You must have a highly developed moral sense,' the Inspector said warmly. 'I've known all kinds of crooked types, but I've never met one who tried to do himself in over such a small matter—unless, of course, there were other things to be taken into consideration. Before you made this admirable moral gesture into the water, did you have something else on your mind?'

'No,' Everton said sullenly. 'You're a queer kind of policeman,' he added, more loudly.

'I'm not a queer kind of policeman,' Leigh said patiently. 'I'm just the usual kind of policeman. That is, I can see when a story hangs together and when it doesn't. Now, when you were in jail, you said you thought it all over. And what conclusion did you come to?' he asked conversationally.

'It wouldn't interest a policeman,' Everton said angrily. 'I decided to change my social habits, that's all.'

'Falling head first into rivers. Being in sudden need of three hundred pounds and helping yourself—did all that arise from being one of a set?' the Inspector asked.

'It must have been an interesting crowd. And Mrs. Bath was one of it. Now, how did you get to know Mrs. Bath?'

'I knew her niece by marriage. She introduced us. I hadn't seen either of them—the niece or Mrs. Bath—for about three years until I ran into them both to-night. Mrs. Bath asked me here for a drink.'

'Knowing your history?' the Inspector asked gently.

'Knowing a great deal of it.'

'And you hadn't met any of the other people in this house before?'

'No,' Everton said.

'And your statement about being downstairs with the other three when the shot was fired holds good?'

'I've already told you about the rest of the evening. May I go now, or am I to be arrested for murder because I once passed a bad cheque?'

'You may go,' the Inspector said, and Everton, whom practice had made sensitive to contempt, felt despair closing in on him. 'But first you must give me details and dates of your Embassy and prison service. I don't suppose we shall turn anything up against you, but it would be a joke if there was an atom bomb mixed up in it somewhere after all. Or drugs. You've never touched the morphia trade, I suppose?' he asked with pretended hopefulness. 'God knows what you had put in the diplomatic bag with your conscience before you tipped yourself into the river. Now, I'm only joking, Everton, don't take it seriously. I'll just mark down these little facts. Dates.' He made a note on the back of an envelope. 'And now you may go, but not out of the district for a day or two. I think it would pay you to be as helpful as you can in this case.'

'And how would it pay me?' Everton asked sullenly, his hand on the door.

'I wasn't talking about money. I was talking about morality,' the Inspector said. 'I wouldn't waste my breath on the word if you were a different type of person. But suicide! You're the queerest crook I ever met. Could we drive you back to the hotel?'

'I'll walk,' Everton said.

'You look as though you'd sooner go for a ride with a crocodile,' the Inspector said jovially. 'Well, we'll have our little talk later.'

Everton, who had hoped that the little talk was over, left the room in misery, but although his mind was filled with emptiness and darkness, the relief of leaving the house was so great that the level of his despair sank a little as he walked slowly along the grey road beside the sea.

A light still shone in the house next to the Bath's. Lucy had said that a mad woman lived there. Perhaps she had shot the judge with an airgun. And Jan? Where and how did Jan come in? She had said a lot about asking the right questions.

"I'll get on to that in the morning," he told himself, when he was back in his silent hotel bedroom.

He lay and thought about the past.

It had been a splendid but anachronistic gesture to ruin himself to save a woman, although he had not precisely intended ruin to be the outcome of the affair.

If he had made his gesture forty years earlier, he thought, staring at shoes that had to be untied, he could have found redemption planting sugar-cane or coconuts in some empty island where the natives would rapidly have learnt to worship him. But there was a waiting list now for all islands and plenty of vacancies in the seedy jobs at home. He was a beachcomber who had taken society as his beach, but one day he would rejoin the community. He was determined to build himself up again into a man who held no grudges, desired no revenge, felt no bitterness, hated no human being. A few hours ago he had been not unhappy, he had at least been suspended in a neutral state, not far from the hope of a future where he might face some of his old world without embarrassing it. The old world, or part of it, had intruded too soon. He had collapsed into misery at the sound of Lucy's voice, and when he saw Atkinson, who might, who must be, Ronson, security had moved round a bend in the tunnel. That might be where security lived. The tunnel was circular.

He realized now that sleep was a prize that lay somewhere further along the night. In bed he would find nothing but the magnified horror of his own ruin. Shivering, he put his feet to the ground and went to the window. He drew the curtains and looked out over the sparkling black water, thinking of the yacht he had seen from Lucy's house. Despair would become a negative, even a dead, emotion, if he could cast out to sea and sail alone for hours or days or years. The lazy softness of the sea wind, the emergencies of the storm, these carried the message of eternity and allowed the present to settle down inside its grain of sand.

He stared along the shadow of the moon, trying to let his mind sink into the depths beneath the golden stream. He was falling back into quietness when he saw, or thought he saw, the black shadow of a ship sliding across the moon-path and along the coast. Was the yacht, the purpose and business of the yacht, one of the questions Jan had said he was afraid to ask?

He had loved Jan once. She had wrapped him round in faith and loyalty until it became imperative for him to break away. His emotions were settling down in a feather bed: safety and certainty were maddening him. Then he had met Lucy and the excitement had wakened him up again. Now he felt ready to welcome safety with a bunch of flowers, hand-picked at dawn. But that was now, in the small hours; to-morrow was as likely as ever to offer a complete change of performance.

What had Jan said? She had accused him, although in more words, of being a piece of sealing wax that melted when Lucy held a match to it. Lucy? He thought she had been offering him shares in a limited liability company where the shareholders were not allowed to ask questions. The Inspector had told him he had a moral obligation to be active on the side of the police. He did not feel himself to be in debt to the police. Help might come to him from someone, some-where, but none would come from the police. He had been lectured to all the evening, he thought, self-pity rising with exhaustion. Even the judge, with his talk of accounts to be balanced—the judge had been a drum, and when one conventional thought hit him he had reverberated until he was hit by another. But the judge was dead, and death was as fatal to pride as to flesh. There was nothing left of him now but a little space in the world that would soon be filled. Everton, fixed in his irrational guilt, thought of his conversation with the dead man, and realized that the pomposity had been a paper shield held before a sad emptiness. Had the judge suspected his own mortality? Had he thought of himself as a man who could stretch out his hand and touch death? Everton heard a car murmuring along the road and suddenly shuddered.

'A lot of activity goes on around these parts at night,' he said aloud. 'But it's not my business. Leave it to the police and lift your hat to everyone.'

He went back to bed, determined to think of nothing, but screw-ing the murder round and round in his mind. He was sure only of the fact that Lucy, Atkinson, and Cady had been with him when the shot was fired. "Look elsewhere," he told himself. "Look at Jan, or the mad waiter, or the perfect manservant, or even at the woman poet who lives next door. Look at no one. Keep your head in your own sack. The view is better."

When he fell asleep he dreamt of a dog lying across his face.

5

HE WOKE LATE THE NEXT MORNING, AND HE HAD THE IMPRESsion that he had been wakened by silence. The sea was still; there was no noise of wind or of rain. There was no noise of clattering dishes, humming lifts, snarling vacuum cleaners. An hotel without the morning noises it arranges to disturb the guests seems as menacing as a condemned cell. He washed and dressed slowly, and went downstairs to a dining room deserted by everyone but a resolutely smiling manager.

'I am sorry. I am afraid you have missed breakfast. It is over. It is eleven.'

'Some coffee will do,' Everton said.

'I am sorry. There is no more coffee.'

'You seem to be organizing a real drive to keep visitors away,' Everton said in a mild tone. 'You'll never get your gold star from the tourists' association this way. Do you often refuse to feed people?'

'After breakfast the staff went on strike. It is very unusual,' the manager said, 'but also it has happened before. I tell you what I do. I fire the lot.'

'That must make you popular with the Caterers' Union. And what do the guests do until you get some more staff? Sign up with a fishing boat, or cook herring over a candle in their bedrooms?'

'You think it is a joke,' the manager said, smiling painfully. 'The guests all but you are already on the beach. If they come back there is no lunch.' A new thought struck him. 'I shall be ruined.'

'It looks like it, unless there is a tidal wave,' Everton agreed.

'But I might already have obtained some new staff from the agency. Then less money, although some, will be lost.'

'You won't lose any money over me,' Everton said in a kind voice. 'I'm on an expense account. And I'll cook myself some breakfast.'

'Guests, alas, are not allowed in the kitchen. The Caterer's Union would object. A powerful body. One would not care to offend it.'

'You've offended it already, or why are they striking?' Everton said. 'I'm going to the kitchen.'

'I'm sorry, sir.'

'How do you know what union I belong to? I might be a powerful member of the Association of Agents Provocateurs, for all you know.' He brushed the manager gently off his arm and pushed his way through the swing doors. He had always been attracted by doors that said Staff Only.

There were four men in the kitchen, sitting round the great wooden table, and they were engaged in what seemed the fascinating occupation of dealing out pound notes like cards. The short-sighted waiter, wearing glasses about a quarter of an inch thick, and looking familiar, as though he had once been a Cabinet Minister, was holding a bundle of notes in his left hand. With his right hand he was dealing a note to the melancholy barman. He was looking, not at the notes, but at the faces of the other men, and the other men were looking at the money. When Everton entered, all four men set like fired clay.

'You look like a film that has stopped,' Everton said chattily. 'Why not go on with your game?'

He was measuring them carefully, with a dismayed feeling that they were ready to burst into violence. Three of them wore overcoats. They had the appearance of men who were leaving in a hurry. The fourth, a pale, fat, short man, was in a blue jersey and flannel trousers. He was the kind of man who should have been smiling, but the smiling muscles seemed tired, and his face was not pale, but grey with exhaustion.

There were some cups and a coffee pot on the table, and while Everton still surveyed the men, the short-sighted waiter put down the note he held in his right hand, picked up the coffee pot, and threw it at Everton's face. The manager, standing behind Everton, caught him as he staggered back, and dragged him out of the room. The men round the table plunged out of their picture into a blizzard of action: Everton tried to lash free of the man who held him, but his arms were being wrenched back in a police grip, coffee was running down his face, and his head felt as though it had been hit by a bus.

The manager dragged him back through the dining room to the lounge, dropped him on a sofa, and stood over him.

'The man was wrong to do it,' he said softly, 'but I have explained that guests are not allowed in the kitchen. The Caterers' Union forbids it.'

Everton felt the lump on his head and said nothing. He was having his usual second thoughts, and he found that it was not, after all, so desirable to fight his way back to the kitchen to beat the others up single-handed.

'These men are in an ugly mood. Trades Unionists. You know what they are like,' the manager said.

'And I suppose they were writing to the Branch Secretary,' Everton said. 'And the money—just counting out their tips?'

The manager looked aloof. 'Good waiters are hard to find. I take what I can get from the agency.'

'You've got something very odd there,' Everton said. He sat up and took a handkerchief from his pocket and wiped some of the coffee from his face. 'Tell me, what's the name of the agency?'

'The Coastal Universal Service,' the manager replied automatically. He was listening, and his energies were concentrated on what he heard. Everton, too, began to listen for something other than words.

'The agency will perhaps send me some others to replace those who are leaving,' the manager said absently.

'Those who have left, I think,' Everton said, listening to the car that had started up outside. 'It's safe to let me go now.'

The manager, who had been bending over Everton, straightened and moved away. Everton suddenly twisted over the back of the sofa and jumped to the window. A small green van was moving down the road.

'I thought I heard a car,' he said, turning and grinning at the manager, who had an ugly, pouncing look on his face. 'But it's only a lorry. Now I think I'll go and wash the coffee off, unless the water in my room has been unionized.'

He turned and walked out of the lounge, shutting the door behind him with terrible relief. "XXB 9847," he whispered, and he repeated the number again and again until he reached his room. Then he wrote it in his notebook and sat down to think. He felt the lump on his forehead, and his submerged truculence began to rise.

He went out in the corridor and called loudly for the manager. He heard the man pounding up the stairs, and he stood and waited for him.

'I thought I'd better tell you,' he said loudly. 'There's been a murder round here and I've been asked by the police not to leave. You can't throw me out unless you're prepared for a series of long, long chats with the police. You'd better go down to the kitchen and get me some coffee now. I'll have it internally.'

The two men looked at each other, then the manager bowed.

'Certainly, sir,' he said gravely. 'But I hope it is understood you do not interfere with staff matters.'

He turned to go.

'Wait a minute,' Everton said. 'You'd better get your Trade Unionists to call the strike off and come back. The police will want to see them. That waiter with the glasses and the barman were present at some of the murdered man's last conversations on earth. I shall certainly remember to mention this to the police, although, you understand, I don't intend to interfere with staff matters. If your men have vanished, the police will search for them. The quietest thing will be to get them back.'

'It is true that we all wish for quiet,' the manager said, smiling.

'I also want to be left alone,' Everton said, as the manager went downstairs.

Was that true? he asked himself, as he turned back to his room. If he'd wanted to be left alone he shouldn't have gone with Lucy the night before. Everything that had happened since had proceeded from that error, even although he now felt there to be a gratuitous malice on the part of everyone he met. Resentment was slashing into the control he had set on his mind, and a rage for action was bursting through. Once before in his life rage had surged up; his months in prison had given him the opportunity to press it down again. This time he would let it mount. For the last fifteen hours he had been treated like the clown in some brutal medieval palace. Lucy, the judge, Cady, Jan, the police—in their different ways they had all insulted him, and a member of some sort of waiters' gang had thrown a coffee pot in his face. And Atkinson—had Atkinson threatened him, tried to bribe him, or been content to use him for a secret, malevolent purpose? Whatever Atkinson had done, it could be added to what the others had done. Now all the insults merged together, and he found his mind black with anger. The reasonable man was in the whirlpool again. Instinct must be allowed its turn.

Now that he had decisively cast aside the passive role he felt happy and relieved. He would go and dig in the laundry basket with the rest of them. The first thing was to see Jan and convince her he was ready to ask some questions. But when he stepped into the corridor and found the hotel still silent, he moved Jan back to second place. The first thing was to look at the rooms that the violent waiters had lived in.

It was a small hotel. There were only half-a-dozen bedrooms for residents; the waiters' rooms would be on the floor above.

He went up the stairs quietly, opened the first door he saw. An unmade bed; dirty water in the wash bowl; a chest of drawers, empty; a cupboard that contained only two soiled white coats. Had the waiter decided to give up being a waiter? He had left in a hurry. The next room was larger, neater, as empty of apparent clues. The third had a brass bedstead with tumbled linen on the floor beside it, a stench of strong tobacco; a mixture of cigarette ends on an ashtray—not all, surely, smoked by one man. On the floor there was a bowl with a little moisture in it. A spittoon? There was another smell, on the whole unpleasant, fighting against the tobacco. He left the room and went downstairs.

On the first floor he met a chambermaid, playing in what looked an aimless manner with a vacuum cleaner.

'If it's the gents you want,' she said without much interest, 'it's not up there, sir.'

'Do you always start work so late?' Everton asked, lingering.

'I turned up as usual,' she said sourly, 'but the manager sent me back again. Said there was some guests wanted a nice late sleep without noise. Honeymoon couple, I'll bet.'

'You clean all this floor by yourself?' Everton asked sympathetically.

'Oh, it's grind the work out of you now the hours is limited,' she said. 'Honeymoon couple! He'll have to pay the proper hours whatever story he tells.'

Everton went downstairs slowly. Naturally all the work in the hotel could not be carried out by the very peculiar little gang he had seen in the kitchen. The innocent, although unalluring, woman he had spoken to was certainly a daily; there would be other dailies, probably fobbed off with other stories. The gang had needed a little peace and freedom from interruption. They had obtained it crudely and inefficiently. The woman who did not believe in honeymoons was also free from loyalty to her employers.

In the dining room he drank his coffee slowly. The manager had once again achieved a smooth face.

'You will be pleased to hear, sir, that I have been engaged in successful negotiations with the Caterers' Union. The staff will probably return,' he said.

'I hope you get your cooks and scrubbers back too,' Everton said. 'What did you tell them? That there were some cockroaches in the kitchen who wanted the morning to themselves?'

The manager turned away abruptly, and Everton smiled. He was glad of the chance to hit back. Now for Lucy—and, of course, Jan. He went out to hire a car.

When he reached the Colonial house he saw that there were policemen in the garden and men on the beach. They were searching the innocent soil for the body, although they had only the word of four people that the body had existed. Four unreliable people.

He walked round the house, hoping in a moderate way that he would find Jan without having to see Lucy first.

Two men at the back of the house were struggling with a ladder, and a policeman watched them with the disapproving air of a man whose hands were tied, but only temporarily.

'Mending the balcony,' he said in amazement. 'You can't mend a balcony when there's been violence.'

Lucy appeared on the verandah beneath.

'Of course they can mend the balcony,' she said in annoyance. 'They've started the job and naturally they must finish it. I don't want policemen falling to the ground on all sides. You can stay and see they don't take away any smoking revolvers in their pockets.'

Everton felt cold and quite unmoved by Lucy's slightly ravaged beauty, for so it seemed in the sunlight.

'Hello,' he said cheerily. 'Let the balcony stay as it is. Unless you feel you've passed the Juliet stage of your development.'

'Hugh! How can you joke now?'

'It's through my tears,' he said. 'Now tell me something. Why did you ask me here last night?'

'I was so surprised to see you,' she said in calm, conventional tones. 'And don't try to twist it into anything else,' she added in quiet warning. The policeman, with an English diffidence that seemed out of keeping with his uniformed role, had turned away. 'I didn't ask you to be in the hotel last night, did I? I was just overjoyed to see you.'

'And now?'

'I'll be overjoyed to see the last of you if you hang around making insinuations.'

'I'm going to hang around with my insinuations for a long time,' he said softly, with his eyes on the policeman's back. If the man had good hearing, he was probably using it. 'Do you know why, Lucy? Because I can't stay away from you.' He thought the policeman's neck was darkening.

'I'm not used to hearing you talk like this,' Lucy said suspiciously. 'What's happened?'

'Nothing,' he said. 'Will you ask me in?' He jerked a thumb towards the policeman's back. 'I want to match a knitting pattern.'

He stepped on to the verandah beside her. 'Tell me, Lucy, how long have you known Atkinson?'

'He's a neighbour of ours,' she said. 'We've been here about two years and he lived around when we came.'

'And who pays for his drinks? Or, if that's unfair, what pays for his drinks?'

'He's just a man,' she said. 'A man with a private income.'

'A gentleman. The question I always ask about gentlemen is what they do with their leisure.'

'I don't know much about his leisure.'

'Is he always busy when he comes here?'

'He was a friend of my husband's,' she said, turning away.

'Is he going to help you choose your widow's weeds?'

'When I knew you in the past the nicest thing about you was that you went away without being asked to go,' she said, but she smiled at him in a different manner. He caught his heart as it rose and carefully pushed it down. He was never again going to jump for the cardboard biscuits Lucy held out to him, and he thought she had a handful of them behind her back.

'I must go,' she said, with a smile that was the equivalent of a long-distance kiss.

'Oh, wait, please,' he said, and she looked gratified, but not surprised, like a cat that is given its usual dish of cream after it has mewed.

'How would you like me to wind up my mechanical brain and set it at this murder?' he asked.

'I shouldn't like you to get into trouble, Hugh,' she said, and this time there was no gratified purr in her voice. 'Now I must go.'

'Tell Jan I can give her a lift back to town if she's here and not in irons,' he called after her, and then waited with some confidence for Jan's appearance. He felt that Jan would always come when he called her.

While he waited, the policeman approached him, without being called, and he gave the man his name and the address of the hotel.

'I feel you have details of part one of the conversation,' he told the man. 'If you want to make notes about part two, just summarize. Say I called to pay my respects to the widow.'

Jan appeared, looking a little less pretty than usual. A slightly haggard appearance added to Lucy's dramatic charm, but Jan was a girl whose attractions depended to some extent on healthy habits, like going to bed early, walking in the fresh air, and eating something green every day. She probably hadn't been able to fit them all in since her uncle was killed. He kept these thoughts to himself. He wanted her to think of him with friendly respect.

For the first few minutes in the car, the conversation was stiff and the meeting unrewarding.

Halfway back to the town, just before they reached the splash of boarding houses, he stopped the car.

'Now,' he said, 'for all I know, this is a straight A equals B therefore C case. What gives you the idea it's algebra for senior students only?'

'First,' she said soberly, 'I don't want you to discount what I say because I don't like Lucy. You can dislike someone and still see the truth about them.'

'Not if the truth is pleasant. But I don't for a moment suppose it is,' he added quickly.

'Very well. I've known for months that something was wrong. First of all there's the company. Atkinson and Cady have been at the house all the time. They're not the types my uncle would normally have chosen as friends.'

'Your uncle was about seventy. That isn't the age he would normally have chosen to be.' She looked puzzled. 'I mean there were many things about your uncle's age and condition he would not have chosen. He'd lived for years in a position where he could order eminent counsel to change their green socks for black ones because the eye of the court was offended by colour. He could tell defendants that they lived in a moral swamp and plaintiffs that their minds were deficient. He could insult his fellow mortals with more impunity than a fish porter and take a stronger moral line than a bishop. And all the time he had the satisfaction of knowing that he was in the right—the impartial administrator of the law. Then suddenly it's taken away from him. He is probably nettled by income tax, afflicted by old man's meanness, cut off in this seaside town from cackling legal wit—and from minds trained to the special intelligence of his own. Then you complain he associates with people he wouldn't normally have known. He had to associate with someone, or die.'

'So he associated. And he died,' Jan said sharply. 'You always go on talking until you disprove your own case, Hugh.'

'You're getting to be like your uncle,' he said sourly. 'Now tell me about these people.'

'You've met Cady. He's so stupid that he'd try to sell eggs to a hen. There's a theory that he has some kind of business interest, but it would pay any employer to bribe him to leave the country. Cady is interested in sailing. So is Matthews, another friend of theirs. He looks like a sea captain who has lost his certificate for drowning his passengers for the insurance. Atkinson—he has a quiet voice. I've never heard him say a word out of place, but when you add up his conversation there's no result. It seems unnatural. Even disquieting. I think they're a gang and Lucy knows what they're up to.'

'Were they up to murder?'

Jan looked away from him. 'My uncle was very heavily insured,' she said.

'Since when and how much?'

'I don't know since when. He took out heavy insurance in favour of his first wife, I think. She died so long ago I can't remember her. I think he increased the insurance after marrying Lucy. He's insured for about forty thousand pounds. It may be natural. He wasn't a rich man.'

'That's one of your relative terms. But I suppose if his bank account hit my bank account there would be the kind of battle that occurs when a steam roller passes over a mouse.'

'He had probably about sixty thousand pounds,' Jan said. 'I think half goes to Lucy and half to me.'

'I hope you've been able to give a ladylike account of where you were when the shot was fired.'

'I was at a dance,' Jan said, in a very controlled manner. 'Miles away. The police are probably interviewing my partners now. It's probably lucky that I wasn't brooding alone on the beach.'

'I hope you didn't spend too much time in the ladies' room adjusting your corsage,' Everton said moodily. 'Now, don't be insulted, Jan. In a murder the first voice the police listen to is money, and when there's sixty thousand pounds to be divided up, money shouts.'

Jan was very quiet, and when she spoke it was in a subdued voice. 'There was something wrong with my uncle before he died. He's been behaving queerly for weeks. He's always been a smooth man with no crevices for dirt to get into. No crevices for new ideas, for doubts, either. But something in his texture seemed to change. The surface cracked, and he was full of uneasiness and amazement. He used to be very direct and always sure he was right, and suddenly he was full of double meanings and uncertainty.'

All she meant, Hugh thought, was that the old man was beginning to crack up. Later than most people, he had reviewed his life's work and found it unsatisfactory. Even the young, with their opportunities for redemption in battle, business, or bed, could be attacked by misery and emptiness. A man of seventy in exile needed a solid store of complacency.

'How was he on hobbies?' he asked. 'Did he collect flint arrow heads or criminal statistics? Was he fond of sailing, or is that Lucy?'

'He hated boats, and I think Lucy does too. She likes to sail on things the size of the *Queen Mary*. Smaller boats disarrange her hair.'

'In the midst of sorrow what cats we are,' Everton said approvingly. 'So it's Cady and Matthews who sail. Can you tell me any more about them?'

'No. Except that Cady is the kind of young man who has a girl in a hat shop. I think he reads poetry to her. He is interested in things of the mind.'

'Is that why he likes Lucy?'

'A man can't be thinking all the time.'

Everton started the car again. Jan's attitude to Lucy was excusable, but monotonous.

'What hat shop?' he asked. 'Cady's girl friend?'

'It's called Jane or Ann or Diana or something like that. Susan's, that's what it is. It's in the High Street. Why?'

'The only way to a woman's head is through the hat. Here we are, my dear. I'll see you to-morrow.'

He stopped the car, and she sat waiting. He knew that she wanted a gesture of affection, but he thought with sudden malice that women had too easy a time, playing the passive rôle. It meant they could always console themselves afterwards by the thought they hadn't been the initiators of trouble. If he kissed her now she would be pleased, then later on she would be able to tell him it was all his fault.

He smiled at her briefly. She looked very gay, and with a casual good-bye stepped out of the car.

6

FOR A SEASIDE TOWN, IT WAS A VERY ELEGANT HAT SHOP. THE window was swathed in dark blue satin. From the centre of this rose an elongated, plaster model of a woman's head and shoulders. The shoulders were narrow, the neck was long and thin. With eyes half-closed for mystery, she looked down a nose that had been lengthened to show contempt for possible customers. She wore a scarlet skull cap with one feather curling over the back of her narrow head. It looked like a Red Indian head dress, plucked. There was no price ticket. Its absence would certainly frighten away women looking for ten shilling bargains, and might inspire the rich with confidence.

Inside, the shop continued its hostility to the thin-pursed by containing only three hats, all too insubstantial for economy. A girl in a black dress, who had modelled her facial expression on the plaster cast in the window, was looking in austere distaste at her one customer, an elderly woman whose clothes suggested a habit of rushing at fashion like a gallant old horse approaching fences it knows it cannot take.

'It's not how I look that matters,' she was saying. 'Looks are unimportant to the developed personality. But I do feel that hats can put you out of touch. Without a hat, there is nothing,' she stopped, in apparent doubt, 'nothing but a few mathematical conceptions between your head and the stars. With a hat, you might as uselessly be under the red tiled roof of a bungalow. Space has gone. You understand?' She removed from her head a pink hat trimmed with one white flower the size of a clenched fist and returned it to the girl. 'You do understand?' she repeated.

The girl's face was pinched with suspicion.

'And if I'm to be shut off from space,' the woman said, 'I think I would prefer the small consolation of losing the stars in something that took the weight off my chin.'

'Madam wants something plainer,' the girl said hopelessly.

'I think I surrender too much in a hat shop,' the woman said. 'When I sit untrammelled on my cliff, watching the emanations come and go, my mind is far from hats. Usually. Sometimes I think of people, and then I see them. If they are frightened, I feel them. I want to cry out, Go Back. Stay Away. I sit on the cliff at all hours,' she added, in a very practical voice. She picked up the hand mirror, and, for the first time, saw Everton, who had been standing quietly just inside the door.

'I'll look in again,' she said, glancing sharply at Everton as she gathered up her handbag. Her large, flat brown eyes tried to sum up his purpose, but he remained silent and composed until she had left.

'Dopey,' the girl said, relaxing from the pose of austerity that had already become strained.

Everton approached her. 'I want to buy a hat for a friend,' he said brazenly. 'Medium height, medium-sized head, medium looks, always wears medium hats. Do you have one?'

The girl turned slowly towards him. She had a commonplace, narrow face, but her eyes looked dramatic. They were needling with suspicion now, but as she studied Everton's melancholy, friendly face they softened into amusement.

'Wouldn't your friend—ladies usually like to choose their own hats.'

'Not this one,' Everton said confidently. 'I know what she likes. And I know what she looks like. A bit like you, only—well, never mind.'

The girl looked down, although not soon enough to hide her small, pleased smile. Everton noticed she wore too much eye-shadow.

'If you tried on a hat or two,' he said, 'I'd have an idea.' He pointed. 'What about that blue straw thing?'

The girl, smiling a little distantly now, like a woman of many affairs, sat in front of the mirror and pulled on the blue straw hat. Everton stood beside her and gazed admiringly.

'It looks delicious,' he said. 'Could you try another?'

She turned away, languorous, lost in the pleasure of being loved. Or so he hoped. He was sure that her cautious instinct had slipped, and when her back was towards him he leant forward and gripped her shoulders.

'Let me go!' she cried stiffening, not in a dream now.

He let her go at once, and she turned towards him, shaking.

He smiled at her sourly.

'The two women have turned into one,' he said. 'Now tell me what you were doing in that garden last night. And don't say what garden? If you want to try out your voice, say Let me go! Do you remember saying it last night?'

'I'll tell you what I'll say,' she said to him, her narrow face lengthening into shrewdness. 'I'll say What garden? What garden? You can't prove I was there.'

'I could leave the proving to the police,' he suggested. 'Someone will have seen you. Someone always does. Did you walk both ways? Did you take a bus? Get a lift from a car? Murder brings out the public spirit in the worst of us. Witnesses will pour forward like the water from a fire hose. So stop saying What garden and think of something better. Who told you to be there? Cady?'

She was thinking hard. 'Not Cady,' she said. 'No one told me to be there. I knew something was going to happen and I went. And don't ask me how I knew. Something someone said.'

'Cady?'

'Yes, Cady.'

'And what did he say?'

'It won't do,' she said sharply. 'There's no reason why I should tell you anything. You get out of the shop or—'

'Or you'll call the police,' he said, smiling. 'You tell me a little more or I'll call the police. And make it the truth. I can smell lies like garlic in my shaving water.'

'All right,' she said. 'I knew from Mr. Cady something was going to happen. I went there to see if I could stop it.'

'Those two strong arms against fate,' he said, looking at her. She was probably over twenty, but she seemed immature, undeveloped, as though she had been brought up on bread and jam instead of the meat and milk of prosperity. 'You went there to see if you could stop it, but you didn't. And what exactly did you do?'

'Nothing. I hung around. Then someone came. I suppose it was you. Then I went home.'

'It sounds like a thoroughly innocent evening. But it smells like—garlic.'

'All right,' she said sharply. 'I don't want to get anyone into trouble. But if you must have it you must have it. You take some of your questions to that old woman who was in the shop now, acting crazy, pretending she'd seen me. I don't know what she came here for. But how did she see me, that's what I want to know. Where was she, to see me? Perhaps she was in the garden, with the dog.'

He heard the doubt in her voice, as well as the defiance.

'You don't think she was. You don't think,' he said slowly, 'that a woman brought the dog.'

'Well, Mr. Clever. No, I don't. I think it was a man, but I don't know what man. And there's no garlic on that one,' she added impertinently. 'And that's all I can tell you.'

'Get it in order for next time,' he suggested. 'Next time should be to-night. Say half-past seven. We'll have a drink and get to know each other. I'm terribly respectable, and your mother wouldn't mind. I won't blackmail you,' he said carefully, and watched her narrow face droop again. 'I'll meet you outside the shop.'

He smiled at her and went through the frosted glass door.

Cady was waiting on the pavement outside. Everton would have walked on, but Cady blocked his path.

'Been buying hats?' he said, smiling and shaking his head. 'Odd sort of bloke, aren't you?'

'I didn't know you were interested in hats, too!' Everton said in amazement. 'I saw a nice little girl in there,' he said in a rich voice. 'And I thought I'd like a little company to sweeten my troubles.'

'If you really want company, let's walk down together and look at the beach,' Cady suggested.

Everton found himself irrationally averse from looking at the beach. He thought of making a run for his car, but to run in daylight from another man would have separated him from his own sanity.

Cady took his arm and guided him across the street to the promenade, where the old men sat muffled in tweed with newspapers over their faces, and children squirmed as their bare feet touched the hot stone.

'Let's have an ice cream,' Cady suggested. He bought two ice cream cones from a kiosk, handed one to Everton, and began to eat his own with great enjoyment. His round face shone with greed.

'I don't want to interfere with you, old man,' he said, 'but the little girl in that shop is a friend of mine. There's a code in these matters, and I suppose you subscribe to it.'

'I'm only a humble grammar school boy,' Everton said. 'I don't know what the code is.'

'I'll tell you what it is. You're not to hang around my girl friends,' Cady said, still in an amiable voice. 'Keep away from them.'

'I'll need a list, or I might offend unwittingly.'

Cady's ice cream was trickling down his chin, and he licked as far after it as his tongue would go.

'You talk too much,' he said. 'You know what I mean, all right. I'm not trying to order you about. I just want you to do the decent thing.'

'Come out of your schoolboy dream,' Everton said. 'You've mixed with too many rough types to play prefects and fags now. You're too big a boy even for Borstal. And don't look so frightened. You may be mixed up in this murder, but you can't be more than an accessory after—or perhaps before—the fact.'

Cady suddenly grinned. 'Clever, aren't you?' he said. 'But there wasn't any murder. You take it from one who knows.'

He had finished his ice cream, and now, with a broad, silly smile, he turned and left.

Everton had a chilled feeling that he had been threatened. Cady was stupid, but there was no comfort in that. He was stupid enough to do as he was told, and it was Atkinson who was telling him.

He looked down and saw that he still held the ice cream cone in his hand. He swore at it, and threw it down on the beach. Then he went slowly back to the hotel, gazing stiffly in front of him. He knew that Cady was following him.

In the hotel's small dining room he surrendered himself to melancholy confusion. The short-sighted waiter who did not wear glasses was moving clumsily across the room with covered plates. After this morning he could not be there, he should not be there, he was there. The manager was eating at a corner table. He looked mildly at Everton as he passed, but he did not speak. They knew, they all knew, that Everton had not the courage to expose them.

Everton sat down and looked around. An adolescent girl spoke impatiently to her silent parents; the old lady who knitted and who in winter would always take the seat next the fire was wheezing over her food. The strange woman who had been in the hat shop was talking either to herself or to the pale pink mess, with its slight suggestion of forensic medicine, that lay untouched on her plate. There were some small children, who rocked with laughter at their parents' timid requests for silence and good manners. And there was Inspector Leigh, who waved to him in a friendly manner.

The waiter came. 'Food,' Everton said, without looking at the man. 'Whatever you recommend. I'm sure you know what's best. Something simple, like lettuce with the arsenic washed off. Some tinned salmon, Group Three. Don't bother to put cochineal with it. I don't want my palate spoilt.'

The waiter brought him sausages and mashed potatoes, and Everton kept his eyes down as he ate. When he looked up, it was always to see someone else watching him.

When he had finished the meal, which seemed to have been planned with the help of some cookery book for imbeciles, he felt hostility drawing nearer. He looked up, to see Inspector Leigh standing beside his table.

'I'll join you for coffee,' he said, 'if you don't mind. You don't, do you, Everton?'

Everton smiled drearily.

'What's been happening to you since last night?' the Inspector asked, sitting down.

The ugly waiter stood over them with a coffee pot.

'Nothing,' Everton said. 'Nothing's been happening to me.' He wasn't afraid, but explanations, explanations to the police, seemed too difficult.

The waiter poured their pallid coffee and went away.

'Do you know the people at this hotel?' Everton asked in a casual voice.

'If you mean the management, I don't. But you should ask your friend Atkinson. I think he owns the place.'

'Oh,' said Everton. 'Then…'

'Then what?' the Inspector asked, sipping his coffee without appearing to notice its tenuous connection with the coffee bean.

'Nothing. Nothing at all,' Everton said in a worried voice. The Inspector lit a cigarette and began to smoke contentedly. After a minute Everton felt obliged to speak.

'It's only that last night he was agreeing with the—the judge— about what a terrible hotel it was. Inept staff, and all that.' He waited for a comment. There was none, and he found himself adding reluctantly. 'They seemed rather inexperienced—and foreign.'

'They look all right to me,' the Inspector said peacefully. 'You always get foreign waiters in these classy places.'

'Classy?'

'It's got a cocktail bar,' the Inspector said in calm explanation. 'The body hasn't come up yet,' he added, without much change of tone.

'Up?' Everton asked in a sick voice.

'Up. It's bound to be in the sea, you know. It might not come up for a week. It might come up right here on the beach among the sand castles or it might be washed up twenty miles away. Bodies are always behaving differently. But it will come up in the end. What else could be done with it? There's no other place to bury a body half as safe as deep salt water.'

'Well, what about it,' Everton asked truculently. 'You think I moved—moved the—moved it?'

'Oh, you didn't move it,' the Inspector said gently. 'You didn't have a car and you didn't have a boat. Atkinson, now, he had a car, but he was using it to fetch us.'

'There was a boat in the bay below,' Everton said, and he wanted to add that Atkinson might have taken the body out and down to the boat before he fetched the police, but caution and fear held his tongue.

'A boat in the bay below. I'm glad you mentioned that. It corroborates what I've already heard. In fact, what I saw for myself. But that boat wasn't moved. It stayed there all night. However, there are plenty of other boats. It's the facilities for sailing that keep the prices up round here. Still, Atkinson was in the lounge with you when the shot was fired. It was your own watch,' the Inspector said, 'by which you were checking the time? Not a clock on the mantelpiece or something like that?'

'My own watch,' Everton said. 'And the clock on the mantelpiece. And other people's watches. And they were all the same.'

'Now, what do you mean by other people's watches?' the Inspector asked quickly. 'Do you usually tell the time by other people's watches?'

'No,' Everton said. He knew he would have to go on. 'It's nothing. But while we were playing bridge I thought the others kept looking at their watches. I thought they were jumpy about something. I was probably mistaken.'

'Probably,' Leigh said. 'And we haven't found where the dog was kept. It was a home-loving dog. Lazy, spoilt. Wouldn't be interested in rabbits if you pulled a hole over its head. Not a wanderer. I've a feeling we're going to discover it was locked up somewhere.' He stopped speaking for a moment. 'Do you like the food here? Would you have said the judge was a gourmet? I'm forgetting you didn't know him in the past. Only his wife. Still, it's funny he should have eaten here so often. Atkinson may have fed him at cut rates.'

Everton did not know how much of this conversation was intended as direct attack, but he listened intently. Communication was indirect, but it existed. He wondered why the Inspector should communicate with him at all. He was dealing with this slowly when a shadow slid across the table and he looked up, for the second time that day, into the flat, brown eyes of the woman who had been in the hat shop. She wore no hat now, and her greying hair looked as though it had spent an hour in a wind tunnel.

'Inspector,' she said, and nodded to Everton. 'You're the young man I saw in the hat shop.'

'In the hat shop,' the Inspector repeated absently, and Everton flushed. It wouldn't be any help, he realized, to say he had seen a dream of a hat in the window.

'You'll probably think I'm eccentric,' he said defiantly, 'but I wanted to talk to the girl.'

'And so did I,' the woman said. 'But I was interrupted. And now I'm going back. Hat shops, tea, bus, home, bath. I like to respect conventions, but conventions, I've noticed, don't respect people. They're a cage. Like hats, they are opaque to the infinite. They don't suit my temperament. There is another thing that doesn't suit my temperament,' she said, sitting down. 'And that is to have secrets on my mind. The secrets of the soul are innocent, but the secrets of the mind I prefer to share with you, Inspector.'

'Now?' the Inspector asked gravely.

The woman fluttered. 'Not now. Secrets are multipliers. In a few hours mine may have bred. To-morrow I may be able to interest you.'

'I could call on you this evening. Say around nine,' the Inspector said, looking thoughtfully at Everton, who stood up as a polite prelude to leaving them alone.

'No,' the woman said to Everton. 'You mustn't go to the hat shop first. I shall go there, and pull my ideas down to earth.' She turned away from him. 'Inspector,' she said in a tired voice, 'you think I'm a foolish woman. I am sure you have never read my poetry, you can't understand my feeling for nature, you have probably been told I am queer. But I have eyes, ears, and a sense of justice. Nine o'clock this evening. Did you say the name was Everton? Good-bye, Mr. Everton.' She gave him a gaunt smile and edged her way out, dropping parcels as she left.

The manager rose from his table in the corner and picked up the parcels. He called one of the waiters and spoke to him. The man took the parcels and went out in pursuit of their owner.

'She's called Leonard. Don't be in too big a hurry to think she's a silly woman,' the Inspector said placidly. 'The people who give evidence for us very often aren't intellectuals. Still, perhaps she is. Poetry! Well, it takes all sorts to write poetry. I know a bit about her through my wife who's a great hand at knowing a bit about everyone. My wife's view is that she isn't entirely satisfied with the stars and the infinite. You'd think if you went to all that trouble about Nature, Nature would give you something back again. However, so long as she's not certifiable she'll make a witness.' He looked at Everton, measuring him, it seemed, for sanity. Everton was glad to leave him.

He was also happy to leave the hotel. He had told Leigh nothing of the events of the morning. It would always be too late to tell him now. He was very nearly committed, in his own mind, to investigating the secrets of the hotel by himself. Was the ugly waiter's face familiar? Had he seen the barman before? He stepped out on the pavement, his thoughts spinning like a roulette ball, and found that Cady was standing beside him, blinking in the sun.

'Would you like to walk along the promenade with me?' Cady said.

Everton stood still.

'Oh, yes, you would,' Cady said. 'Shall I tell you something? I like you. I like you so much I'm going to stay beside you. We two shall see the sun go down, as the poet says.'

'I hope we shall,' Everton said. 'Anyway, what poet?' He turned and walked away quickly, but he found that Cady, holding his elbow, was still beside him.

His mouth was drying up. He was getting on the wrong side of the situation again. He didn't want trouble. He wasn't even prepared to knock Cady down. The reasonable man went through life without making enemies. If enemies had to be made, it would be better to choose less dangerous ones than Cady.

'All I want to know,' Cady was saying, 'you've been with the police Inspector and that—that woman Leonard. I want to know what she said, and when you've told me you can forget my dear familiar face.'

'She didn't say anything,' Everton said. 'She just gabbled.' He turned suddenly and jumped from the promenade towards the beach. A ball rolled towards his feet, and he picked it up and tossed it back to the little girl who had thrown it. This was a child of about seven, who, from her face, knew enough about human nature to keep other children of seven in their proper state of subordination.

Everton walked towards her and said with an ingratiating smile: 'Throw it back and we'll have a game.'

She gave him a staff manager's look, but said, with some uncertainty, 'Nanny says I'm not to play with strange children. I don't know about strange men.' She looked at him with piercing innocence. 'But I know what she'd say about you,' she shouted, and ran away.

'Since there's no help,' Cady said, 'let's take our walk now. Earth,' he said, waving towards the sea, 'hath not anything to show more fair. What was that old woman saying to the policeman? Take your time. We'll wait here by the harbour. There's something up.'

A policeman was rowing a small boat up and down, while another stood in the stern holding a rope. The harbour was small, and there were many boats moored in it. Every few minutes the drag anchor caught in the moorings of another boat. A thickening crowd stood on the promenade and on the little pier, eating oranges, ice cream, and sandwiches out of paper bags. None of them knew that a murder had been committed and the body lost, but they knew the policemen were not fishing for mackerel, and hopes of drowned bodies naturally came to every mind. The crowd had already reached the size that automatically attracts every passer-by who is doing something less positive than trying to win a bicycle race.

Cady held Everton's arm and pushed him forward through the crowd. A man in trunks was diving from the boat. Each time he went under there were groans of expectancy from the nervous; when he came up there were cries of advice from the ribald, mainly about frogmen and midget submarines.

'We'll see what comes up,' Cady said, breathing hard. It was a hot day for September. 'And while we wait you can be thinking what the old woman said.'

'She said nothing. And I don't want to stand here watching the police drag for a body.'

'So you know it's a body,' Cady said, his soft face relaxing. He looked excited and childish, and Everton told himself again that this man was the opposite of sinister. "Probably if I offered him a stick of rock he'd go away," he thought, then he saw that the stupid grin was fixed. The hand that held his elbow seemed inhuman, as though it had been made in a factory. While the rest of the crowd watched the boat and the policemen, Everton stood looking at Cady. He saw the sweat on his brow and the tongue running greedily over his lips. He looked around, and saw faces that were intent, morbid, fearful, excited. They all waited in the same spirit, but with the others the appetite would drop away, satisfied; in Cady it would remain. He was in love with the visible forms of death.

A stiffness was sweeping through the crowd, and Everton looked back at the boat. The man in trunks, holding a rope, was preparing to dive. He went over the side, and it seemed minutes before he came up again. Everton remembered that his own body had been rescued from the Seine, and he turned his head away as the man came up. The two policemen began to haul on the rope. Cady, bending forward, was rigid as a dancer holding the final pose. Everton heard several women scream.

'Fainted,' a man said in disgust. 'Shouldn't have been here if they're going to faint. They've got no right, pretending to be equal. I've got no use for women,' he said aggrieved.

Several others reluctantly devoted themselves to crying, 'Give her air!' but they kept their eyes on the boat and did not move. There were angry cries of 'They've covered him up. Trust the cops!'

'He's been murdered. Pushed in. It's a disgrace!' the man next Everton shouted, and several women began to cry.

Everton shut his eyes. Something in a blanket was being carried up the beach. Something, someone, had been carried out of the Seine years before. He was sick and he was afraid.

'And now tell me what the old woman said,' Cady repeated. He sounded tired, and his eyes were watering. The crowd had trickled away after the policemen and their bundle.

'Nothing.' Everton breathed. 'Still nothing.'

'We'll go on with our walk,' Cady said. 'It gets very quiet farther along the beach. Isolated, almost, now the big summer crowds have gone. We won't be interrupted.'

Everton, numb, realized his own dreadful anonymity. The crowd, of course, would care. The idle hand would light a cigarette, the eyes would stare at the bundle coming out of the sea, perhaps a child would dig in the sand and his spade would strike a shoe. There was a death that would bring interest to a million readers in the morning trains.

Suddenly he saw the affair in perspective. It was unimportant, and it was only his anxiety not to give in to threats that had magnified it. He was so anxious not to be intimidated that he was letting himself be driven into a nervous stupor.

'She talked,' he said. 'About the murder, I suppose. She had something to tell the police but she didn't want to tell them right away. She arranged to see the Inspector. This evening about nine. At her house. But she was going back to the hat shop first.' He stopped.

'All right,' Cady said. 'All right. Care for an ice cream before we part? No? Then bye-bye.' He lumbered away, leaving Everton alone.

Everton stood still, looking at the sea, and trying to decide if he had been a reasonable man. If he had made any mistakes, he told himself, he could correct them quite simply by going to the police and telling them what he had done, what he had told Cady, under duress. And under what duress?, the police would ask. And with what, indeed, had Cady threatened him? It would be impossible to explain to the police. It was also unnecessary. The information he had given Cady was entirely useless. There was always the chance, he told himself, that he had done no harm.

7

INSPECTOR LEIGH DROVE SLOWLY ALONG THE SEA ROAD, LOOKING appreciatively around him as he went. The appreciation was habitual, rather than spontaneous.

Rigid exclusion of the usual amenities had kept the town quieter than its neighbours. There was no cinema, the bus service was unreliable, instead of a car park there were many notices forbidding the parking of cars, the railway station was inconveniently placed. Nature had come to the help of the citizens by providing only the thinnest strip of gritty sand with a steeply shelving beach, attractive to suicidal infants, but discouraging to the normal parent. The ring of brittle cliffs that surrounded the bay kept most of the houses at a decent distance from the sea. A small, safe harbour brought a few sailing enthusiasts to the town: these were welcomed, as they tended to put the rents up and keep the rates at a comfortable level. A generation of rich people had built large, comfortable houses around the bay, but time and income tax had seen their defeat, and the biggest of the houses had been turned into schools, nursing homes, and those dreary, padded retreats known as private hotels. Meanwhile, everyone was able to congratulate everyone else, in the Tudor, Queen Anne, and occasional post-war, coffee shops that the place was unspoilt, and that it was still possible to hire a horse and ride it through the woods, although not for long, for behind this respectable English dream the small mean houses grew like thistles in an abandoned field.

It remained, however, a town whose capital was quietness and respectability. Murder might bring trade, but it would be of the wrong kind. The Inspector's duty, he realized sourly, was to produce the murderer in the minimum number of newspaper inches. The worst thing that could happen was that some enterprising newspaper would think of some ghoulish point—a pun, perhaps, on the name of Bath—and rush into speculation and banner headlines. Everything must be played down.

The Inspector sighed as he passed the small, boxy house of Mrs. Leonard. She was the Bath's nearest neighbour, and if a newspaper ran some of her poetry, or photographed her on the cliff in a smock, getting close to nature, watching murderers creeping about by moonlight, the publicity would be the ruin of the town. There was the dog, too, and the widow was photogenic.

The widow proved to be even more beautiful than she had seemed the night before. She was dressed in black, black that was filmy and graceful rather than dreary and downcast. How old was she? If she was forty, she had spent the years without borrowing from her beauty. But even if she was forty, and it seemed ungallant to advance the estimate, she was a young woman to have been the wife of the man whose body he had just inspected. She was probably less than forty. A well-poised thirty-five. The age of maximum charm, for a woman needed a few years of maturity to develop her talents, her intelligence, and her knowledge of men.

'Mrs. Bath,' he said gloomily, 'a body has been found in the harbour. I'm afraid it's your husband's.'

Lucy screamed. She reeled, and seemed about to collapse on the floor, but instead she backed towards the nearest armchair, and fell into it. The Inspector watched her carefully, his sympathy dimmed a little by his officially observant eye. He stood over her, offering her glasses of water, and gradually her sobs subsided.

He decided that the practical note was the best to sound. 'Mrs. Bath,' he said carefully. 'What we have to do now is avoid publicity that might damage you. There will have to be an inquest. The more evidence we have to offer the sooner it will all be over. So the less time we waste, the better.'

Lucy sat up. The implication that her grief could easily be quelled was clear enough, but if she felt anger she did not show it. The Inspector, making his judgment, felt that he was dealing with a direct, although perhaps unsophisticated, mind.

'I know we've been through this before, but last night was a difficult time for you,' he said. 'You are sure you know of no enemy of your husband's who might have attacked him, perhaps not deliberately, but in a moment of rage. Good. Do you know of any enemy that he might have attacked? It's possible that he was killed by someone acting in self-defence.'

'He didn't really know anyone well, except legal people. He was at the age when many of his friends had died or—vanished. And enemies usually are made out of friends, aren't they?'

'No enemies arising from his former position as judge? None of these criminals who swear vengeance after heavy sentences?'

'Not in my time,' Lucy said. 'We'd only been married about six years, you know.'

'We can look into it,' the Inspector said doubtfully. 'Six years. Some disparity in your ages, then, Mrs. Bath?'

'That's what everyone thought,' she said with a sad smile. 'I married him because he seemed the most charming, the most civilized, the most intelligent human being I had ever met. Also, in a way, the most worthwhile. He was a useful man,' she said, dabbing her eyes.

'And what did you do before you married him, Mrs. Bath?' the

Inspector asked, mentally deducting six, first from thirty-five and then from forty.

'Most of the time I lived quietly at home,' Lucy said in a sad, dreamy voice, as though she were casting her mind back to some quiet, grey rectory.

'And where was home?'

'Budapest, Sofia, in Warsaw for a short time,' Lucy said, with a magnificently vague gesture. The Inspector looked interested. 'My father was an agent,' she added in explanation.

'Perhaps we needn't go into all that,' the Inspector said in a slightly hopeless voice. He had not failed to notice that Lucy's former homes were situated in capitals where, for the moment, detailed investigation would be difficult. 'What was your father, Mrs. Bath?'

'He was an agent,' Lucy said firmly. 'Wheat, wine, fruit. You know. A business man. His name was Johnson.'

'All right,' the Inspector said, abandoning Lucy's past, although not because he felt it to be without interest. 'Now for a more personal question, Mrs. Bath. There isn't any acquaintance of your own who might have been—inimical to the judge.'

'Oh, dear no. I should think not. When I was younger,' Lucy said sadly, 'naturally one or two men were attracted by me. But the attachments were never deep, nor in any way permanent.'

Inspector Leigh considered the radiance that even her pale and heavy make-up could not conceal. A jury would scarcely like a witness whose pockets were so full of under-statements. But that would be her lawyer's business.

'This man Everton,' he said. 'Is he an old friend?'

'Friend?' Lucy raised her eyes in wonder. 'Perhaps you could call him a friend,' she agreed doubtfully. 'I knew him years ago. I don't think I would say I had ever known him well. I was once rather sorry for him. He got in some kind of trouble about money,' she said vaguely. 'He used to be quite pleasant, but I think he mixed with the wrong sort of people.'

'Where?'

'In Paris.'

'You've lived in Paris, too?'

'Oh, yes,' she said, an impatient line appearing briefly between her eyes. She smoothed it away at once, probably in the interests of her complexion. 'When I saw him last night,' she said rather quickly, 'I was a little shocked by the way he had changed. I asked him here just on a sympathetic impulse. And I wondered, too,' she said absently, 'if Jan would like to get to know him again.'

'Jan—your husband's niece—she wasn't at home yesterday evening, was she?'

'Not until late. She was once a great friend of Everton's. Is that all, Inspector?' Lucy said, rising. 'I feel rather—well—shattered.'

'That will be all, Mrs. Bath. We have a statement for you to sign, but I don't think we need go through any of that again. You all seem agreed about time and so on. Remarkably agreed, in fact,' the Inspector said in a wondering tone. If Lucy flushed, the colour was lost under her make-up. 'I should like to speak to your servants again.' He dug his foot gently into the thick pile of the carpet. 'It will be a change for me, you know. Most of the cases I run into nowadays are more of the old women in the back shop type. Money in the tea caddy, you know. Servants! I think I'll speak to them in their own quarters. There's a housekeeper, isn't there? It will be like the old days with H. G. Wells. Do you read much, Mrs. Bath? Not much time for it, is there, what with worrying about the corned beef and the smoked haddock.'

Lucy was stung at last. 'Do you think I'd have better service from the police,' she murmured, her eyes glinting, 'if I dressed myself in a dirty wig and sat over an oil stove in the scullery?' She seemed to realize that she had let the mask of sorrow slip too far, and she collapsed again into dignity.

When Inspector Leigh reached the kitchen he found that Baxter the dog, who was too large for the normal basket or soap-box, was lying on a kind of camp-bed beside the fire. His left hind leg was in plaster. A piece of mangled meat that looked like the haunch of a small horse lay beside him, and a lean woman in a white overall sat by his bed, fondling his beard, which was wet. Baxter dribbled.

'He seems to be having a happy convalescence,' Inspector Leigh said. 'How is he, Mrs. Simmons?'

Mrs. Simmons burst into tears and left the room. She was a sensitive woman. Her husband appeared, and said that his wife was very upset about the dog, and that the woman who came to do the rough work had been away all week. Looking after Baxter was too much for his wife if she had to wash the dishes as well.

'I have a statement for you to sign, Simmons,' Leigh told the man. 'Just what we went through before. I might want a little information from you about the dog, as well. He wasn't in the habit of wandering at night?'

'He was usually let out in the evening for sanitary purposes.'

'And when his mission was completed, how did he come back in?'

'Sir?'

'I mean by what door? Did he ring the bell, or did you wait for him?'

'If it was raining or cold he was against leaving the house at all. In and out like a piece of elastic, making another duty for me in the morning,' the man said with resentment. 'If the weather was all right he'd stroll off, and I didn't stand around waiting for him. Then if he was shut out by mistake,' he said, looking viciously at the great creature on his sick-bed, 'he'd come and kick up a fuss by the late judge's window. Being his pet, not mine. I'm afraid I sometimes spoke harshly to him if he came whining round here, late,' he said with hypocritical sorrow. He laid a gently loving hand on Baxter's forehead, and the dog bared its teeth in noiseless disapproval.

'His leg was broken, as we all know,' Leigh said. 'But what's that mark on his head?'

On the monstrous, woolly head there was a red stain that might have been blood. Simmons touched the spot with his fingers and Baxter winced. 'He's been hit,' he said. 'It's blood.'

'Wash it off.'

'Me?' Simmons asked, retreating from the bed.

'Florence Nightingale not being handy, you.'

Simmons, with the air of a man about to resign, soaked a rag in warm water and bathed the dog's head. After a few minutes he announced in triumph that the mark wouldn't come off.

'Then we'll leave it. And now tell me about the men working around the house.'

'They've been mending the balconies. With a licence. The late judge was very correct. Wouldn't have nothing done without filling in forms number one to a hundred. So we all went in risk of our lives until we had the official Go Ahead, just to save his reputation. He was a very strict man, legally speaking. We could have had the work done a dozen times by now if it hadn't been for the licence. But he drove the men on. One of them was here last night after six.'

'That seems unnatural,' Leigh agreed. 'I think I'll have a word with this work-eater.'

He went into the garden, and spoke to the constable who lingered under the judge's window.

'Microscopes and cigarette butts, my lad,' he said briskly. 'What have we got?'

'There's this ladder that's lying on the grass. We've had it all photographed, measured, sir. I've let the men go on with their work, but on the other side of the house. Under the dead man's room, as you can see, sir, there are seven marks where the ladder has rested. Four to the left of the balcony, three to the right.'

'It's a pity it didn't snow last night,' Leigh said sourly. 'Although even without that convenience I would incline to the view that the ladder had lain on the grass all night. I hope the papers don't call it the Case of the Dancing Ladder,' he said, still obsessed by the dangers of publicity. 'Now go on with your observations. I'm sure you've seen everything, including the possibility of promotion,' he added with dreamy malice.

'Well, sir, it's true the balconies were very shaky indeed. They're not well-built. It's this colonial style, they call it, and we haven't got the climate. You can see how they're made. A bit of zinc to stand on with some rusty iron bars underneath to keep them from caving in, some wrought iron in front to make them look pretty, the whole thing held up by a couple of struts from the wall underneath. Even at their best, they'd hardly take a couple of heavy-weights having a friendly fight. The struts should have been mended long before the war. They'd be forgotten then, and they've probably had licence trouble since. The iron underneath the zinc should be mended now, but they haven't got a licence for that. Just for new struts. The men seem to have done this one. You can see the struts are in place and painted with red lead. Oxide, they call it. Keeps out the rust. It's still wet, I think, but no one's been up. We've been waiting for you,' he said, with oblique reproach. 'A man called Everton's been here, being on friendly terms with the ladies of the house. I've got a note of as much of the conversation as was audible.'

'And what did Mr. Everton seem like to you?'

'He seemed to think he was smart,' the constable said, raising his gentle eyes. 'But I thought he was jumpy. The kind of man who keeps going on benzedrine when he ought to get to bed with a nice sedative and a hot water bottle.'

'We'll see what we can do for him,' the Inspector said savagely. 'Now we'll speak to the man who's been dancing with the ladder.'

The workman was a middle-aged man with a shrewd, reticent face. A man who would always be omniscient about Them and what They would be up to next, but who would convey his knowledge to others principally by a series of well-timed silences.

'Well, let's see, what's your name, Peters? Tell us what you've been doing to this balcony,' Leigh said.

'Mending it,' the man said shortly.

The Inspector leant against the wall and stared at his hands, while he smelt carefully around this non-co-operative attitude.

'Tell me about it,' he suggested finally. 'It's not, you know, unreasonable to be interested in what's been happening with ladders around the window of a man who has been murdered.'

'I was mending the balcony.'

'Alone?'

'There's a lad. You can't count him, unless you wonder how he got his hands tied in his pockets.'

'Go on. In fact, try to go on for quite a bit,' the Inspector said in his usual mild, dreamy voice.

'The balcony is in a bad way. They all are, round this house. So Mrs. Bath rang Green's, that's the firm, and said they had the licence and would they send some men to fix them. That would be months ago,' he said with deep satisfaction, 'but not being urgent, it wasn't done till now.'

'And about this particular balcony. When did you start on it?'

'Yesterday morning.'

'And what did you do?'

'Took out the struts and put in new ones.'

'The balcony was dangerous before this was done?'

'It wouldn't have fallen down by itself.'

'Would it have fallen if someone had stood on it?'

'No.'

The Inspector waited, this time with an irritated tightening of the lips. For a minute the menacing official silence wrestled with the stubborn private silence. The official silence won. Peters spoke.

'It was safe enough, but rusting, see. It might have stopped being safe.' He waited a few seconds, but his obstinacy had lost strength. 'So I changed the struts.'

'How? With the balcony standing out like a shelf the struts would have to be strong.'

'Well, you can see, can't you?' Peters muttered. They looked up. The struts were bolted into the wall about two feet beneath the balcony. They came up at an angle and were screwed to the underside of the balcony at its edge. Leigh looked dissatisfied by his own observations and waited again for Peters to speak.

'I took out the old struts, see, and put in the new ones. Bolted them to the wall, screwed them to the balcony, painted them with red oxide, went home. I'll do them over green, when I'm let alone.'

'How many times did you move the ladder?'

'How should I know?'

'Oh, I think you could know if you tried,' Leigh said, sighing. 'You must have a system. You wouldn't begin to take out a bolt on one side and give up halfway and move to the other. It's a natural thing to move ladders as little as possible.'

Peters was scowling again. 'O.K. I put up the ladder. On the left. Took out the old strut. Put in the new one. Fixed one side before taking the other off, see? Don't want the lot on my head. Then I moved the ladder, did the same on the other side. Then? Well, it's likely I left the ladder there, on the right. Red-leaded that side. Moved it back. Red on the other.'

'That's twice on the left, once on the right,' Leigh said, without surprise. 'Then did you leave it up or down?'

'I put it down. On the path.' He kicked the pebbles with his foot. 'Here. Under the window.'

Leigh turned to the constable. 'You following this?'

'Someone else moved the ladder,' the constable suggested.

'Oh, very bright,' Leigh said angrily. 'A mysterious assailant went up the ladder, looked in the window, went down the ladder, moved it, had another look in the window, down again, moved it, up again. Now where were we?'

'He was shot,' the constable said sullenly. 'He didn't fall off the balcony.'

Leigh was calculating. If the witnesses had spoken the truth, Bath was found in the middle of the room. If the hole in the head of the corpse also spoke the truth, he had been shot from closer range than the balcony. The post mortem would probably settle that point.

'When did you leave work last night, Peters?'

'Five thirty.' He looked sardonically at the notebook and pencil the constable held. 'If you're writing my life story, call it five fifteen.'

'The man, butler or what he is, said you were here after six,' Leigh commented.

Peters laughed hoarsely. 'Working late? Me?' He laughed again.

'All right,' Leigh said. 'Now you get up that ladder, touch as little as you can, and tell me if the work you did yesterday has been disturbed.'

Peters nodded glumly. He stood the ladder against the wall, and they waited while he peered at the struts.

When he came down he wore an expression, rare for him, of emotional content. Something had gone wrong, so all was right with his world.

'It's loosened up,' he said. 'Safe, but not safe enough. It's been tampered with. Someone's been at those bolts with a spanner. Paint's been scraped off, see. It's screwed up again now, all very nice, but not a real tight job. You can see the screws have been off and on again. Screws on the balcony that is, not the wall.'

'How do you know?'

'It's clear to me if not to you,' Peters said with contempt. 'That after the paint's gone on you don't go unscrewing and screwing up again. But that's what happened, and the paint's scraped off, see?'

'How safe would the balcony be with the screws off?'

'All right for cats. Not for bricks. A decent hundredweight might bring it down.'

Leigh became abstracted, and after a minute he told Peters to go. Then he turned to the constable.

'What happens round here between six and half past? Have you been mixing with the staff?'

The constable flicked through his book. 'Baths,' he said smoothly. 'Baths every night. At least, that went for the judge.'

'He was a clockwork man,' Leigh commented. 'And the others— they didn't all bath together, did they?'

'Mrs. Bath often bathed at that time,' the constable said gravely. 'And the niece, Miss Deverell, if she was around, had hers a little earlier. But so far as I know, they were all washing like mad around six last night. Going out. To that hotel.'

'You'd better check on that. Do it now.'

Leigh, left alone, stared absently at the grass. Everything might have been simple. It might have been the end of the case. But all he was left with now was an intolerable complication and a new set of alibis to check.

8

MRS. LEONARD'S HOUSE, FROM ITS POSITION ON THE LOW cliffs, seemed likely to be called either Sea View or Bella Vista, but the name on the gate was Via, a brevity that had puzzled many postmen. For a solitary woman, the house was in a lonely position, and if she had been in the habit of wearing mink coats instead of smocks, and, in the winter, leather jackets from Army surplus stores, she would probably have been visited by one of those sharp, violent men with a nose for the vulnerable.

The house was grey, square, and practical, but with the disheartened air that comes to houses of every rank when the tenants look on them as weather-excluders rather than indicators of income and morality.

When Everton, tired and timid, knocked at the door, Mrs. Leonard opened it almost at once. Her face was as strained as a watchdog's just before it barks. She looked at him, trying to speak, then over his shoulder at the reassuring sea.

'Come in, Mr. Everton,' she said finally, in a calm enough voice. 'I was expecting you.'

'I don't see,' Everton said wearily. 'Well, how could you have been expecting me?'

He followed her through the plain, empty hall into a sitting room that was pale with a middle-class chintz expression that looked as false as a wedding photograph. She had probably taken the house furnished.

'I'm a great reader of character,' she was saying. 'I've often thought it a pity I wasn't trained to do something with other people's minds. There always seems the chance that they will be more interesting than one's own. I write, you know, but not in the usual way. Not for money, Mr. Everton, and not for an audience. The words drop from my heart on to paper. Sometimes they lie there, sometimes they rise again and crush the disorder in my soul. But I was talking of mind. You have an evasive hungry mind that must perpetually destroy the road beneath your feet. To hide and to seek at the same time frustrates progress.'

'Yes,' Everton said blankly.

'I don't believe you are afraid of words.'

'I'm very easily frightened,' Everton said. 'In the last twenty-four hours I've been afraid of almost everything.'

'Still, you came,' she said. 'I knew if I kept talking in front of you that you would come.'

'How did you know that I'd be interested?'

'You were mixed up in it all,' she said sharply. 'You found the body, didn't you?'

'I only dead-heated for third place,' Everton said.

'When I get some tea you can tell me all about it,' she said. 'You can read some of my verse while you wait. Printed at my own expense, naturally.' She went out to the kitchen. It was difficult to imagine her doing something efficient and normal, like pouring boiling water into a teapot. She seemed a harmless, silly old woman, but if she was as she seemed, what had she been doing in the hat shop, why did she want to talk to the police?

He looked at his watch. It was just six o'clock. It occurred to him that if he stayed there until the police came and she had passed on her information, she was safe.

He opened the book, which was bound in white parchment, and read:

"Naked and terribly afraid,
I unbolted the door.
Six men in black came in,
They laid me on the earth's cold floor."

Everton shivered, and turned over the page quickly.

"Eat ggr
Meat bbr
Pray to the offended sheep
Who in a million stomachs sleep.
On your knees before the cattle
Defeated in the eating battle.
And if you've robbed the humble hen
Of all her sons, pray then, pray then."

This verse seemed to Everton less melancholy than the first, but he thought it might have been written without sitting in the dark on a cliff, watching murderers go by, which was what he suspected Mrs. Leonard of doing.

He turned a few pages, looking for verse about nature and the sea. He found:

"Bent with infinity my soul swoops high,
But body drags forever down from grace,
Too far the falsely flattened star
Too wild the winds of space."

He was deciding that this might have been written on a cliff when Mrs. Leonard came back, carrying a rusty tin tray with a silver teapot on it, a cracked Crown Derby cup and saucer, and a thick white mug.

'You look sad,' she said. 'Is it noble sorrow or pity for my poetry? Most of it is written on the cliff. I dream there, and sometimes verses come out. In the high summer I take my carrots to the beach and have my lunch in spiritual communion with the sea.'

'You are a vegetarian?'

'Not entirely,' she said cautiously. 'I have written some vegetarian poetry, but only when I have been swept away with the mood of the moment. I don't positively like eating meat. I keep my own form of Lent. That is, it seems hardly necessary to fast, but I need to indulge the sackcloth spirit. So for six weeks every year I eat meat every day. There is another—oh, do excuse me, my teeth have slipped again.' She covered her mouth with a handkerchief. When her face was once more exposed, her teeth were in place.

This is a fine damsel for St. George to be rescuing, Everton thought angrily, but he remembered that this St. George had done his best to deliver the damsel into the dragon's jaws. The problem could also be solved without swords. If he kept the conversation going until nine o'clock and the arrival of the police, she would be safe enough. Two hours' discussion about Druids would carry them through.

'Did you know the Baths well?' she asked abruptly.

'No. Did you?'

'My soul rejected them. They suffered from what I call infinity-blindness.'

'Oh.'

'They were earth-bound, but to different earths. They hated each other,' she added in more explicit tones. 'I am sure that he was lured into marriage and that she wanted him not as a true husband. The emanations of hatred that came from them affected me like heart disease. Fascinating,' she said, distributing some tea between the cups and the tray. 'I saw as much of them as I could. And sometimes,' she added, 'more than they supposed.' She swept the thin tangle of hair out of her eyes. 'I have had conversations with them both. Mrs. Bath has vitality. Misdirected.'

Everton realized that women never did like Lucy. He let Mrs. Leonard's voice wash over him while he thought about women. Lucy moved so fast that other people could never quite catch up with her. No one now would ever try, emotionally at least, to catch up with Mrs. Leonard. He thought she was conscious of this, although she might be more troubled by her failure to bring the infinite down to earth. Probably beneath the knotted hair and behind the false teeth Mrs. Leonard retained considerable respectability: Lucy was rash. She kept such queer company that many people assumed she kept some of it in bed. He supposed this to be untrue. Her vitality was not so narrow.

He tried to shut his ears to Mrs. Leonard, who was explaining how she breathed on the cliff in warm weather. 'You must inhale until the ribs are pressed out, then exhale with a great heave of the diaphragm and concentrate on reaching moon-high. Then the breathing must come faster and faster, until the moon is passed.' She sat on the couch, heaving up and down as she breathed with her eyes shut, and Everton looked past her. He listened to the sea stroking the shingle beach, the gentle sea, that waited without interest for the enraging wind. A few miles out the wrecks of centuries lay piled against the bar. On calm days the fishermen would take the visitors out to the bar at low tide, and sailing over the flat green water they would peer down at the filtered green shadows of the wrecks, but they would never see the Viking ship that lay beneath the sand with the tramp steamer pressing from above. The little fishes would swim incuriously through the stripped ribs of the dead men. The judge's body had been dragged back to earth.

Still listening hard to the muttering sea, he thought he heard the soft protest of the wooden gate. There was one step only on the shingle path, then silence. Whoever had come in the gate was standing still, or walking as quietly as a hunting animal along the edge of the lawn.

He slipped the book of poems into his pocket, and carefully moved the cup of cold tea to the mantelpiece. No one could reach the house without making a noise on the pebbles. But before the noise was heard, it would be advisable to go to the door, throw it open, and ask the intruder what he wanted. Boldness would win, Everton thought, sitting very still.

He heard himself say, in a carefully unalarmed voice, 'There is someone in the garden. If we talk very loudly he will know you are not alone.'

Mrs. Leonard stopped breathing deeply. She looked as though she might faint, but her head would naturally be in a strange condition when so much oxygen had been pushed into her blood stream.

'I could read poetry aloud to you,' Everton said, 'or we could sound as though we were having a row.' He added, almost in a whisper, 'But if you know anything about this murder do remember that if the information is shared it will make you safe. Tell me if you can, what you know.'

'I think you are very wise,' she said loudly. 'Certainly I will consider what you say.' She stopped for a second. 'I saw the man with the dog,' she breathed, 'a short thick man with glasses. He came to the house on foot, leading the dog.'

'Do you suppose that was all?' Everton asked conversationally. There was still no sound from the garden.

'He left again on foot without the dog,' she whispered, and added in most unnatural tones, 'More tea?'

'No more tea, thank you. Before or after the shot?'

'The tea is still quite hot,' she said, with a desperate lack of invention. 'He came just before, he left just after.'

'You haven't told me when you started to write poetry, or even why. Do you think he went up the ladder into the judge's room?'

'I don't know,' she murmured, 'I couldn't tell you.' She was staring in fear at the window. 'I suppose I started to write poetry because I was unhappy. Happy people have no need of desperate resources. Unhappy people often do not adopt them. But people aware of internal discords must struggle to resolve them.'

This seemed more like genuine conversation, he thought, nodding approval. 'You think the poet writes to crush his misery? There must be other reasons. Why were you in the hat shop? Where does that girl come into it?'

'She was in the garden, too. But I don't know when she came nor when she left. There are other reasons. The soul climbs with poetry. But it is the soul that has been battered down by life that feels the need to climb.'

'If you don't know when she was in the garden, do you know why?' he asked, and added clearly, but in a gentle voice: 'And how have you been battered, Mrs. Leonard, or is it wrong to ask?'

'Deserted. Hated. Betrayed. Rejected,' she cried with sudden force. 'To need love, to deserve love, to win the vilest hatred, to watch the ruin of the soul. No, don't look afraid. Don't withdraw. You have been down in the craters of the mind. You have met violence and hatred and nearly met destruction at the hands of that man. Oh, why can't I forgive! He is a dangerous man. Perhaps it does seem clever to know him. I must order my thoughts,' she said with her hands to her head. 'I wonder how the sea would look. Tell me,' she said in a hungry voice, 'how does water look as you sink through it? No. You asked a question. I can't tell you why she came,' she murmured in despair. 'But long afterwards, she waited outside. Then she walked away. A few minutes later a car left. I thought I heard it stop.'

Her voice had diminished to the smallest of whispers. He answered her loudly. 'The police will be here soon. May I use your phone?'

'It's in the hall,' she said, in a very rational voice.

'Will you show me?' He felt strong, capable, unwilling to leave her alone.

She led him into the hall. There had still been no noise from the pebble path that ran round the house. Could a man walk soundlessly on loose pebbles? Everton imagined a foot going down very gently, not with the weight on the toes, but heel first, so that the foot was firmly placed before the weight was transferred. It could be done, he decided, and felt the telephone receding.

'Wait here with me,' he said to the woman. 'Please.' His voice was unemotional as he dialled the police station. 'I'm speaking for Mrs. Leonard,' he said, 'in that house along the coast road. 'It's called Via. Inspector Leigh was coming to see her at nine o'clock. She would like him to come immediately. Yes. Important.'

He put the receiver down just as he heard the soft footstep on the path, the softer step at the door. It was too late now to talk his way out of trouble.

He ran to the door and wrenched it open. Cady stood on the step, not smiling now, but with sweat on his pale, fat face.

'Too late, Cady, too late,' Everton said. 'What she knows, I know too. You can go away and tell your boss there's nothing for you here.'

'But I'm not going away,' Cady said, smiling softly. He put one hand in his pocket and walked forward. Everton backed away, watching the hand. He saw the gleam of the knife blade and kicked at the hand that held it. The knife dropped and Everton drove his fist into Cady's soft face, with the terrible happiness that comes from violence released at last. Cady went down, and Everton snatched the knife from the floor. Cady swung round at his legs and brought him over sideways with his head on the step. He crawled up, with blood in his eyes, but the knife still in his hand, and moved slowly towards Cady, who was rocking clumsily on his knees.

Something whirled in between them. It was Mrs. Leonard, and she hammered on Everton's face with her fists. 'Let him alone,' she cried in fury, 'let him alone!'

Everton pushed her away and wiped the blood from his eyes with his sleeve. He stared at her stupidly and saw beyond her that Cady was on his feet. She hit him again, and Cady pushed her violently out of the way. As she fell, Everton changed the knife to his left hand and hit Cady on the temple with his right. Cady went down, and he was unconscious before he hit the floor.

Everton leant against the wall, thinking about the knife in his hand. It was an ordinary pocket knife. It might even have been a Boy Scout knife, but the short blade had been ground down on each side to dagger sharpness. Someone had ground it with care, and perhaps with love, but the blade was still clean. Everton snapped it shut and threw it out of the door into the garden.

He looked at Cady, who was on the floor, and at Mrs. Leonard, who was standing up now, with the tangled hair over her contorted face. He moved towards her to help her.

'Don't touch me,' she said. 'Don't touch me, you—you murderer.'

'You're mad,' he said, pushing Cady with his foot. 'He's not dead. Only thinking.'

'Leave him,' she said. 'Go away. Get out of my house.'

'I can't leave you with him,' he said blankly. 'I'll have to wait. Until the police come, anyway.'

'The police!' she said, in terror. 'Oh, what can I do! You must go. You must go now. You mustn't be found here. Either of you.'

Everton was looking at himself in the small mirror that hung in the hall. There seemed to be a lot of blood from a very small cut. 'Get me a damp towel or a sponge,' he said over his shoulder. She looked down at Cady. 'It's all right,' Everton shouted at her in fury. 'I won't touch him.' She went away, and in a minute returned with the towel.

Everton cleaned the blood from his face. Before he had finished, Cady, who had begun to groan, was trying to get to his feet again.

Mrs. Leonard bent down and shook him.

'The police are coming,' she said loudly. 'Do you hear? The police are coming. You must leave now. You must leave by the back.'

Cady wavered on to his feet again. 'Do you understand,' she said, 'you must leave at once. And not come back. The police are coming.'

'Nine o'clock,' he mumbled.

'No. Not nine o'clock. They are coming early. Go now.'

'I'm staying,' Cady said.

'No. He knows everything. The police must know too. There is no safety for you here. No harm you can do here.'

'I'll go,' Cady said, and she pushed him across the hall and through another door. In a moment she had come back to Everton.

'And what do we do now?' he asked drearily. 'Talk about poetry again?'

'You must go too,' she said, sweeping the hair desperately from her eyes.

'I'm not going out the back way to be murdered by that maniac,' he said angrily. 'I'll stay here and explain to the police what happened.'

'I'll tell them you're lying,' she said simply. 'I'll say you dragged him in here and attacked him. They'll believe me, you know. I've never been in prison,' she said savagely.

Everton's head was spinning. He tried to understand what he should do. 'We're all mad,' he said in despair, and ran from the house.

9

THE GIRL FROM THE HAT SHOP WAITED MOROSELY ON THE pavement. Everton had said he would meet her at seven thirty. Now it was eight o'clock, and he had not come. She had not wanted to meet him, but she wanted even less to stand on the pavement, pretending not to be interested in the time, displaying to everyone who passed the humiliating truth that she was the kind of girl who could be kept waiting. Popular and successful girls were never left standing on pavements. She was not unpopular: she knew several young men who would have been glad to meet her. She avoided most of them: she had her ideas about the future, and these did not include marriage in two furnished rooms in a back street. She lived with her widowed father in a council house: her need, her desperate need, was escape.

She looked at her watch again. She had told herself she would leave at ten to eight, but she could not face the bus and the warmed-up stew, the over-warm kitchen and her silent father in his prim, dark suit.

She was surprised, too, by the non-appearance of Cady. He had warned her earlier in the day to avoid Everton's company. The least he could have done would have been to try and make trouble. She was not in love with Cady, but she liked him for his superior education. He talked with the right accent, sometimes about culture, sometimes, even more vaguely, about business and money. He was queer, but he was going to be useful. And now even Cady had failed to come. She was in desperate need of proof that she was sought after.

A man in thick glasses who had been lounging on the promenade, staring at the colour-drained sea, now turned, and with a rather lumbering step crossed the road and began to walk rubber-footed along the pavement. Zoe stared at him, oppressed by a sense of familiarity. When he reached her, he stopped, and she watched him with a stiffening of the mind. His own peculiarly flattened face wore an expression of playful sympathy. He was a toad trying to laugh.

'He has not turned up,' he said to her, wagging his head. 'I should wait no longer.'

Zoe looked at him with careful calculation. She had schooled herself to wear a starched, uninviting face when spoken to by strange men in the street; she despised girls whose ideas were limited by the hope of a few hours' entertainment. She was attracted by his oddly familiar appearance; five minutes of his company might rescue her from depression.

'I haven't been waiting long,' she said, her voice quivering like a gramophone needle. 'And I'm afraid I don't know you,' she added, with a return to hauteur.

'No one knows me here,' the man said roughly. 'I do not wish it. I am an exile. My feet are rooted to the English soil,' he said, softly this time, 'but my obstinate heart struggles to be free. If I could master my heart—but I cannot do that alone.' He looked at her wistfully, and Zoe's ego healed immediately. It was a pity he wore glasses.

'You must teach me how to speak to a young lady,' he went on. 'I have never before been attracted to talk to one. Since I left my own country.'

'And what are you in your own country?' she asked. 'A Polish count, I suppose?'

'That is what I am,' he agreed. 'A Polish count.' He looked at her sharply. 'Why do you smile? Are you thinking a Polish count is small cheese to-day?'

'Very small cheese,' she said. 'Let go of my arm.'

He took his hand away at once. 'The young lady is particular,' he said sadly. 'The young lady has an ideal. Tell me of your ideal.'

'I like men who are not common,' Zoe said promptly, 'and who have interests beyond the films.'

'There,' he said, 'I am an uncommon man, and not at all interested in films. Let us walk a little, and I will try to be the ideal.'

They began to walk along the promenade as though they were old friends.

The man told her of his life as a Polish count, and Zoe listened, her interest mingled with biological caution. She knew that the man thought his triumph had been easy, she knew, too, exactly how far she intended to walk with him. Where the promenade ended and the houses thinned out and retreated from the sea, where the beach became lonely under the cliffs, was at least two hundred yards too far. She would walk to the last bus stop on the front, and then she would leave him abruptly. For the present she adopted an air of extreme inno-cence, even to the point of pretending to believe in his Polish count nonsense. She told him about her life, in a rush of careful chatter.

'People don't feel in much of a hat-buying mood,' she said, 'when they come to the seaside. And the trouble I had with my father to let me work in a hat shop! He wanted me to do something quite differ-ent. I should have continued with my education and had a career.'

'There are many careers where personality counts,' the man said. 'Have you thought of managing an hotel. I have a friend—'

'In Poland?' she asked, rather too sharply.

'I must not interfere,' he said sadly. 'Tell me about your young man. I have seen you with a Mr. Cady, have I not?'

'He's a bit odd,' Zoe said casually. 'Always talking about poetry and death. Really out of the ordinary.'

'And Mr. Everton. Is he out of the ordinary, too?'

'Fancy you knowing about Mr. Everton so soon,' Zoe said in simple wonder, and the man, who had been leaning towards her, drew back.

'I only try to make conversation,' he said meekly. 'We talk about more agreeable things. You would not like a drink, no? An ice cream, and I tell you about my friend in the hotel business? There is a career for advance. The whole of England is talking about hotels and how they must be bettered.'

'Is there much money in it?' Zoe asked doubtfully.

'Hotel managing girls in a few years make two, three, four thousand each year. I give you my friend's address,' he said. He had taken her arm again, and they were walking quickly now. Soon they would have passed the end of the promenade and reached the lonely corner of the beach. For an English resort, isolation came quickly. He pressed closer to her, describing with quick, heavy words the charms of the hotel business.

'What is your friend's address?' she asked. 'The Coastal Universal Service,' he answered quickly. You come to see him to-morrow, yes, at three. A very nice man. His name is—Young. Mr. Young.'

She was looking past him, to the bus stop. A beach photographer, who had finished his day's work, was waiting there. She smiled and signalled to him, and he looked at her in surprise, for the daylight had begun to fade.

He took out his camera, and held it to eye-level. As they drew near, he handed Zoe a numbered ticket. She smiled and put it in her handbag.

'What is this? I don't understand this?' her companion said, stopping.

'It is a photograph,' Zoe said. 'You send the ticket with the money and the man sends you the photograph.'

'Give me the ticket and I will send.'

'I collect photographs of myself,' Zoe said coldly. 'For my album. I don't know if I want this one. The light's not very good. It doesn't matter if you want it now or later,' she said cheerfully. 'They keep the photograph for months in case the person wants it.'

The man, for the first time, seemed abstracted. His grip on her arm slackened, and he stood for a moment, irresolute. 'I think it will be late soon,' he said. 'Dark will come. We should walk back. We might discuss further your hotel career.'

'This is where I get the bus,' Zoe said. 'I've had enough walking for to-night. And I have your friend's address.'

'You see him, yes? To-morrow?'

'To-morrow's my half-day. I might try to nip along to see him,' she said amiably. 'Good-night.'

She watched him go, still trying to trace the familiar in his appearance. She was glad she had been able to shake him off without a scene.

The photographer showed himself willing to talk about the hardships of his life but Zoe's interest was in success. She made a slight response in a tone that revealed astonishment that he should have spoken to her; and he moved away, downcast by this further proof of failure.

Zoe, strong in her competence, watched the cars roll slowly past to the sea front. She had no envy of the occupants. Mum and Dad had brought the kids from their back street boarding-houses to have a look at the sea before Nature closed down for the night. They wouldn't stop here. But at the next town, where there was a bandstand and what was usually described as a little life, the kids would have a last ice cream, Dad would have a drink, and Mum would knit till the light faded. Thoughts about the sea, its depth, emptiness, and refreshing qualities, would enter their minds while they talked about other things. Zoe would soon have a car, a better car, and she would secure it on different terms. Money, she knew, clutching her handbag more tightly, money was the secret.

The touch on her arm froze her thoughts for a moment. She turned round quickly, and smiled as she saw Everton. The evening was assuming rotundity. Home was not now at the end of a short, straight line, but somewhere on a curve.

'Hello, Mr. Punctual,' she said, betrayed by surprise into the common touch. 'Did you come out of a trap-door, or something?'

'I saw you from a bus,' he said. 'About ten minutes ago, with a man. So I jumped off. Is there someone I can knock down for you, or was it just your brother?'

'It was a gentleman offering me a job,' Zoe said stiffly.

'Oh. Where?'

'At the Coastal Universal Agency. A Mr. Young.'

'What kind of job? Film star?'

'Hotel manageress.'

'But you shook him off,' Everton said approvingly. 'That's a clever girl.'

Zoe, who had until now successfully crushed her misgivings, began to feel the need of someone else's alarm.

'He wanted me to walk to the end of the beach,' she said. 'But I got the photographer there to snap us. Then he didn't seem so keen.' Her tone invited comment: she was no longer sure of her ability to play a lone hand.

'I recognized the man,' Everton said, at once assuming authority. 'A shy type. I'd like to have that photograph.' He held out his hand, and she looked, furtively, he thought, in her handbag, and then gave him the numbered ticket. The photographer was still dreaming of his misfortunes. He brightened a little when Everton gave him five shillings and invited him to send one copy of the photograph to the hotel and one to Zoe at her home. 'In fact,' Everton said, 'for another five shillings I'd like to have my copy to-morrow.' The photographer's day, dominated as it was by considerations of petty cash, had now been successful.

The bus appeared, swinging out of the night like a lighted ship in a heavy sea.

'I'm coming home with you,' Everton said suddenly to Zoe. 'Don't argue. I don't know what you've done, but you've moved into some kind of danger zone.' He knew she was in a mood, which might be no more than temporary, to welcome the presence of a masterful man. He recognized that his own mood, too, might pass quickly, but for the moment he had defeated Cady, and he was no longer afraid.

'You can come on the bus,' she said weakly, 'but not in the house.'

'Frightened of what Dad will say?'

'Dad won't say anything,' she said bitterly. 'He'll be at his books. He never does say anything.'

Everton, anxious to improve his position, began to talk quickly of Paris, and she listened to him dreamily. It was her own future he was describing, although it might be a few steps away.

When they left the bus he walked with her through the orderly rows of tiny grey houses. There were no shops, no pubs, no cinemas: the houses might have been outcrops of rock in the desert. Here and there groups of boys stood, silent, like animals, on the streets, although when a group of girls passed noises were exchanged. It was a relief, a sign of life, when a fish and chip lorry sent its smoke to the moon.

'Civilization without the amenities,' Everton said gloomily, and Zoe, who had dwelt for years with discontent, looked at him with sharp approval.

'Before I come in or don't come in to your house,' Everton said firmly, 'I want to know what you're up to. You're nurturing something. Murder has been done. It isn't safe to wear too many secrets next your heart. Now, understand. I don't think you've been murdering. But if you know anything about how that old man was killed, you must tell what you know. It's safer for you. Safer physically. And legally imperative. There's something very unpleasant called accessory after the fact. And people who know about murders and keep their knowledge to themselves sometimes end in jail.'

'That's not how I'm going to end,' she said obstinately. 'I don't know how the murder was done.' She stopped abruptly.

'But,' he said. 'There was going to be a "but" on that sentence, wasn't there. Go on. And don't forget what I said about the law.'

'The law,' she said in contempt. 'You come in and see for yourself. That's what.' She ran up the short path, and he followed her.

The house was small, the kitchen was tiny, and smelt as though kippers had been cured in it recently, and an effort made to drown the smell by burning oil. Sitting at a table by the stove was a small man surrounded by large books. He was smoking a pipe, so that the last odour could be added.

'Hello, Dad,' Zoe said wearily. 'This is Mr. Everton. This is my father, Mr. Stokes.'

The man was dressed neatly in dark grey, but there were stains down the front of his coat. He was probably an absent-minded eater. He greeted Zoe vaguely, and Everton with slight surprise.

'I've come on something very close,' he said to Zoe. 'Willis versus Hodges. 1903. It's very close indeed. I think we'll have them there. I've been busy on the notes all day. I'm afraid I've done nothing about your supper, my dear, but there's still a bloater and some jam from last night. My notes, you see. They take a lot of time, Mister,' he said to Everton, waving an exercise book. 'You're not a lawyer, I hope,' he said with sudden suspicion.

Everton shook his head.

'Then you wouldn't know about Willis and Hodges, 1903,' Stokes said with relief. 'It's a very clear parallel to my own case, I think. I've made notes. I've got something to go to court about at last. I conduct my own case, you know. It will cost very little. Zoe, would you like to warm up a bloater for the gentleman? We have to keep living expenses down,' he said sadly. 'Those law books, you know, they're not free. And if you get them up-to-date, you know, they cost a little more. I don't go beyond 1911, so far. But I'm saving. Little economies, you know. The case will be cast iron when I go to court. Zoe, why don't you get some fish and chips for the gentleman?'

'We'll go into the lounge for a minute, I think, Dad,' she said. 'You want to get on with your work.'

She led Everton into another tiny room. 'Now do you know what I think about the law?' she said. 'He used to have a sweet shop, but there was some trouble about the lease and he got himself evicted. Just a legal point, he said, and he's been trying to clear it up ever since. I've been brought up on the law, and you can keep it.'

'It would be an expensive pet.'

She patted her hair. 'Now you'd better go and leave me to my bloater.'

'You're not safe here,' he said slowly. 'You're up to something and I smell trouble. A quartet of Shakespeare's murderers could come in and your father would only ask if they had any 1919 law books. Don't go for lonely walks with strangers and tell me now if you saw Mrs. Leonard at the house last night.'

'I didn't see anyone,' she said sharply. 'Except… except, I'm not sure, but I've just thought the man to-night reminds me of a man I thought I saw with the dog.'

Everton hesitated. 'I'll see you to-morrow,' he said finally. 'I'll come to the shop and clinch the deal about the hat. And now I'll say good-night to your father.'

He went into the kitchen.

'Good-night, Mr. Stokes. No, don't get up. Look, there have been burglaries round here recently. That is, not burglaries in the true sense. There's a rumour about spies. Government spies, naturally. You understand me, Mr. Stokes? I shouldn't let any strangers in the house.'

He looked at his watch on the way back to the hotel. It was just half-past nine. Too late, in an English seaside town, to be permitted the luxury of eating even the scraps from other tables. Unless one asserted oneself. He grinned. His fight with Cady had taken years off his introspective habits.

He went into the hotel. The manager was sitting in the small lobby, reading the paper with his eyes on the door.

'I have news for you, my friend,' Everton said. 'I'm hungry, and I wish to eat.'

The manager looked piously at his watch.

'The staff will like it,' Everton assured him. 'They are not very good at waiting, the practice will help them. You'll find me in the bar when the meal is ready.'

In the bar a fat man sat whispering to a polished blonde. He was certainly smoothing the way to his divorce or hers. In the other corner, at a small table by herself, Jan was waiting. Everton went to her, and the fat man, who had stiffened a little, relaxed again. He clearly thought that the couples were running, or at least sliding, on parallel lines.

'I've been waiting to see you,' Jan said. 'I thought you'd like to know what's been happening.'

He ordered a drink, and she told him of the Inspector's theories about the balcony. 'And now he thinks everyone has been climbing up and down ladders, and he wants to know what we were all doing at half-past six.'

'So you had a lovely alibi and it's broken,' Everton said sympathetically. 'At least I suppose you had a lovely alibi. Or were you sitting out in a moving car at eleven o'clock and you slipped away to pick up a powder puff at home? Thirty seconds for the shot, and back to the car. Escort still dead drunk or lying loyal. I've read about these alibis.'

'Naturally, I don't murder people,' she said, flushing.

'Come and sit with me while I eat and you can tell me what you do when you're being unnatural,' he suggested.

She followed him into the quietened dining room, and Everton spoke to the waiter in surprise.

'You've changed a lot since I last saw you.'

'Yes, sir, I am not the same man. It is his evening off. I am the overtime.'

'A nice bit of beef,' Everton said conversationally. 'It has been mellowed by its long sojourn at the docks. Have you?'

'Sir?'

'I took a roundabout way of asking if you had trouble getting into England?'

'No, sir. I am a war refugee.' He slipped away from the lighted table into the shadows by the wall.

'Interesting face that man has,' he said to Jan. 'Unforgettable, in a way. It looks as though he had been constructed in a perfectly normal manner and then had all the flesh and blood removed. Perhaps he's the rough model for a statue. They are all rather queer here. But they are foreign waiters.'

'They are foreign.'

'You mean they haven't been to a waiters' school. Don't be a snob, Jan.'

'Oh, don't go on talking about the waiters,' she said in some kind of desperation.

'Yes, I will. I want you to draw me a picture of that bony boy.'

'I'm not an art student now. I don't want to be conspicuous.'

'You need an audience to be conspicuous. There isn't one.'

'I haven't any paper.'

'You can use my notebook. Come on, lightning sketches in the café. We can get a living in Soho, or move to Paris and pick up a few sous in Montmartre.'

'Sous are out of date. And so is sketching in restaurants.'

'If you don't play I'll burst into tears and say you've broken my heart. That's out of date, too, so choose your anachronism. Please, Jan.'

He felt in his pockets for the notebook and pencil, and handed them to her.

It was true, he decided, watching her, that she disliked attracting attention. It took someone with Lucy's manner to blaze through oddity. But even if Jan was a small fish artistically, it was certain that she swam in the sea. As she drew, the air of calculated respectability on her face fell away, she looked first furtively and then with absorption at the waiter who stood on the edge of the shadows. The strokes of the pencil became sure, her face settled into lines of tranquillity, the sketch she handed Everton had the confident, settled line of the assured craftsman.

'Now you shall have a liqueur for your trouble,' he said approvingly. 'I can't afford it, but I'll put it on expenses. I'll say I had to return the hospitality of a rich Argentinian. I was pumping him to get his views on English hotels.'

'And what were they?'

'Too much frozen beef. Not enough frozen water. It's what they all say in the summer. No iced water. In the winter they complain of the cold. There is no hotel in England where any foreigner can get past the barrage of very old permanent residents who squash around the fires in all public rooms. And central heating is so rare in the provinces that if the local authorities find any they take it to show in the county museum, science section. There are sometimes tiny shilling-in-the-slot gas fires in the bedrooms, but if the weather is cold shillings are withdrawn from circulation at once. Was it an Argentinian you left me for, Jan?'

She looked at him steadily, and he thought her eyes were made of iced water.

'I left you to avoid the ignominy of being left. Your pretence of loving me had worn so thin I could see Lucy through the gaps.'

He knew that there was no consoling answer. 'You shouldn't jump to conclusions,' he said miserably.

'I didn't jump to this one. It fell on my head. It knocked me out for months.'

'But you are very conscious now. I think you have acquired some philosophy that excludes me.'

Jan fiddled with her handkerchief. 'It needs money to sustain my philosophy,' she said. 'Hugh, I can talk to you because I'm not in love with you any more. You were an example of what happens to me. I don't attract men. Not thoroughly. And I don't with my heart believe that a woman can live alone. When she is very young and trying to learn what life is about, when she is full of ideas about Tolstoy or Van Gogh, then she can live alone, or just bounce off people and be happy. But when she is older—just old enough to be aware of mystery and force—then she can't be alone. If everyone had to keep to his separate cell no one would want to live. I'm glad I shall have some of my uncle's money. Think of the rich women who have had husbands and—and full lives, because they had money to offer.'

'Honey for the bees,' Everton said. 'Shouldn't they get their own?'

'I said you were an example. Even you thought I had money. All I had was an allowance from my uncle, and he had to stop that when he retired.'

'But I wasn't attracted to you because I thought you were rich,' Everton said, in a shocked voice.

'Didn't it help? Didn't the fact I lived in agreeable surroundings and dressed expensively and gave parties where rather charming people who liked the best drinks were glad to come, didn't all these things make me rather nicer to know?'

'You might have been even nicer if I'd met you in a milk bar and you'd admired me for my mind,' Everton said angrily. 'You only need money because you think you do. You're so damned uncertain of yourself that you're frightened to move a step without some stick to lean on. You're just a negative character.'

'Thank you,' Jan said, preparing to rise.

'You're frightened to be positive about anything. What about those waiters here? You know something. But you're not going to tell. You've all the faults you accuse me of. Except perhaps being too fond of Lucy.'

'So we're back to Lucy again,' she said dangerously. 'If you want to know anything about the waiters, ask Lucy. I'm not interested in politics.'

'Nor is Lucy.'

'Perhaps not. But she's much, much more interested in money than I am.'

'You don't understand her,' he said.

'Oh, I'm not going to stay and have Lucy explained to me again.' She glared at him and rushed out.

He stayed on his feet until she had gone. He had left the notebook lying open on the table.

'Your liqueurs, sir,' a voice said. It was the bloodless waiter. His hand shook, and the glass of Cointreau he held slopped over the edge.

'I am sorry, sir, I have spilt it on your address book.'

'That's all right,' Everton said. 'The address is still perfectly clear.'

He lay sleepless in bed for hours that night, and in the end he heard the footstep outside his door, or thought he did.

'Don't bother to come in,' he said very clearly. 'I'm playing cops and robbers, and I'm the side with the gun.'

He thought he heard the man outside the door go away, although, of course, it was always possible that there had been no one there.

EVERTON HAD CULTIVATED LONELINESS FOR YEARS; NOT MANY letters had turned corners to reach him: he was surprised to find himself once again waiting for the post in an hotel lobby. The short-sighted waiter also seemed surprised. He was holding an envelope very close to his face when Everton appeared behind him and lifted the bundle from his hand.

'I'm expecting an important letter,' Everton said blandly. 'It won't make my fortune, but it may help humanity.'

He shuffled rapidly through the letters and picked out the one addressed to himself. It was in a cheap, buff envelope, and looked like a circular.

He returned the other letters to the waiter and strolled into break-fast. This was one of the traditional English dishes: a fish painted to resemble a kipper. Everton pushed it away.

'I'll have a continental breakfast,' he said. 'I mean the kind they serve in cafés, not concentration camps.'

The waiter hovered while Everton slowly opened the envelope.

'It's a photograph,' he said in surprise. 'Fancy!' He looked absently around him until his glance settled on the waiter. 'If you're allowed to take your eye off me for a moment, waiter, bring me an envelope.'

The waiter at first did not move, then he stood on one foot, debating. He came down on the side of service, and walked ungra-ciously away.

Everton stared at the photograph that had been taken the night before beside the bus stop. It was clearer than he had hoped. Zoe's meagre little face was pale as a paper flower; the man who was with her was recognizably the short-sighted waiter, but this time he wore glasses.

When the waiter returned with the envelope, Everton tore a page from his notebook, wrote a few words quickly, and slipped the photograph, the note, and Jan's sketch of the bony man, inside the envelope. He sealed it, and dangled it before the waiter, who still stood beside the table.

The man held out his hand.

'I shall post the letter?' he asked.

'No.'

'It would be faster, perhaps.'

'I haven't addressed the envelope, you see,' Everton told him, and looked directly into his face.

'You should practise a winning expression,' he said. 'You look like murder. And people who mean murder should never look like it.' He rose quickly to his feet. 'I'm going to post my letter now, so don't bother going to my room to tidy my shoes. I'm wearing them.'

He paused, tapping the letter on the table. 'I tidied your shoes yesterday—yesterday morning. You were out. The bowl of water you drink from was still on the floor.'

'I don't understand what you mean,' the man said, speaking in a tone that was not a waiter's.

'I mean I didn't know you kept a dog. But you kept this one for a very short time, didn't you? Now I'm going out to post my letter. By the time you decide how to stop me it won't be worth your trouble.'

He left the room, whistling a little, and posted the letter at the first box on the street. Then he wandered along in the morning sunshine until he came to the hat shop. No one had bought the Red Indian head-dress in the window, he noticed.

Zoe was in the shop. She was alone, but she looked happy and excited as though she had a big man from the milliner's world gazing at her from a corner. She was wearing a blue-and-white striped cotton frock that made her seem immature, and some make-up that added at least five years to her age.

'You look gay,' Everton said suspiciously. 'You've settled something in your mind. Perhaps you have decided to embroider a Duchess set. Or is it something deeper than handicrafts?'

'I'll tell you what it is,' Zoe said. 'At least, I'll tell you something. You're not on the side of the police, are you?'

'I'm not on anyone's side,' Everton said. 'I sometimes try to knock up a little score for myself. I'm the third team.' He looked at her, thinking of her simplicity. 'What do you expect me to say?' he asked irritably. 'If I were on the side of the police naturally I'd lie about it. If you want to confide in me, go ahead and confide, without pretending to be cautious.'

'There's just something I'd like you to know without doing anything about it so that I could let someone else know you know,' Zoe said.

'Well?'

'I have something they don't know I have.'

'Well?'

'I don't see why I shouldn't tell you,' she said. 'I've got the glasses.'

'The glasses?'

'Yes, that's all.'

'So if someone asks me I've to say you've got the glasses?'

'Yes. But they won't ask. I only want to be able to say you know.'

'Why me?'

'You're supposed to be interfering already. They'd believe I might have told you.'

'I'm not going to play,' Everton said firmly. 'Unless you tell me one thing.'

He watched her face sharpen. 'I only want to know if you're in love with Cady,' he said.

Her face relaxed again.

'He's rather sweet and romantic and exciting. He makes life seem—oh, as if it mattered more.'

'Like putting arsenic in your coffee instead of sugar,' Everton suggested. 'Is it Cady you're going to tell you've told me about the glasses?'

'No.'

'I'm glad. He has wonderful reflexes. He'd probably recoil and knock me over a cliff. Or out of a boat. Are you another of those people who like boating?'

'I can't sail. I'll be able to afford it one day. But I like swimming.'

'Five yards from the shore and scream when it gets to your waist?'

'I've got my club badge,' Zoe said. 'And I was the champion over all lengths in school.'

'You must teach me doggie paddle one day,' Everton said. 'When I've bought a new bathing cap.'

'Silly,' Zoe said. 'Now do go away. I've lots to do, if I'm going to see someone later.'

'Cady?'

'No.'

'Detectives?'

'No.' Zoe patted her hair. Then she opened her handbag, took out a lipstick and mirror, and tried to apply the lipstick without putting down the handbag. She sighed, and glanced at Everton. He was looking out of the window. She put the handbag down and concentrated on the lipstick. Everton turned suddenly and picked up the handbag. She lowered her hands slowly and turned to face him, the pink of her lips showing here and there through the dark carmine of the lipstick.

'Finish what you're doing,' Everton said. 'You can't go to meet a murderer with your face in that state.'

He flipped through the handbag, passing quickly over the usual oddments. At the bottom there was a packet wrapped in brown paper. He unwrapped it slowly.

'Why,' he said. 'I thought you meant brandy glasses. You should have told me you were short-sighted, Zoe.'

'I'm not short-sighted,' she said.

'Possibly not in every way.' He unwrapped the paper and looked at the thick lenses and heavy black frames. 'These seem very odd glasses for a young girl. You can have them back.' He wrapped them up and put them in her handbag. 'You should have your eyes tested. Or if you don't want to do that, why not have your mind tested? You'll get into trouble, you know.'

She sighed deeply as she took the handbag. 'I might get into money,' she said.

'Reward for catching murderer? Or do you mean something more direct?' He looked at her narrow young face, her eyes so nearly empty of experience.

'I don't care what happens,' she told him. 'I want to see some life, and you can't do that without money. I want to buy the clothes I read about in the magazines, and winter on the Riviera and meet Indian princes. I wouldn't mind being a film star, but it takes too long. I want to be like one of the people they make films about.'

'The girl the G-men get in the end as she's doing in her third lover—or the virtuous type with an Indian arrow through a non-vital part of her blouse and the hope of being a pioneer's wife?'

'I mean someone with one of those long cars and a newspaper reporter and some rich society people in love with her.'

'These girls often marry the newspaper reporter,' Everton warned. 'And blackmail doesn't necessarily lead to a long car and a boudoir the size of Liverpool Street Station. It's a crime. It's wrong.'

The obstinate, stupid film dropped over her face. 'Don't talk to me of right and wrong,' she said. 'I've heard too much of them in my time. However I do it, I'm getting out of this place. Now please go away. I've a lot to do if I'm to meet my friend in time.'

Everton left her. He was worried. But it was like being in hospital and worrying about the sickness of a stranger. She was free, depraved, and old enough to go to prison. The list of things that might influence her was short. It included only force, money, and a man.

When Everton arrived at the Bath's house he found that the police, in their undramatic way, had deserted it. The lawn was empty, the balconies unguarded. When the full account reached the newspapers, the sightseers would arrive. If the murder was never solved, the National Trust might take over. Murderer's corner. A little money could be made, he thought morosely, by the purchase of all the houses where murders had been committed. Just a small charge of sixpence to defray expenses. The thought of the silent figure on the floor, the floating form in the bath, would draw the crowds more certainly than the quill in the empty ink well, the knowledge that forgotten poetry had been composed in the room that had looked on the lake before the garage was built. This way to the room where he cut her up. Threepence extra admits to the kitchen where the poison was mixed. Why not be photographed with a gun at your head, in the chair he sat in while he bled to death?

He stepped softly on to the balcony and looked in the window of the living room. Lucy sat on the couch, her graceful arms behind her head. She was very still, and she was looking across the room at Jan.

'My dear child,' Lucy said softly, 'I don't pretend to understand. For God's sake try to be clear. What is it that you want?'

'I want money,' Jan said, in a harsh voice that Everton had not heard before. 'I want money. I want it now.'

'I've told you. The rotten little insurance company won't pay till after the inquest. And then—well, if the coroner decides that Gregory fell out of the window into the harbour five miles away just by accident, we might see the money sometime. But if he decides on suicide or murder, the insurance won't pay.'

'The insurance is lost because my uncle was murdered?' Jan frowned. 'I don't believe it. I can see that perhaps they won't pay now. But I didn't kill him. They can't prove I did. They can't stop the money coming to me. They can't even stop the money coming to you, Lucy.'

'I might take offence at the word "even",' Lucy said smoothly. She picked up her glass and sipped carefully. 'You know I couldn't have killed him. Even the police know that.'

'Do they know you weren't an accessory?'

'Don't be rude, little one. Maybe it was suicide, and then we lose the insurance anyway. They don't pay out on suicides.'

'My uncle didn't commit suicide,' Jan said. 'No matter how strong the provocation,' she added in a grating voice.

'Are you sure?' Lucy asked. 'The professionals never saw the body.'

'He didn't commit suicide. He wouldn't. It was one of his moral prejudices. He didn't commit suicide.'

'I'm sure I never gave him reason to,' Lucy agreed equably. 'So we're back where we were. You want money. You'll take offence, I'm sure, if I suggest that there are ways of earning it. Would you know what I mean?'

'Yes, Lucy. I know what you mean.'

'You're a priggish little thing. You may find it difficult to be priggish—and get the money you want.'

'You are so stupid, Lucy,' Jan said coldly. 'I was once a priggish little thing. Your great, clumsy mind simply can't contain the thought that people change. I'm not a priggish little thing any more. I'm a dangerous little thing. I think. You're so pleased with yourself. You were brought into someone else's racket because you were useful, and at once you begin to think you're a master mind. You think up the poorest plot on God's earth to get rid of your husband and drag the others in to help you, and they do it, because they know if it goes wrong they can get away and leave you to do the explaining, and if it goes well they can take your money and still get away. Of course it went wrong, and you and your silly little gang are left with nothing but trouble and no money at all. Don't think you're going to drag me in now.'

Lucy's beautiful face was immobile. 'And if you don't mean to be dragged in, just what are you suggesting?'

'I'm suggesting a little payment of debts,' Jan said coolly. 'You persuaded my uncle to stop my allowance. You owe me something. I'd like a cheque for a thousand pounds. You can call it an advance on the insurance. If neither of us was concerned in my uncle's death the insurance will come through in the end.'

'And what do I get for my thousand pounds?'

'Nothing,' Jan said. 'I'm not bargaining. I'm asking for a thousand pounds.'

'It sounds like blackmail,' Lucy suggested, in a lazy drawling voice.

'But it can't be blackmail, because you have nothing to be blackmailed about, have you, dear? It's an advance on the insurance.'

Lucy slid off the couch and put her glass down carefully. 'You little wretch,' she said quietly. She held her strong hands in front of her and walked forward. She caught Jan round the neck and shook her, then she flung her away and stood rigid.

'You're in a very dangerous position,' she said, her voice trembling. 'Get out!'

Jan had fallen back against a chair. She stood up. She was very pale. 'I'm in a dangerous position?' she said. 'Think, Lucy. Use that slow, stupid mind. Who's in the dangerous position? Will a charge of assault help? I think I probably have the marks of your fingers on my throat. I'll get out when I have the cheque for a thousand pounds.'

Lucy's wonderful eyes were blazing.

'You can put that idea out of your head,' Jan said. 'Don't get in too deep, Lucy. And don't think that I'm being stupid, too. All I want is a thousand pounds. I'll write you an acknowledgment that it is an advance on the insurance. I shan't want any more advances. I need this money, now.'

Lucy hesitated. 'Some women can't get a man unless they buy him,' she said in a coarse, grating voice. She went to the desk.

Jan was very pale now. 'And some women can't have a man without ruining him,' she said flatly.

Lucy waved the cheque in the air, drying the ink. She was in command of herself again. 'I hope he's willing to be bought, my dear. You must be in a desperate state. Will you write the receipt now?'

'It's written already,' Jan said steadily. 'I knew how your mind would work. I even expected to be assaulted. If anything happens to me it will look queer, won't it? You'll be the sole surviving legatee. But you like to be the centre of attention, don't you?'

She took the cheque and walked out of the room.

Everton, on the verandah, had remained very still. He thought he wanted never to see either of them again. He found hatred the most shocking of the passions. He thought of leaving very quietly, but instead he sat down and stared across the lawn at the sea. After a few minutes he looked up to find Lucy beside him.

'How long have you been here?' she asked abruptly.

'I wanted to give you an agreeable surprise,' he said. 'I thought if I waited here long enough you would appear.' He stopped, and seemed to become absorbed in the contemplation of her hands. 'And you did appear,' he added.

Lucy tried to measure the situation. Everton's carefully blank expression did not help her.

'I think you heard something,' she said finally. 'That—that niece of my husband's has been trying to blackmail me. I gave her a thousand pounds.' She looked at his face again. 'Damn you, Hugh, you might listen to me when I speak.'

'I was listening,' he said vaguely. 'I can tell you just what you didn't say. You didn't say you were frightened, and you didn't say you were angry, and you didn't say you wanted me to reassure you. But that's what you meant, isn't it?'

Lucy held out her hand to him and he took it with a shiver. 'I can't reassure you until I've reassured myself,' he said softly. 'When I met you the other night I spilt a drink in the bar, and interrupted a conversation. Your husband asked me why I spilt the drink. Why did I, Lucy?'

'Antipathy to judges, perhaps,' she suggested.

'And sympathy for liars,' Everton said. 'The barman was lying when he said he came from Genoa. I stopped the conversation before he was exposed. Not because I cared about the barman, Lucy. But because I knew you cared. You were like a cat with its back arched, and I wanted you to be a nice cosy puss again. Why was that barman hired, Lucy?'

'How should I know?'

'The night your husband was murdered he said you'd been writing a lot of references. Nice of you to try and help strangers into jobs.'

'What do you think I am. The quaker girl? Do stop playing comic strip detectives, Hugh.' She rose, panting. 'Stop it, I tell you. I won't be interfered with. If I'm not interfered with I'll do no harm. Don't force me to do something I don't want to do. Keep out of this, Hugh, and it will end.'

He stood staring at her blankly. Her rage was not smothered and thin-lipped. With her eyes glinting, her cheeks flushed, her full lips trembling, Lucy looked magnificent.

Suddenly, deliciously, she melted into tenderness. 'Hugh,' she said, 'don't be like this. Be as you used to be.' She held her hands out to him and he found himself moving forward. Then he remembered that only a few hours before the waves had fumbled the swollen body of her husband. He shuddered and moved away from her.

She gave an enraged cry and hit him hard on the face. He caught her by the shoulders, his fingers digging in the soft flesh, and kissed her angrily. He knew that he was doing what he wanted to do, and while he kissed her his obstinacy and terror faded.

When he let her go he felt for a moment clear and happy in his mind.

'I shouldn't come near you without someone to tie me to the mast,' he said softly.

'You make your own bonds, Hugh,' she said sadly. 'Why not break them—and stay? We could be happy, Hugh.'

'For how long?' he asked harshly.

'For to-night, to begin with.'

He stood looking at her, measuring, wavering. He felt his mind crumpling and his knees beginning to shake. He let his thoughts slip backwards, in the desperate hope that they would come to some source of strength. He was back in prison, in hospital, in the Seine, in Ronson's car. It was through Lucy that he had met Ronson, through Lucy that he had met Atkinson. He went back farther, to the supper table with Lucy, delicate and deadly in white lace and scarlet, Lucy's large hand closing on the money, Lucy's soft voice talking first of nothing then of more money. Why had she needed money? Had she been softening him down for Ronson? In the Embassy he was useful and she loved him, in prison he was better forgotten. And now? And now she was offering him happiness again. It was too large a gift to refuse. She waited, smiling, and a voice behind her said in cold surprise: 'Why, hello, Everton.'

Everton began to laugh. 'Ronson! I mean Atkinson. You're the last person I'd have expected to tie me to the mast. But now the boat has passed the danger point,' he said cheerfully to Lucy. 'And I shan't need to be tied up again.'

He nodded cheerfully to them both, and walked away across the lawn.

EVERTON, WALKING BACK ALONG THE SEA ROAD, CONSIDERED the time he had spent apart from his fellow men and women. He knew that he had finished with that part of his life; the hermitage was abandoned for ever. He intended never to see Lucy again, he regretted ever having met the late Mr. Justice Bath; Atkinson and Cady and Mrs. Leonard were frightening people; both Jan and Zoe were better left alone. But amongst them they had set him in motion again. Life was ready to begin. The first thing was to get another job. The world was full of people who had never heard of him; probably most of them wouldn't be very interested in his conscience.

He was still trying to revel in his freedom when he reached the town.

He intended to walk past the hat shop without a sideways glance, but this was too high an ambition. He allowed himself the glance. The shop was shut.

It was late for lunch, and the hotel was part of the life he was abandoning. He went to a café and ordered a meal, thinking idly of the past and earnestly of his future, which was to begin by writing to the travel agency, resigning from his ridiculous job.

He walked back to the entrance of the hotel, composing the letter in his mind. At the door he hesitated, and then walked on. The sun was shining, and he was free. Or nearly free. He turned to look at the hat shop as he passed it again. It was shut. Although it was against his new plan, he stopped, and tried the door handle. It was locked.

He looked around him in the sunshine. Other shops were open. He walked on again, uneasy, and not so free.

He walked to the end of the beach, where first there was a blank stretch of pebbles, then the sea rolling up against the soft cliff. He stood there for a long time, thinking vaguely first of Zoe, then of Cady, then of Zoe again. Finally he walked back again, and this time he went straight to the hat shop. It was still shut. There was no reason why Zoe shouldn't have taken the afternoon off. Or was there? He remembered that she had been going to meet someone. For the purpose of blackmail. She might be having a very happy time, blackmailing away.

He went back to the hotel to write his letter. When he had written it he went out again. The shop was still shut. Perhaps Zoe was already on her way to London, Paris, and other centres of gaiety, pouring champagne into her slippers and driving about in one of those glossy cars fifty-four feet long.

He went slowly back to the end of the promenade to catch a bus. He remembered the address that Zoe had written the night before to give to the photographer. He left the bus at the housing estate, and wandered through identical streets for half-an-hour before he found the right one. The house was a little less trim than its neighbours: it was easy enough to recognize the front door of a man whose mind was given to litigation.

Mr. Stokes himself answered the door. In the light of day the spots and stains and wrinkles on his dark suit wrote the brief obituary of respectability. He led his visitor into the kitchen, which seemed smokier and smellier because of the sunshine that scratched against the grimed windows.

Mr. Stokes seemed genuinely confused by the suggestion that he might have seen his own daughter. 'She's a good girl,' he said vaguely.

'But I wouldn't know where she is. I hardly expect her back at any time, to be precise. I get absorbed in my work, you know, mister. I'll make you some tea,' he said hopefully.

He put the kettle on the oil stove and stood in front of it, holding an aluminium teapot. He turned his head occasionally to peer wistfully at the volume that lay open on the table. The pages were heavily stained, probably with grease from a bloater.

'My case isn't going well at the moment,' he said sadly. 'Zoe's a good girl, but she takes no interest in the case. Now, I wanted her to do something more fit than working in a hat shop. If she'd taken up typing she could have been a help to me. With the case. I'll show you my notes. They'd be easier to follow, typed.'

He left the kettle, which very soon boiled over into the oil stove, and went to a cupboard. He brought out three cardboard boxes, and plunging in, came out with armfuls of foolscap paper, written very closely on both sides. 'If you'd like to tell me what you think of it,' he said. 'But don't take it away,' he added slily. 'Look at it here on the table, *if* you don't mind.' He pushed the teacups away and put some of the piles of foolscap on the table. Everton looked at it vaguely.

'Mr. Stokes,' he said, 'are you quite sure your daughter hasn't been here since this morning?'

Stokes shook his head blankly, looking in sorrow at his spurned notes.

Everton, making the noises of departure, stopped at the door to say: 'Wouldn't you like to walk to the bus stop with me, Mr. Stokes? A little sunshine would do you good,' he said, trying to be benevolent.

'Sunshine,' Stokes said bitterly. 'I know what that's worth.'

There was a letter addressed to Zoe on the table in the hall. Everton lifted it casually and put it in his pocket. Stokes was not a comfortable man, but he had the advantage of being the type who would not notice a little petty pilfering. The letter contained nothing but the photograph of Zoe and the waiter that had been taken the night before. Its presence on the table proved nothing but that Zoe had left home before the morning post and had not returned since.

When he had reached the sea front again, he left the bus and walked. This time there was no point in going to the hat shop. It was after six o'clock. Nevertheless he walked to the shop and tried the door again. When he turned round, Cady was swaying on the edge of the pavement.

Everton looked at him curiously. Since the fight, he was not afraid of Cady. Twenty-four hours earlier, the sight of Cady would have dried his mouth out like a desert wind. He was not afraid now, but he was not enthusiastic. Cady's attitude towards the death of his fellow men was one of loving curiosity: this gave him an advantage when violence was blowing along the streets like paper.

'Here,' said Cady, 'have you time for a word?'

'No,' Everton said.

Cady's freckles stood out. He looked earnest, like a boy scout studying a compass. 'Do you know,' he said, 'there are some things decent chaps do and some things decent chaps don't put up with.'

'I hope that molesting me is one of the things decent chaps aren't going to do any more,' Everton said. He felt unfriendly. He wished he had a gun.

'I think,' Cady said, with his air of malignant stupidity, 'that if a man has to die, well, he's passed on, but decent chaps draw the line at women being pushed to—passing on.'

'I'm glad you draw the line at female mortality,' Everton said drily. He recognized in Cady's words the pulped version of what used to be called a code, and wondered if they had accepted many mental defectives at Cady's public school.

'We must play the game as we see it,' Cady said, with enormous gloom. 'There are only two lots I know on the other side. You and the police. It doesn't seem to be playing the game, quite, to go to the police. Theirs not to reason why, and all that. But I want,' and for once his stupid eyes looked desperate, 'to get out of this. Zoe. You've been looking for her, haven't you?'

'And have you any other ideas about where to look?' Everton asked gently.

'I think she went for a swim this afternoon,' Cady said, moving his rubbery nose up and down. 'Yes, that's it. She went swimming.'

Everton let the silence grow around them. 'She didn't mean to go swimming when I saw her,' he said, in a carefully unalarmed voice.

Cady began to swing from one foot to the other. 'Well, old boy, that's what she did. They told her to. "You're going swimming," they said.'

'And then what happened?' Everton said, speaking very quietly.

'And then I went away,' Cady said quickly. 'It was nothing to do with me, old boy. But afterwards I thought about it. I can't go peaching to the police. But I thought I'd like to tell someone.' He took out his handkerchief and blew his nose.

'When was this?'

'Oh, I don't know. Two o'clock. Three o'clock. Hard to say. I've been walking about since. Thinking. I'd like to get out. It might be all right, you know,' he said pathetically. 'She's a good swimmer, Zoe. But I think I'd like to get out of it. Try something new. Africa, perhaps. Must be somewhere a chap can go and make a decent living. I wonder if there's anything to be done with the Indians?'

Everton didn't mean to let Cady go. 'Why don't you get your share of the money before you pull out?' he said. 'You probably think you've had your share, but I know some people in this racket who can write four-figure cheques several times a day.' He stopped to feel his way. 'I should go to—to the office, and run your eye over a few of the things that have been going on. They almost certainly keep a record, you know. You see what's owing to you. Write down a few facts and exchange them for money.'

Cady looked embarrassed. 'Never paid much attention to that kind of thing,' he muttered. 'Leave the haggling to the tradesmen and trust the other chap. That's my motto about money.'

'It seems a very old-fashioned one,' Everton said. 'Anyway, don't clear out until you have a few bundles of notes. You'll need them when it comes to buying false passports.'

'Oh, I can pick up a passport easily enough,' Cady said. 'Why, that's—well. You can take my word that end's all tied up. Very cosy. I've got a passport on me now, and I can change it for another easily enough.'

'Perhaps you can't—now,' Everton said. 'And the ports may be watched.'

'I'll take my boat,' Cady said. 'Atkinson's boat. Any boat. Whither, Oh splendid ship! Out of the country, that's whither. Well, good-bye. You'll look after the Zoe end, I take it.'

Everton watched him lurching off down the street. Cady now appeared to him as a man of so much simplicity that he wondered if he took some intellectually corroding drug. It was a mistake to credit half-wits with a charming innocence. Their deficiencies could include both charm and innocence.

Sickness and panic trickled into his mind as he tried to think what he might do about Zoe. Obviously he must go to the police. And he would tell the police—what? He would tell them a story so thin that its clothes would fall off halfway through. A girl had a pair of glasses that didn't belong to her. The shop she worked in had unaccountably shut. Cady said she had gone swimming. The story looked very malnourished indeed. Reluctantly, he moved towards a telephone. At the box he wavered. An unfriendly voice would certainly say What, and Who. It would end, he recognized, in a pretence of anonymity. He would refuse to give his name, the police would try to trace the call, a dust storm of suspicion would blow up, and most of the dust would settle on his shoulders. He stood irresolute on the pavement, forcing himself to understand how the reasonable inaction of the moment would appear in an hour or a day. Then he walked briskly to the police station.

He found Inspector Leigh sitting with a pencil in his hand, looking as dreary as a dog that hasn't been taken for a walk.

'I've been having a go at *The Times'* crossword puzzle,' he explained to Everton. 'Sharpening up my reasoning powers. Like Sherlock Holmes. But this thing is for literary types. I can't get on with it at all. A man of your type, now, could probably do it in five minutes before breakfast.' He folded the *Times* neatly and dropped it into the wastepaper basket. 'People who are used to wasting time, get good at these things.'

'That's it,' Everton agreed, 'they call it culture. You notice it particularly in jail, where the men have a lot of time on their hands. Convicts are a very cultured crowd. You should talk to them about Epstein one day.'

Leigh, forestalled in malice, scowled at Everton.

'I'll tell you what I've come for,' Everton said. 'I want to describe a mountain to you, and I hope you manage to turn it into a worm-cast. This girl Zoe—Zoe Stokes—works in a hat shop. She's Cady's girl friend. I think she was near the house the night of the murder.' He stopped, to think about the glasses in her handbag. He decided to leave them out of his story. 'I saw her this morning, and something she said suggested to me that—that she knew something about the murder, and was going to confront the murderer with some evidence. Since then the shop has been shut, and she hasn't been home.'

Leigh was moving his head from side to side, like a man with a stiff neck. Everton waited.

'Finish it, finish it!' Leigh said sharply. 'And don't ask me what I mean. You always leave half your story out. The way you've told this, it's a fascinating gap with a lot of dull stuff in between. The girl shuts shop and takes a day off in the sunshine. What am I to do? Arrest her?'

'I think she went swimming,' Everton muttered.

'How do you know?'

'Cady said they told her she was going swimming.'

'They?'

'He didn't say who They were. People never do, of course. He told me that and he said he was worried, then he went away.'

'Could she swim?' Leigh asked quietly.

'She told me she was a very good swimmer.'

'And how do you know she was near the house that night?'

'She just happened to tell me.'

'And that's another story with a long gap in it,' Leigh said with distaste. 'If I had some of that famous Russian truth drug in my drawer I'd stuff it down your throat. Now I'll tell you we've found a driver who went along that coast road late that night. He was going away from the town, and where the road is quiet he saw a girl walking in the middle. He was just pulling in to the side at the time. He had a friend with him and they wanted to look at the moon. His view is that the girl was walking in the road because she wanted a lift. A car came behind and she stayed in the middle of the road and the car stopped. There was some kind of discussion that lasted a few minutes and looked from a distance like a pick-up. Then the girl got in and the car went on to the town. He looked at it when it passed and there were two men in the front. I had the time from this driver. It was getting on for two o'clock. It was just about the time I'd have expected Atkinson's car to pass. When we'd finished questioning him and Cady he gave Cady a lift back to town. This driver didn't see any other car around that time. Naturally we thought of Cady's girl. Her father doesn't know when she got in that night. He was in bed. Did you know all this?'

'No.'

'Then what the hell did you know to make you so interested?' the Inspector said, in the voice of a belligerent.

'She was in the garden that night because I nearly caught her when I went out to look for the dog. I recognized her voice afterwards.'

'All right,' Inspector Leigh said savagely. 'We'll cut your explanations of why you didn't tell me this sooner. Now we've got to find the girl. I'll send a man to her home—one after Cady—pass on her description to the police cars.' He picked up the telephone. 'Got any other ideas?'

'Only one,' Everton said. 'If she did go swimming, where would she change her clothes?'

'At the sheds on the beach, I suppose.'

'You keep your mind in a bear pit, don't you? Why shouldn't she change on the beach?'

'Because it's draughty and indecent. You're probably not used to a high-class place like this.'

Everton groaned.

'All right,' the Inspector said. 'It's humiliating for me, working with someone like you who knows everything and says nothing. I'm glad you reminded me we should have the beach searched. Without you, I'd never have thought of it. Oh, God!'

Everton followed him to the outer office and listened to his instructions. On the pavement outside, the Inspector suddenly turned on him.

'What was she wearing this morning?'

'I—I can't remember,' Everton said. 'If—if I saw her again I'd remember. It was something blue—I think.'

'Get in the car.'

Everton got in.

'Someone else is searching the beach. We'll go first to the swimming sheds.'

The swimming sheds were large, ugly, white, concrete, with a few arches to remind the suggestible of Morocco. Under one of the arches an old man sat at an old card table, nodding over rolls of green tickets. The sun had set, the sand looked wet and grey, the sea was deep and still. The family parties had gone home, the deck chairs were folded up, the sand castles were yielding to the crawling tide. No one was swimming, no one was bathing, no one was paddling. The old man, loyal to his working hours, evidently meant to drowse his time out by the empty sheds.

He blinked and stared at the policemen.

'Girls,' he said, 'women?' He shook his head. 'I've seen plenty bathing beauties in my time,' he said cryptically. 'I take no interest.'

'But you'd know if someone had gone swimming and hadn't come back,' the Inspector said patiently. 'You wouldn't just let them drown.'

'Oh, I'd find their clothes in the end,' the old man said contentedly. 'Then I'd know. But it's never happened. And I've had a long time here. Lost children, now. We have lost children sometimes. But their mothers usually come for them,' he said, losing interest again.

'Are there any clothes here now?' the Inspector asked with less patience.

'We'll have a look,' the old man said peacefully. 'That's what we'll do. But there haven't been many swimming to-day. It's thinning down. There have been no women in since 5 o'clock, about. A few weeks more, and I'll have nothing to do till next year. You got any nice winter jobs I could do in the police, without descending to uniform?' He stood up, creaking, from his table, and led them into the empty concrete corridors of the swimming sheds. 'When it's busy, we make them put their clothes in those wire baskets. If it had been busy to-day, we'd have seen at a glance if there was any clothes left. But, oh dear, it hasn't been busy at all. I'll be out of work soon. It's a long, slow winter, and the summer's been long and slow, too,' he added with a yawn. 'No clothes in here, either,' he said, peering into another empty box.

'If things were so quiet, you might have noticed her, if she came in here,' the Inspector suggested. 'Did you see a dark, thin, young woman, probably in blue?'

The man chewed something that probably wasn't in his mouth. 'If the Queen of Sheba was to come in with Solomon I'd notice just enough to say Gents to the left, Ladies to the right. I don't notice women.'

They were nearly at the end of the second row of boxes.

'Do you notice women when you don't like them?' Everton asked.

'I don't notice any women. But as you say, if I don't like them I feel them in the air. I believe,' he said, stopping, 'that I felt one in the air to-day. But she wasn't in blue. I think she was in green. I couldn't tell you what her face was like, but I didn't take a fancy to it. And here we are,' he said with satisfaction. 'Here's something that will please you.'

He had opened the door of the end box, and now he pointed with pleasure to the few garments that hung from the hook. There was a frock of blue cotton striped with white and two flimsy undergarments.

On the seat lay a pair of white sandals and a white handbag. And that was all.

The malice and boredom dropped away from Leigh's face, and he stood staring emptily at the garments. Everton put a hand towards the frock, and dropped it again, hopelessly. The old man, looking from one to the other, suddenly seemed sharp and furtive and alarmed. 'There's something wrong, then,' he cried. 'It isn't my fault. I didn't know she'd go and drown herself, or I'd have noticed her. I'd certainly have noticed her if I'd known she was going to get drowned.'

'You've made up your mind quickly,' Everton said to the Inspector. 'Why are you so sure now that she's not coming back? She—she might have gone for a long swim.'

'If she went swimming from here before five o'clock she must be walking back along the bottom,' the Inspector said, picking up the handbag and opening it. He shook the contents on to the seat. 'You amateurs. Amateur detectives, amateur murderers. You make me tired.'

Everton, looking at the scattering of coins and lipstick and powder on the seat, saw that the glasses she had carried in her handbag had gone. Zoe had kept her appointment.

'Amateurs,' the Inspector repeated. 'Can't you see what should be here and isn't?'

'You mean—you mean from her handbag?' Everton said. He remembered he hadn't told the Inspector of the glasses.

'I don't mean from her handbag,' the Inspector said. 'We'd better go.'

Everton followed him from the sheds.

A T THE POLICE STATION INSPECTOR LEIGH SPOKE INCISIVELY to a sergeant. 'I want all the people connected with the Bath case. I want them here. Now.' He turned to Everton, who was standing numbly by his desk.

'You'd like to stay, wouldn't you?' he said in a menacing voice. 'You've been pushing your nose into everything. Don't take it out of the room now. And if you have the idea I want that great ice-cold brain of yours to guide me, get rid of it. I want you here because you're one of the people connected with the Bath case. Just sit around and think of all the lawyers you know. You may like to call one of them in to help you.'

Everton waited. The Inspector appeared to be engrossed in his notes, which occupied, so far as could be seen, about half-a-page in a small notebook. One of his subordinates was probably ghosting in a few hundred pages for the official report.

Everton waited. He thought he heard the voice of polite outrage in the ante-room. That would be Atkinson. If he had given up being Atkinson he would have shouted, like Ronson. If Zoe had been drowned, Ronson would have been the man to do it. He liked wet graves.

Everton waited. Female voices could be discerned. Deep, middling, and high. Big bear, middle-sized bear, little bear. But all of them were bearesses. Lucy was the big bear, and big bears were always frightening. Jan's was just a character part, and Mrs. Leonard, with her high voice, moved into squeaking farce. Cady should have been droning somewhere, but he didn't appear.

Everton waited, and the sergeant brought them all into the room. They gave an impression of collective wariness.

Inspector Leigh's politeness was so thin that an autumn leaf would have fallen straight through it.

'A girl, Zoe Stokes, has vanished,' he said curtly. 'If you want to tell me you know nothing about her, just keep quiet, and we'll save time. Everton knew her. He thinks she had some information about the murder of Mr. Bath, and that she intended to blackmail the murderer. Cady, who has not responded to my invitation to come here, said that she was going swimming.'

Atkinson's eyes flickered to the door and back again. Lucy wondered aloud if she could smoke. Jan seemed frozen, and Mrs. Leonard withdrew into one of her private worlds.

'The girl has not turned up,' the Inspector said. 'Her clothes have been found in a box in the swimming sheds. Wait. I don't want comments. When she left Everton she said she was going blackmailing, not swimming. I'd like to know what made her change her mind. And I'd like to know if she went swimming alone.'

'I don't quite see your point, Inspector,' Atkinson said in a shocked voice. 'People can't be forced to go swimming when they don't want to. Not that way, anyway. Not into swimming sheds and out again—to vanish.'

'But if they could be forced,' the Inspector said gently, 'it would take a woman to do the forcing. A man couldn't walk right through the women's section, to the far end, where the clothes were found, without attracting more attention than a murderer would want. You three,' he nodded towards Lucy, Jan, and Mrs. Leonard, 'you are the only women remotely connected with this case. I want to know what you've been doing all day. You can refuse to answer if you like,' he added drearily.

'Oh, I can answer,' Lucy said readily. 'But I can't prove what I was doing every minute of the day, you know, Inspector. I think I was at home all the morning. I had a row with my niece-by-marriage, didn't I dear?' she said to Jan.

'What kind of row?'

'About money. She wanted money, and she didn't want to wait for wills and lawyers and inquests and the insurance company to make up its mind. That's right, isn't it, Jan?'

Jan's hands lay still on her lap, under perfect control. 'That's quite correct,' she said. 'So I was at home, in that house, all the morning too. Lucy and I have long rows.'

'And in the afternoon,' Lucy said, 'I went and had my hair done. In a subdued style,' she said in a bereaved voice. She turned her head slightly, so that the Inspector could see her in profile. 'Then I went home again. The appointment was for four. And I don't know what else I can tell you,' she said, in a tone of touching appeal.

'I had lunch in the town,' Jan said. 'And in the afternoon I went for a long walk to pull myself together. I'm always very shaken after rows with my aunt-by-marriage.' She allowed one hand to creep up to the scarf round her throat. The Inspector's eyes followed the movement, and Lucy dropped her bag on the floor.

'And I spent the day regretting and writing,' Mrs. Leonard said dimly. 'On my cliff, staring at the sea.'

'You stared at the sea all day?' Inspector Leigh said, showing that he thought this implausible.

'At one point I took a bus into the town to buy some sausages. Vegetarian sausages. And some nut roll. And a little box of cress. And then I took a bus back again.'

Inspector Leigh had difficulty in holding down his movements of impatience. 'You're fond of the sea, Mrs. Leonard,' he said. 'Do you ever go in it?'

'Yes,' she said simply. 'One's thoughts are sometimes grander, freer, when one's body is buffeted by waves. I am a steady, but not a fast, swimmer.'

'I never go in the water,' Lucy said, shuddering. 'I hate the sea. I lived here only to please my poor husband,' she said sadly. 'But Jan's a splendid little swimmer. Aren't you, Jan?'

The Inspector looked from one to the other, then back at his own hands. 'This girl knew something,' he said, 'and I should tell which of you is concerned that we know something, too. This balcony business, now. That was a child's trick. The girl knew about it, of course. She was in the garden that night.'

'Did she tell you so?' Jan asked in a low voice.

'Our friend Everton bumped into her. She knew about the dog,' he said, his eyes moving quickly from one face to the other. 'She may have known about the ladder, too. Yes, I said ladder,' he suddenly snapped at Atkinson, whose eyebrows were already rising courteously. 'I've spent a lot of time and thought on those ladders, and I'm not going to have any of you people look supercilious about it.'

Atkinson's face closed up into a very good imitation of an honest soldier listening to a corrupt politician.

'I'll tell you what happened,' Leigh said slowly, 'and then we can all get together and decide which of you people was going to be the most embarrassed by this girl's knowledge.' He looked at them all, very slowly, in turn, and Everton saw, or thought he saw, the mask settling on every face.

'The balcony outside your late husband's room, Mrs. Bath,' Leigh said, addressing Lucy, 'was in dangerous disrepair. But until you arranged to have it mended, the danger was a threat, rather than a fact. Your husband very often stood on the balcony, and always did so late at night if his dog came and barked under his window. The dog was a spoilt brute, and it was probably common knowledge that your manservant hated it. The dog was let out into the garden last thing every night by the servant, who was also supposed to let it in. If the dog didn't reappear when he called, he rather enjoyed shutting the door. The dog was then in the habit of barking under your husband's window. He may have found this irritating, but when it happened he would step on to the balcony, call the dog, and go down and open the door for it. I suppose if he hadn't called the dog from the balcony he might have had to go in the garden to let it in. This happened probably about once a week. Anyway, often enough for everyone in the house to know about it. Then, like a good wife, you, Mrs. Bath, arranged to have the balconies repaired. The man, Peters, who finally came to do the job, discovered that the iron struts that supported the balcony were rusting away. He procured new struts and new bolts, and on the day of the murder he mended the balcony. He put the ladder up on the left side, took out the old strut, and fitted the new one, screwing it firmly to the wall and the balcony. He moved the ladder to the right side of the balcony, fitted the new strut there. He went down the ladder, got his tin of red lead, and without moving the ladder went up again, on the right side, and painted the strut. The red lead was to prevent the new strut rusting. He then moved the ladder back to the left side, painted that strut, and went home about five thirty. The dog, of course, was missing, as you all remember, and the judge was very concerned about its loss.'

Lucy put a large hand to her mouth and yawned quickly. 'Oh, I am sorry,' she said, 'but your story does seem to go on for ever, Inspector.

But I know you have to be thorough. Have you found out something new, something we haven't heard before?'

'I don't know if what I'm saying is new to you,' Inspector Leigh said in level tones. 'The man who was working on the balcony, Peters, went home at five thirty. That has been checked. Your servant says a man was working on the balcony after six. That servant of yours is an old-fashioned type. Too high class to get friendly with workmen in overalls. So he didn't pay much attention, just enough to register a little surprise, when he heard the noise, that the man was working later than usual. To be perfectly open about the matter, he can't tell us exactly to the minute when the man was working on this strange overtime, nor can he be sure what you people in the house were doing while what he supposed to be the repair of the balcony went on. He thinks you were probably having baths. It's a fact that some of you may have been looking for a little moral refreshment by then. I think myself that a hot bath is very soothing. Nothing much can happen to you when you're having a bath. Unless you're a bride in a million.'

He stopped and waited for the effect, but no one smiled.

'Anyway, you can't do anything much while you're having a bath. Whatever clock you've wound up is going to go on ticking. The judge, I think, probably was having a bath. Mrs. Bath and Miss Deverell may have been having a bath, or, rather, one or other of them may have been having a bath. There are only two baths, excluding a low-grade one for the servants, in that house. The story is that Miss Deverell had the bath first, quickly, and you,' he looked towards Lucy again, 'had it afterwards, slowly. I don't think it's important. It's ten to one it was a man up that ladder.' He looked at Atkinson, whose face remained expressionless, as though he were setting an example to recruits under fire.

'We'll leave that for the moment, and go back under the judge's window with the ladder. The workman, if you remember, used the ladder twice on the left side, once on the right. But when I examined the ground I found seven sets of impressions, four on the left of the balcony, and three on the right. So I think the mysterious six o'clock workman climbed up the ladder, unscrewed and removed the nuts and bolts from the balcony, and pushed the loosened struts outwards, so that they swung free of the edge of the balcony. To do this he first of all put the ladder on the left side, then moved it to the right to get at the other bolts, then laid the ladder back on the path, where he had found it. So the ladder had now stood for the third time on the left side and for the second time on the right. The nuts and bolts he made the mistake of putting down on the grass, with the spanner. He wanted to be able to get at them quickly afterwards. He had forgotten that as they were covered with wet red lead, they would leave a mark on the grass. They did. We've taken some of the blades of grass, after our little bit of colour photography, and we're holding them as one of the exhibits.'

He glared at Lucy. 'Please don't get impatient, Mrs. Bath.'

Lucy sat up with a start. 'I'd forgotten where you were, Inspector. I'm sorry to be so exhausted.'

'He's still under that window,' Atkinson said curtly.

Lucy lit a cigarette with her eyes shut, and dropped it almost at once on the Inspector's little strip of carpet. He leant forward, picked it up, and put it out at once on his tin ashtray. Lucy lit another cigarette, and the Inspector watched it carefully as he talked.

'I'll tell you where we were, Mrs. Bath. We were standing under a balcony that is now without support, and that would collapse under the weight of an ordinary man. Your late husband was large and at least fifteen stone. He thinks the balcony is safe as usual. He doesn't know that the whole thing will come down with a crash if he steps on it. His dog is missing. If it barks under his window, he is in the habit of stepping on to the balcony to call it. What actually happened was that the dog howled under his window. But it howled a minute too late. He had already been shot. That might be lucky for someone,' he said with mock benevolence. 'If he hadn't already been shot, he'd have stepped on the balcony and died that way, and then the people who made the arrangements about the balcony and the dog would have been in very serious trouble. However, he is shot. Mrs. Bath finds the body. Time passes. Mr. Atkinson goes to her support. A long time elapses. They reappear. Mr. Cady and Mr. Everton go up to look at the body. They see it. They come down again. There is some business about telephoning the police, and a telephone that doesn't work, although it does. So Mr. Atkinson has to go in his car for the police while Mrs. Bath has hysterics and Mr. Everton has to wait until they are over before he goes out in the garden. There he almost catches the missing girl, Zoe Stokes, and does in fact, find the dog, under the window, injured. So it wasn't surprising if it howled. When the police come, the body is missing, and that's all.' He stopped, poured himself some water, and took a long drink.

'Surely not all!' said Jan.

'All?' Atkinson asked in surprise.

'The body turns up in the sea, and it has a hole in its head. But you know about that.'

Atkinson put one of his hands on the desk, looked at it, then put it back in his pocket. 'You've left something out,' he said anxiously. 'The fourth ladder mark to the left, the third to the right. You haven't told us about that.'

The Inspector looked at him, while the silence grew until Everton could hear the blood in his own ears.

'That hardly needs to be explained. By the time the police came, the struts under the balcony had been screwed up again. Very soon after the murder, someone who was interested put the ladder up again, once on the left and once on the right, and very inexpertly put the nuts and bolts back on. It wasn't a good job. The nuts weren't tightened, so that the balcony moved a little if anyone stood on it; and it wasn't a clever job, because the wet paint was rubbed off while he was doing it. But it was certainly a quick job. Unfortunately, there wasn't any safe, rapid, and quiet way of getting rid of the dog, so he gave it a tap on the head with the spanner, still wet with red lead, and hoped to do something about it later. Not every one of you had the opportunity to do this last bit of ladder moving. Mrs. Bath, Atkinson, or Everton, who was actually in the garden when the police came, might have done it. But I don't think Everton could have moved the body. He didn't have a car—like you, Atkinson—and even if he had borrowed Mrs. Bath's car, he wasn't out of the house long enough. And he certainly walked back to the town when we'd finished with him. We checked on that. Miss Deverell seems a bit vague. She was certainly at a dance most of the evening. She was driven back to the house late, more than an hour after the murder. But we haven't been able to fill in every minute of her evening.'

'She was probably sitting out in the cloakroom, concealing her lack of partners,' Lucy said, opening her eyes very slightly.

'We can't make it more than half-an-hour gap, and it may be less,' the Inspector said, frowning. 'From something after eleven to something before quarter to twelve. If these times are right, it would have given her a chance if she had been very quick, to borrow a car, get to the house, stay for about two minutes, and drive like hell back again. She would have had to borrow a car of course. But we can't be dead sure of the time. People remember who they danced with when the band was playing what, but no one remembers how long the numbers lasted.'

'There was a Paul Jones,' Jan said in a dead voice. 'I hate them. I can't bear to dance with strangers. I went in the cloakroom to avoid it. I think I stayed longer than I meant to. When I came out it was a tango, and I waited until it was over before I danced again.'

'Precisely,' Lucy said.

Mrs. Leonard stood up very slowly. 'There is poison in this room,' she said wildly. 'When you speak to each other it's like murder all over again. I have no car. I do not climb ladders and work with spanners. I didn't drown this girl. Why am I here, with hatred beating against me like nettles, when I had nothing to do with the girl?'

'But you did have something to do with that girl,' Inspector Leigh said softly. 'You went to see her twice in the hat shop yesterday. You and Cady seem to be the links with the girl.'

'I saw her going to the house. She stayed a long time. I told you.'

'It would have been enough to tell me, perhaps. What did you tell her? Or what did you want to ask her? Were you trying to find out how much she had seen?'

'Yes,' Mrs. Leonard said simply. 'She was there before the murder. I didn't think she knew the—the late Mr. Bath. I wanted to know how she came to learn that something was going to happen to him, that night. But everything is clear to me now. I feel it.' Her shallow brown eyes flickered upwards, met the Inspector's professionally sombre gaze, and dropped down again rapidly. 'The man who brought the dog told her.'

'He's a new character,' Atkinson said with a sudden, astonishingly harsh laugh. 'The first man in the case who's not me.' His hands had wandered out of his pockets again, and he pushed them back.

'Cady's in the case,' the Inspector reminded him. 'Although Cady didn't remove the body.'

Atkinson appeared to recognize the provocation, but did not act upon it.

'You gave the girl a lift back in your car that night,' Inspector Leigh said smoothly to Atkinson.

'No,' Atkinson said shortly.

'You were seen by witnesses whom I could produce in court. If the case ever gets to court. Did you give her a lift?'

'Yes. I gave her a lift. Is it a crime to pick up a girl who is walking in the middle of the road late at night, looking over her shoulder in the hope of getting a lift?'

'It's not a crime. But it's interesting. You, you now,' the Inspector twisted in his chair to face Everton, 'what did the girl tell you about her blackmailing intentions?'

'She didn't positively tell me anything. She had arranged to meet someone, she said she meant to get some money.' Everton found he had a desire to avoid Leigh's glance. He lurched into explanation. 'She told me she had the glasses. She had some crazy idea it would help her if I knew. Glasses,' he repeated heavily. 'She had them in her handbag. A man's glasses. Thick, strong. I thought they were the waiter's. A waiter at my hotel. He's very short-sighted.'

'A waiter?' Leigh bent forward, hopeful, detached, but still ingratiating, like a cat that rubs itself against a trousered leg. 'Did you think she was going to blackmail a waiter?'

Everton looked involuntarily at Atkinson. 'Yes,' he said loudly. 'I thought she was going to blackmail the waiter. Because he was the man who had the dog. I went in the waiter's room. It smelt of dog. It's that kind of dog. On a hot day you could smell it from France. The waiter's room is small and hot, and it smelt of dog. There was a bowl on the floor, with some water in it. That must have been for the dog. Mrs. Leonard saw a man of the waiter's build lead the dog in the garden, just before the shot was fired. The waiter tried to pick up Zoe and take her for a lonely walk on the beach. So I thought they must have been his glasses.' As Everton spoke he looked hopefully, not at Leigh, but at Atkinson.

'We'll have the waiter checked,' Leigh said. 'But if he came in the garden with the dog he was part of plot one. The plot that failed. I'm more interested now in the second plot, the plot that worked. Perhaps they weren't the waiter's glasses at all. Perhaps they belonged to the late Mr. Bath. In that case they'd hardly be blackmailing mate-rial—unless they'd got in the wrong place, like the smell of dog. The wrong place wouldn't be in the house,' he slumped back in his chair and shut his eyes. He seemed to be thinking aloud. 'The only wrong place for these glasses would be somewhere not associated with the body, alive or dead, of the late Mr. Bath. And when was that body in the wrong place? When it was somewhere between the house and the sea. In a car, almost certainly, because that was the only way the body could have been moved. Did you say you gave that girl a lift, Mr. Atkinson? Could she have found anything in your car?'

'No,' Atkinson said steadily. 'She couldn't. Nothing that I put there.'

'And nothing that dropped off?'

'Nothing that dropped off anything that I put there.'

'Then we must find out who borrowed your car, and when, to move the body. The girl was in the garden, watching. She probably saw. She rode in your car, later in the evening. She found, or I think she found, the glasses. She was going to use them, or Everton says she was going to use them, for blackmail. Then she vanishes, or appears to have vanished, this afternoon. And what were you doing this afternoon, Mr. Atkinson?'

'I was sailing,' Atkinson said coolly. 'But I'll tell you what I wasn't doing two nights ago. I wasn't shooting Bath. I was in a room with three other people when the shot was fired. No one could blackmail me for a crime I didn't commit. What am I being accused of?'

'You're not being accused,' the Inspector said. 'Just warned. There are too many people in this trapeze act, and I think one is losing his nerve.'

The telephone on the desk rang, and Leigh picked up the receiver. 'Constable Perkins, yes. Send him in.' He put the receiver down. 'We had a search warrant for your house, you know,' he said to Lucy apologetically. 'Perhaps we're using it too often. I've just had some men out there.'

A large, thin, beaky constable, almost oozing suppressed information, appeared in the room.

'The man from the swimming sheds thinks he's identified the green frock, sir. It was in the young lady's wardrobe.' He looked at Jan, and Lucy suddenly burst into laughter.

'You bitch!' Jan said. Then she began to cry.

'You're a savage little thing, aren't you?' Lucy said with deliberation. An expression that might have been cruelty flashed across her face and was gone, leaving it a model of hurt womanhood.

Jan was ordering her mind under control, and the struggle was visible. 'You're trying to destroy me,' she said finally, in a voice that ground out the words as though she were groping her way through a foreign language. 'Destruction is your hobby, isn't it, Lucy? But I don't think you have time to save yourself. You can lash around, but it's too late. Now, I'm going. Good-night.' She nodded to the Inspector. He made no move to stop her, and she left the room, walking very slowly, like someone who has had almost too much to drink.

'I don't know what to make of that,' Lucy said in a puzzled voice. 'She's been behaving very queerly for a long time, now.'

'She lives in a very queer house,' Mrs. Leonard said harshly. She exchanged looks with Lucy, then the Inspector, apparently exhausted, told them they could go.

'Do you want to come back for a drink, Hugh?' Lucy asked pathetically.

'I'm going to bed with my head under the blankets, the door locked, and a brick in each hand,' Everton said sourly. 'Good-night, Lucy.'

He hurried out to see if he could find Jan.

S HE HAD CROSSED THE ROAD, AND WAS STANDING ON THE EDGE of the promenade, looking at the sea. Even in the dusk Everton recognized her by the floating coat and the wisp of hair that was slipping down from the back of her small head.

'I should say you were easy to identify,' he said, touching her hand lightly. She did not turn round. 'But old Drearyboy at the swimming sheds would hardly know the difference between the fat lady at a circus and Cleopatra. Even if Leigh put you in an identity parade with eleven dwarfs Drearyboy wouldn't be able to pick you out.'

'Are you trying to console me by saying you know I was at the swimming sheds but they won't be able to prove it?' she asked. She didn't turn round.

'It sounded like that. But what I meant was that it's all bluff. Drearyboy was trying to prove that he hadn't got to the point of senility where the kindest thing would be to bury him. He had to say he'd observed something, so he plunged into his unconscious, which I should think is the largest part of his mind, and came up waving the fact that he'd seen a woman in green he didn't like. The idea that he could tell the difference between a frock made of dyed sackcloth and a piece of filmy green lace is ludicrous. Leigh was trying to bluff. He hoped you'd burst into tears and dictate a ninety-five page confession, foolscap, single-space typing. I know I'm being hearty and annoying. Come and have a drink.'

She nodded. 'We'll go back to your hotel,' she said, 'then I'll know what I want to talk about.'

The gentle-eyed barman was evidently having a night off. The short-sighted waiter stood in his place behind the bar, his expression defying any customer to ask for anything. One or two people sat at the little tables, holding empty glasses and nervously whispering to each other.

Everton ordered whisky for them both, in loud and peremptory tones. 'Have you decided where you're going when you leave?' he asked the waiter, as he picked up the glasses.

'I do not intend to leave.'

'Oh, yes, you do. You're going to leave this hotel. You're going to leave this town. It may be too much to hope that you are going to leave this country, but for the present I'd like you to leave this end of the bar, so that you can't listen to my conversation.'

The man's hand closed tightly over the siphon he was holding, and there was a moment of complete stillness, of the kind that often comes before violence and confusion. Then he put down the siphon and moved quietly to the other end of the bar.

Everton moved back to the table where Jan waited.

'You see I'm happy and confident,' he said. 'I'm even more agreeable than that. I'm not going to talk about Lucy.'

'But I am,' Jan said wearily. 'I'm going to talk about her. You heard my conversation with her this morning, didn't you?'

'I what?'

'Don't waste time pretending. You were on the verandah. I heard you come. If I went on with the—the discussion, it was partly for your enlightenment.'

Everton felt for his cigarettes. He went through all his pockets. Jan waited. He lit cigarettes for both of them, thinking of several things he might say. But he knew Jan well enough to understand that she would not be deflected. The conversation was going to be long and full of unpleasant revelations, and it was too late now to talk about literary trends. 'Or gardening,' he said. 'You wouldn't like to discuss gardening?'

'Don't play the fool, Hugh,' Jan said. 'You've evaded the issue too long. You heard how Lucy and I talked. You saw her give me a cheque. Do you think she did that out of kindness?'

'All right,' he said. 'You have a story to tell. Tell it quickly.'

'Getting money from Lucy is about as easy as going into a cage and taking meat from a starving lion. She loves money. Why do you think she gave it to me?'

He picked up his glass and drank quickly. 'If you must know, I think she gave it to you because you were blackmailing her. I'll get us both another drink.'

'Not now. I want to talk.'

'I listen better when I'm drinking. Please don't go on talking, Jan. You were blackmailing Lucy because I was listening and you wanted me to believe that she had done something criminal or she wouldn't have parted with the money. And the next time I see Lucy she'll tell me she let you blackmail her because I was listening and she wanted me to know how unpleasant you were. The only thing that comes out of it all is that I'm a good listener but a bad eavesdropper. Next time I think of listening in to other people's business I'll wave a red flag and clash some cymbals together, so they'll know the right moment to begin. If you ask me, you and Lucy were having a fine blazing row before I appeared at all. Maybe you noticed I was there at some point, but only when it was too late to stop. You hate each other. Everything you say about Lucy is coloured by the fact that you hate her. She hates you too, but she can think of other subjects to discuss.'

'I knew it would be the same,' Jan said desperately. 'It's always the same. If you saw her holding someone's head under the bathwater you'd still think of an excuse for her. I don't know if she killed her husband, but she tried to. Who would be behind that stupid balcony plot but Lucy? No, you're going to listen, Hugh. You've been in prison, haven't you? Lucy sent you there. You cashed that cheque for her, because she said she needed the money. It was a thousand pounds, she needed, wasn't it? You were poor. To get the last three hundred of that thousand you wrote the cheque. Why did she need the money? She was the wife of a man who had plenty of money and who was generous to her. She had rich friends. But she went to you. Why?'

'Perhaps I was friendlier than her other friends,' Everton said. He intended to hurt her, but he didn't want to know if he had succeeded. He kept his eyes on the table.

'She went to you because you were friendlier. And because you were weaker, too. Yes, weak,' Jan repeated. 'She went to you because you were with the Embassy, because you could be useful. She went to you because she'd been told to get you into money trouble. She asked for all the money you had and took it and then asked for more. Why?'

'I don't want to discuss this,' Everton said furiously. 'But if you must know why, because she was being pursued by a rotten little blackmailer. She'd been married before, in Poland, and her husband left her and she thought he was dead. So she married again and then he turned up and blackmailed her. She said it would have ruined her husband's—Bath's career. He hadn't retired then.'

'And what was the bait?' Jan asked, with a chilled little smile. 'Even you could hardly have been prepared to go on paying her ex-husband's demands for ever. You must have read about blackmail in books, and known it doesn't stop quickly. I expect she said she just wanted time to think it out and then she'd come away with you and as you knew about it already the blackmailing would end. And my uncle would have divorced her. You could all have lived happily ever after, in Bulgaria, or Poland, or whatever country she was pretending to come from at the time. Lucy and her rich father. She was a chorus girl, that's what she was, and she wasn't a very good one. She worked in second-rate cabarets in places like Budapest. Her father wasn't a grain merchant or a wine merchant or even a merchant for corn plasters or plastic leather buttons. He was a bus driver and he lived in Battersea.'

'How do you know?'

'I don't know,' Jan said, sniffing. 'But it's perfectly probable. You make me so angry I find I'm saying things I don't mean. I don't know what her father was, but it's perfectly true she was a chorus girl. I've been to cabarets with her—in Paris—and she looked at the girls and talked of the turns in a cold, professional way. She knew what she was talking about. When she said a girl had no dash, or criticized the lighting, or sneered at the star, you knew she was thinking about it from inside. When she married my uncle she behaved more like someone who'd left her convent only to look after her widowed mother. I believe she was in some kind of painting racket. She nearly got misunderstood through helping a gallery to sell fake Old Masters. Old Minor Masters. My uncle met her through a friend of his who was investigating the forgeries and was struck by Lucy's innocence and charm.'

'Will you have another drink, or will you stick to vitriol?' Everton asked.

Jan had been talking wildly. Now she suddenly grew calm. 'Lucy didn't want to borrow your money,' she said. 'She wanted to put you in a position where you would need money desperately. She worked on you till you had passed that cheque. Then—then I'm sure someone came to you with a proposition for earning money. Probably someone whom Lucy appeared hardly to know.'

'Why would she do that?' Everton asked, in a carefully steady voice.

'Oh, just a short cut to corruption. How do people who work in gangs get respectable people to help them? They have to undermine the respectable people, somehow. They make them take to drink, or lose money gambling, or help them to develop expensive tastes. They must be made to need money before the money is offered. Think, Hugh. Think back to Paris. Think why you signed that cheque. Think if you weren't made an offer just afterwards.'

Everton went to the bar and bought two more drinks, staring absently at the ugly waiter as he poured them out. He came back with the drinks and sat down beside Jan. He tried to bring his mind up to the big jump again, but it stopped dead, like an unwilling horse. He had never been able to make himself think clearly about Lucy, and the cheque; about Ronson and his suggestion; about that last half-hour before he had been dropped in the Seine and left to drown. But there had been a murder, almost certainly two murders, since then, and the time had come when he must think clearly about Lucy. He brought his mind to the jump again.

Lucy had said she was desperate, she was going mad, she would kill herself, her husband would kill her, if she didn't have the money. She had said she loved him, but she would have to find a richer man, a friend who would be able to help her. There had been tears, hysteria, courage, and resignation. Windows had been flung open, although Lucy had not jumped out of them; guns had been flourished, but not fired. Letters had been written, but not posted, to Mr. Justice Bath—a shadowy figure, who had not appeared in Paris. His arrival, according to Lucy, was imminent, but he had not arrived. He had been on circuit. The blackmailing husband was also a shadowy figure, but letters were received from him. Lucy had alternated between noble despair and womanly panic. Everton had not eaten for days: he and Lucy had sat down together at dozens of tables; they had rushed, weeping or swearing, away from half-a-dozen restaurants. Delirious reconciliations had been sandwiched between savage rows; there had been intervals of exhaustion, but they had enjoyed an unforgettable emotional feast.

He had told her to find a richer friend. The next night she had appeared with a Belgian who had something to do with machine tools. Everton had gone back to his flat alone. He had sat, shaken by remorse and rage, for two hours, then Lucy had appeared at his door, weeping. Money, she had cried, dropping on her knees beside him, would never take her away from him; she had dismissed the Belgian. The reunion had been passionate and pure. Everton had felt a little like Galahad when he left her to cash the cheque. He gave her the money at their last dinner together. She had been gay, enchanting, but not, it seemed, particularly grateful. He had a suspicion that perhaps the ex-husband from Poland was increasing his demands. Everton had been morose and uneasy. He had been trying to sell his car. A friend knew a man who was willing to pay for it; if the friend's friend had the ready money, there would be time to cover the cheque. The dinner had been miserable, folly had suddenly dropped its mask and appeared to him, in a brief, terrifying glimpse, as madness; the chivalrous and the criminal had become entangled; the man who might buy the car had appeared in the more logical form of an agreeable myth. The dinner had ended in the usual storm. And then Ronson had appeared.

Jan was right. Ronson had appeared afterwards. Ronson had made his proposition after Lucy had forced the signing of the cheque. Ronson had made his proposition and offered cash in advance, when there was still time to make good the cheque. Ronson's moment had been chosen with precision. It was not coincidence, Everton thought, driving his weary mind to the jump. Lucy and Ronson had acted together; the corruption had been carefully planned and carried out with exquisite histrionics. And the end of it had been failure. He had declined Ronson's offer. He was a bad debt, a piece of faulty planning. He deserved to be eliminated, and Ronson had tried to eliminate him. He deserved to be abandoned, and Lucy had abandoned him.

He looked up, haggard with thought, into Jan's sorrowing eyes.

'Hugh, I hate to see you look like that. But I had to try and make you think—make you ask those questions. I was right, wasn't I?'

'But why was she pleased to see me again? Why did she ask me to her house? Why did she want to drag me into this?' he said despairingly. 'And Ronson. Ronson must be Atkinson. He must. Then I suppose I was still a dangerous man. If I could recognize him, and know he was with Lucy, I was dangerous. Do you know what Ronson suggested to me, Jan? He wanted me to use my C.D. car to take a few people over the frontier. Just a few honest people that the police were watching for. It must have been intolerable to Lucy, that I should turn up that night. I suppose the quickest thing was to try and drag me into it. And Atkinson—Ronson—was offering me money to keep quiet. A thousand pounds. That sum keeps cropping up.'

'It's going to crop up again,' Jan said, in a stiff, prim voice. 'I think it's time you got out of this, Hugh. Out of this mess. Out of this country. Out of the stupid job you've been doing. So here you are.' She opened her handbag and brought out an envelope. She laid it on the table in front of him. 'There you are. It's yours. It really is yours, Hugh. It's the money you gave her long ago. I took the chance to get it this morning, to get it back, for you. I think you should take the chance to go somewhere else and forget about all this. A thousand pounds isn't much, but it might help you to start again.'

He picked up the envelope, took out the cheque, and put it down on the table between them.

'I can't take blackmail money, Jan,' he said. 'I can't take Lucy's money. I know I spent some money, long ago, but think of the experience I bought. I wish you'd give the cheque back to Lucy. Don't tell her you offered it to me. She—she—' he hesitated, and Jan interrupted.

'She'll despise me for the idea,' she said. 'I know that, Hugh. Softness infuriates her. I suppose she didn't marry my uncle just for his money. He was a very hard man. She liked that. And to a collector of emotions, there would be something attractive in marrying a judge. If you were a criminal. Of course, being a judge, he was incorruptible. So his uses were limited. That's why she got rid of him in the end.'

'Got rid of him?'

'This balcony business.'

'But she didn't get rid of him,' Everton said obstinately. 'He was shot, and she didn't shoot him. Unless she did it by remote control.'

'Very well,' Jan said angrily. 'Of course you defend her, even now. She didn't shoot him, and you and Atkinson and Cady didn't shoot him. Maybe the dog shot him. Or who else?'

Everton drew a spiral pattern with his finger on the top of the damp table. 'And you didn't shoot him, Jan,' he said. 'But do be careful what you say about Lucy. She can prove she didn't, and you can't. You did have that long interval avoiding the dance. Now give her back the cheque. I shall prosper in the end. I shall go to Australia and disguise myself as a sheep and sell my wool.'

'Oh,' Jan said. 'You're so scrupulous. It's maddening.' She picked up the envelope, nodded briefly, and left.

He sat on, drawing patterns idly, and waiting for the water in his brain to turn into wine. He thought of Ronson, and allowed him to become confused with Atkinson. He had not asked Ronson what type of innocent refugee was to be run over the border into Spain. Refugee was a fine word, it automatically suggested the virtuous oppressed, although the refugee might be a villain, escaping from the virtuous oppressors. Even now there were plenty of people on the run in Europe. Communists were chasing capitalists; dictators hounding democrats; socialists hunting fascists. People on top everywhere were persecuting the people who had fallen to the bottom; the old scores were a short list compared to the new scores; the secret police were, as usual, being secret only up to a point; their intentions were frequently public and alarming; the results they achieved gave only slender assurance to the law-abiding. The mass activity of armies was restricted; the private efforts of generals, and even, sometimes, of corporals, were disastrously free.

Everton, absorbed in these meditations, found that a face was rising in his mind. It was a face that had once found its smudged publicity in the newspaper photographs; it had found its power earlier, in the war. It was a face that had been known particularly in France. It had something to do with coal-mining. It had something to do with slave workers. Some members of the Resistance had been captured, once. They had been sent to the coal mines and used up very quickly. A German civilian, a mining expert, they said, had organized the affair. Later, he had returned to Germany and organized recalcitrant prisoners of war and a few dissident Germans in the same manner. The death roll had been long enough to reach the bottom of a coal mine with a few yards to spare. The free German miners had objected, although perhaps not very strongly, but when the post-war trial sent the organizer to prison for a modest twenty years, it was felt that he had gone to the place of greatest safety. Hadn't there been some peculiar, politically-important, escape? And what had the man been called?'

The frog-faced waiter came to the table to collect the empty glasses. He brought a rag with him, and mopped the damp table-top viciously.

'Hello, Ullmann,' Everton said, almost absently. 'No wonder you leave off your glasses. Your picture in those heavy glasses was in every newspaper in Europe. I wonder how you got here? And where you're going next?'

The man dropped the wet rag and stood with his hands on the table, peering through narrowed eyes at Everton's face. He looked swiftly round the bar; everyone else had left. He felt in his pocket, brought out a spectacle case, and put on his heavy, black-rimmed glasses with a sigh of relief.

'Is that your only pair?' Everton asked.

'My only glasses. I protect them.'

He stared again at Everton, and this time his face was powerful and strong instead of strained and confused.

'So,' he said finally, 'you have had your letter.'

'No. I worked it out for myself. There will be a letter to-morrow morning. And probably a flock of military spies. Intelligence, it's called, when it's on our side.'

'But still the spies—the Intelligence—have not come. You are impulsive, Mr. Everton.'

'And you are reckless, to stay here when the police are interested.'

'But you yourself gave the warning to come back. The police you said, and truthfully, would have brought me back if I had vanished so near a murder and so soon. So, in my ignorance of the case, I came back. If you had not given the warning, I should have gone.' He went to the bar, stepping clumsily sideways, with his eyes on Everton. He reached over the bar and brought out a whisky bottle. He put it down on the table beside Everton and then, more rapidly, fetched glasses and a jug of water. He poured drinks for them both. 'We shall be alone,' he said. 'We can talk.'

'What subject can we think of?'

'Money.'

'I thought it could do its own talking.'

'I hope that it can.' Still watching Everton carefully, Ullmann unbuttoned the barman's white coat. He put his hand inside his shirt and brought out a thick packet, wrapped in clean white paper. He threw the bundle on the table in front of Everton.

'Two hundred pounds,' he said. 'Count them if you wish.'

Everton remained quite still. 'Explain them,' he said coldly.

'I like my name and business to be private.'

Everton sighed. 'You are pretending to be slow-witted,' he said. 'I told you I had posted my letter. There is nothing I can give you for the money, now.'

'Was the photograph a good one?'

'Very bad. But not bad enough. You wore your glasses, you know.'

'If I leave and you say nothing it will not be noticed at once—if you do not speak.' He watched Everton's face keenly for signs of weakness. 'You are interested, you see. You are interested in two hundred pounds. You might like four hundred pounds. Something can be done with four hundred pounds, and all I ask is that you shouldn't speak. In two days I can go very far.'

'The police can go farther—in a day and a half.'

'Not always,' the man said carelessly. 'The barman, you see, has already left. It is his day off. To-morrow he is not back again, and at first no one sees. He may have left the country. It is possible.'

'It is certain that he hasn't gone back to his own,' Everton said coldly.

'He had some little excess of loyalty to the last regime that would make his return to Italy awkward,' Ullmann agreed. 'But there are other countries. It can be arranged. England is the best for—is the word "convalescence"? Here even the English waiters pretend to be foreign. What could be noticed less in England than a foreign waiter? It is necessary to stay here a little time, to acquire a good past before moving on.'

Everton encouraged his hand to stray lovingly towards the packet of notes.

'And how do you come?' he asked, his eyes on the money.

'We come by sailing craft,' Ullmann said, watching Everton's hand. 'It is very well organized,' he added with approval. 'One is well looked after, from the moment the money is paid. It is like your Cook's tours. And when we land in the little harbour here, at once we are not strangers. We are waiters, acquired by the agency.'

'And do many people come?'

'Oh, no. It is necessary to have money. And so many worthy men have none. But if you have the money, then, the Cook's tour. And from the time we land in England, we are safe. More important men than I have been waiters in this hotel,' he said with satisfaction.

Everton picked up the package and slipped off the paper cover. He took a note from the top of the pile and ran his fingers over it, feeling the texture.

'You caused the death of hundreds of men, in your time, Mr. Ullmann,' he said.

'They caused their own death,' Ullmann said shortly. 'Only the weak died. The strong men lived.'

'And these strong survivors. They are all in France now? Or Germany? I see why you want to be in England. But we'll think of the weak who died. I'm a weak man myself. But I'm strong enough to do this with your money.' He picked up the bundle of notes, fanned it out, and threw it in the air. Ullmann's shocked gaze followed the notes first up, then down, as they fluttered to the floor. Everton put his hands under the side of the table and flung it into Ullmann's face.

As he fell, Ullmann grasped the whisky bottle and swung it round towards Everton. It crashed against the wall, and the broken glass had not reached the floor before Everton jumped. He landed his right fist on Ullmann's face and then caught him by the back of the neck and crashed his face on the floor. He held him by the back of the collar and shouted, 'Pick it up. Pick up your money.' Ullmann tried to twist round, and Everton bumped his head on the floor again.

'Pick it up,' he shouted. 'Pick it up or I'll break your neck now.'

Ullmann's hand clawed out desperately and closed on a note. Everton let him go. 'It wasn't even a fight,' he said, panting. 'Just a little token from the weak. I'll leave you to clear up the mess. It's your bar.'

He turned and ran out of the room, up the stairs, and into his own bedroom. He locked the door and fastened the window, then sat down on the bed, still panting. It was a long time before he got his thoughts in order.

He was clear about one thing. The glasses that Zoe had carried had not been Ullmann's. So they must have belonged to the late Mr. Justice Bath.

1 4

I T WAS A GLITTERING MORNING. THE SEA SPARKLED IN A MILLION diamonds; children rushed from their houses before breakfast to splash and shout by the edge of the water; seagulls floated peacefully on the gentle waves or rose suddenly in a threatening cloud and shrieked with rage and greed as they fought for the scraps of food thrown from the little sailing boats in the harbour.

Everton woke suddenly with the sun in his eyes and the noise of the belligerent gulls in his ears. He had a headache, and he felt as though he had slept for something between twenty-five minutes and half-an-hour. He thought, looking out of the window at the sea brightness, that a swim would clear his head. He put on his trunks and slipped trousers and a jersey over them and went downstairs and out of the hotel. On the pavement his headache seemed to vanish at once. Perhaps it was only a hotel headache. It was time he moved. He went to the sheds to leave his clothes. Back on the beach he discovered at once that the sunshine was accompanied by a small, cutting wind. He went shuddering into the water until he was waist deep, then dived and swam, counting the strokes at first so that the cold shouldn't drive him out before he had swum a hundred yards. It surprised him that he didn't bruise himself on hard, frozen fish on the way. When the hundred yards was over, the water seemed almost comfortable, and he swam along parallel with the shore for another fifty, and then turned and floated on his back, feeling exhilarated and free. A clump of floating seaweed brushed against his side, and suddenly he remembered

Zoe. She might be lying on the bottom now, a fathom or two beneath him. She had been fond of swimming. He felt panic and despair rise in him again, and he turned and swam slowly to the shore.

On the beach he dried himself quickly, looking at the frolicking, bouncing children. Life didn't stop, and a mind given too much to thoughts of death would create nothing but its own tomb. He had known very little of Zoe, and the little had contained nothing to admire. He had liked her for her smallness and hardness and deter-mination and impertinence. She had been a minnow trying to take a bite out of a shark, and it was natural that nothing more should be heard of the minnow. One could intensify one's feelings about sharks. That was all.

He went slowly back to the sheds. The old man was already on duty, and he scarcely looked up as Everton approached. But when Everton tried to walk past him he made mumbling noises and held out his hand.

'Disc?' he said.

Everton remembered he had been given something like a shiny brass coin to fasten to his trunks before he left. He untied this now, with his numbed fingers, and held it out to the old man.

'Can't I get back in the sheds without this?' he asked. 'Wouldn't you have recognized me? I'm the only swimmer.'

The old man took the disc, looking at Everton angrily. It was certain he didn't recognize him, although he had seen him the night before in sufficiently dramatic circumstances. He would scarcely be a good witness.

'It's against the Council rules,' the old man said. 'You can't get back in here without your disc. Otherwise, people who hadn't paid would take advantage. Come in free. You can't trust people,' he said in the didactic tones of the elderly.

Everton, turning away with a shudder from the Ladies' corridor, walked shivering into his little concrete box and changed quickly. He thought the amenities would hardly tempt the criminal.

He went back to the hotel and ate his bad breakfast cheerfully. It was served by the bony waiter. He had so little flesh that this sunny morning he seemed almost transparent.

'And where is your fellow garçon?' Everton asked. 'I hoped to see him this morning with a bump on his forehead and his nose swollen up.'

'Sir?' The bony man sounded imperturbable.

'He was in a fight last night.'

'To-day he has free. He is probably going to visit his mother.'

Everton reflected that Ullmann was too vile a character to be welcomed even by his mother. It was true, of course, that people did have mothers. Every Lucy had a mother, or had once had a mother. She was probably a very respectable type, who had lived in a small dark flat near a railway line, and hoped to get her daughter into the Civil Service. Even Atkinson had a mother, although she had been called Mrs. Ronson. She would have been a flashy woman, bending slightly and courteously towards dipsomania, pouring herself another gin as her son was finally listed as a juvenile delinquent; drinking bad champagne in obscure night-clubs as he entered his first prison. Even Cady had a mother, although it was hard to imagine how she could have brought him up on such peculiar lines. Ronson would have been a vicious child; Cady had probably been no more than stupid. The war had encouraged his almost professional interest in death.

The manager of the hotel sat eating his watchful breakfast in the corner. Everton stopped to speak to him on the way out.

'You've been having more trouble with your staff?' he said chattily.

The manager glanced up without much obvious interest.

'Good-morning. No. No. My staff troubles are vanishing. I've decided to employ Englishmen. I have two already.' He waved vaguely towards the corner of the dining room, where a man who scowled and another who looked disheartened stood together, immobile and hopeless and black-and-white.

'Two who don't serve although they stand and wait,' Everton commented.

'I'm replacing the foreigners. They're unreliable,' the manager said, and picked up the newspaper again.

Everton strolled out in the sunshine. He wondered where the foreign waiters had gone. The barman he would probably never see again. Ullmann? The police would be after Ullmann. Skin-and-bones might be already packing. Should he be stopped? Should the police be told?

A small green van drove past him and up a side street. Everton, who was walking towards the corner, looked after it without much interest. It turned in to the back of the hotel. He thought it looked familiar, and he stood on the corner and waited for it to reappear. In a minute or two it backed out. He watched it as it turned. The number was XXB 9847. So it was true, and he had seen it before, two mornings ago, when the waiters had decided to go and the manager had brought them back.

The van came very slowly down the street. At the corner it stopped to wait for the traffic. Everton stepped forward, with no intention but to cross the street behind the van, instead he found himself wrenching at the handle on the doors. The back swung open, he jumped inside and pulled the door shut again.

The van was dark, lumpy with old sacks, and smelt of humanity on the way to the police court. Everton sat with his elbows on his knees and his chin on his hands, and leant back against the side of the van. He had the pleasing sensation of having done something daring that involved no risk. He was not in the difficult position of confronting the enemy, but for the present he was the pursuer, and no one knew where he was. If the van had a destination, discoveries might be made.

The van started, slowed down, appeared to turn, and started again. Everton, missing the solace of a window, found that he had no sense of direction. The van might be going to Scotland Yard or over the edge of a cliff into the sea. He did not know. His mind was exhausted, and he was glad that for the moment there were no decisions he could make. He settled himself more comfortably and allowed his mind to wander luxuriously in the pleasant places of his life.

The darkness was a pillow for his tired spirit, he was not disturbed by the rattling of the van. He could see nothing with his eyes, he could hear nothing strange with his ears, but his wandering mind was gradually slowing down and a little chill of alarm entered. His mind groped back to the present and into fear. He sat listening for sounds that did not exist, and his fear grew stronger. He knew he was not alone in the van.

'Who's there?' he asked softly, calmly, feeling the blade at his back, the spanner on his head, listening to the click of the safety catch, sensing soft, powerful hands on their way to his throat. 'Who's there?' he said thickly.

Through the thundering in his ears he heard a faint, an authentic rustle, and he turned his head slowly to the back of the van.

He could see nothing, but he knew that something moved.

'Speak up,' he said roughly. 'I won't hurt you. Who is it?'

'You won't hurt me,' said a low voice. 'But how lucky you will be if I do not hurt you. Sit quite still, and tell me who you are.'

'Name of Brown,' Everton said. 'Just a hitch-hiker.'

He moved back sharply as the light from a torch shone on his face.

'So it is our Mr. Everton,' the voice said with satisfaction, and Everton strained forward, his mind aching with the effort to identify. 'Now that we have you, we must use you. You are a bad job, and the best will be made of you. You have got into such a hole with this van,' the soft voice went on. 'Why do you behave so stupidly? Curiosity? First curiosity, and then trouble. Now let us think how we can make the worst of trouble for you. Do not turn round.'

'I won't turn round,' Everton said. 'After all, I don't want any melodrama. In fact,' he said, trying to speak lightly, 'I'm willing to make a bargain with you. If you let me get out of the van, I'll go.' He waited for the answer with a fierce concentration; he was almost sure that he recognized the voice.

'You will not get out until I say.' Everton sighed. He was sure now that the voice was known to him. It was the bony waiter who was with him in the van. He remembered the man's false air of fragility; he had not tried to assess his strength. His eyes, he remembered, had seemed almost moribund, he looked like someone who had spent a couple of days in a coffin.

'You know who I am?'

'I'm not sure of your name. But you're one of the waiters. One who came in a small sailing boat. I suppose the organization passed you through Europe in the usual way. I'm not sure from what part of Europe, but I think—I think you might be a Greek.'

The van had slowed down again, probably at a main road, and in the new near silence Everton could hear the man breathing. Danger had lashed his senses into a keener perception; he knew that the man was not moving, and hesitation might be prolonged.

'Yes,' he repeated. 'I think you're a Greek. And I think that you were once prominent. A patriot, who made sure there would be no unemployment in the firing squads, until even your own side protested. And then there was a little flurry, a little purge, and you were just another political prisoner. But I can't remember your name. You were released, weren't you, but no one outside Greece was very interested by then. I remember when you were arrested there was a great movement in this country for you, and an even greater one against you. However, you were released, and I don't know why you had to come here.'

The man made noises in his throat, noises of contempt. 'Not all released prisoners were welcomed with flowers and champagne, as it happened in Germany,' he said. 'I was free, but I had too many murderous hands against me. It is unpleasant to wait. For the men with rifles who will step out in the road and stop your car, one sunny morning, for the madman who will spring from the crowd in front of the hotel with a revolver in his hand, for the grenade that will fall from some window at your feet. It was better for me to leave Greece, and the organization passed me through. America, it seemed, would have forbidden my entry, if I had come to England by the usual method I would have been turned back. Your country is less a haven than it used to be. I spent three weeks in Paris, washing dishes; ten days in Calais hiding in an airless cellar; now I am in England, and I will not be a waiter any more. I still have enough money to take me to America. They will let me in now. I have a different name, and I am a waiter. You, Mr. Everton, have done your best to destroy me, and my fellow waiters. Why should you be so callous? Some people are in trouble in their own countries. They wish to leave. But there are consuls, there are visas, there are men in uniform waiting at the docks and the airports. We find there is an organization willing to help men of our sort who are in trouble. It is expensive,' he said reminiscently, 'but it works. We are harmless immigrants. We have no plot in mind, we are not conspirators. All we want is a refuge, and we find it is denied to us by people like yourself.'

'And by people like the late Mr. Justice Bath. He knew.'

'It is safer not to know,' the man agreed. 'And it is also safer not to interfere, as you may find out.'

'I'm not politically-minded, myself,' Everton said in a placatory tone.

'Even Mr. Bath was concerned with legality, rather than politics. And now we have talked enough. All I shall say is that the van is about to stop. In my pocket there is a revolver. You will open the door and get out very slowly, and I will follow you, with the revolver aimed at the small of your back. I am not a light-minded man, and I promise you I would sooner shoot you and be caught, than let you escape and perhaps be caught anyway. I cannot afford to be deported. I do not intend to return to Greece. So you will be very careful. When I am out of the van you will walk beside me, and I will have the gun in my pocket.'

The van had stopped. 'Now,' the man said.

Everton opened the door, slid gently out of the van, and stood dizzily in the bright sunshine. The bony waiter followed him, looking more than ever like a plant that had been grown in a damp basement. 'The door to the right,' he said briskly. 'Walk.'

Everton measured the possibilities of escape as he crossed the pavement. It was a long street, the corner was a hundred yards away, and he was not confident that he could run the distance in less than ten seconds. If he had a lead of twenty yards he would be safe; the man would have to be up to duelling standards to shoot him with a revolver from that distance. He could cover twenty yards in three seconds, but he could be shot in one.

The street was quiet. No one was entering or leaving the small, terraced houses. Fifty yards away two women had put down their shopping baskets to talk to each other at their ease; a very old man and his very old wife were hobbling slowly in the sunshine on the other side of the road; a boy passed on a bicycle, two young children were playing with a ball in the middle of the street. A milk delivery van had just come round the corner, and in the still morning air the rattle of the bottles and trays carried clearly to his ears. A baby was crying in a nearby house. And that was all. They were at the door, and a small brass plate announced that the Coastal Universal Service had its offices inside. It was the kind of street where there would be several brass plates—dentists and doctors of the less prosperous kind, and probably a dressmaker or two.

The door was not locked. When the Greek turned the handle it opened quietly, and he and Everton went inside.

The corridor was dark and odorous. The smell could be divided into five per cent furniture polish, fifteen per cent tomcat, and eighty per cent cooking. All the smells seemed to have been there for a long time. They had no way of escape.

The Greek jerked his thumb forward, and Everton walked past two or three doors, all shut, and up the dingy brown stairs.

'Some of us have to stay here for a few days. It is very comfortable, and quiet,' the Greek said with approval. 'It is an agency, you know. A real agency for providing waiters and barmen, and there are some real waiters and barmen on the books, so it has the semblance of truth. Or so he says. Please to go in.'

Everton opened the door indicated, and walked into a bare room with a small window. The window was black with dirt and grease and the effect of years of winter fog. The only thing to be seen through it, and that was not very clear, was a solid brick wall.

The room was furnished with three wooden chairs and a small table.

'It's quiet, all right,' Everton said. 'Would you call it comfortable?'

'You will wait here,' the Greek said. 'If you come out the door, perhaps I shoot you.' He turned sideways and edged out of the room. He had taken the gun from his pocket and was holding it in his hand. The door shut gently behind him.

Everton looked quickly at the window. If he smashed the glass, he could get through it, and risk the jump. He would be heard, and there would be an unfortunate, and perhaps final, moment when he lay sprawling on the ground. He went softly to the door, and stood beside it, with his left shoulder pressed against the wall. The Greek had made his philosophy clear enough; he would sooner murder and be caught than be caught without murdering. It was a strong position, but his threats had built up an equally strong one for Everton. Death or something approaching it was being planned for him. He had nothing to lose now by taking risks.

Listening, he heard the quiet, deliberate steps of the Greek returning. There was a soft touch on the door handle. Everton seized the handle on his side and pulled the door open violently. The Greek, the gun still in his hand, was dragged forward, and in the moment of his surprise Everton dropped and caught him by the legs. He fell, and hit his head against the door frame. Everton twisted up, and caught the barrel of the revolver with his right hand. The man writhed round and kicked hard at Everton's stomach. Everton fell back, still holding the barrel of the revolver. Someone caught him from behind; Everton thrust a foot backwards between the new enemy's legs and they both crashed to the floor, and the Greek, still holding the revolver, came down on top of them.

Everton brought his knee up hard against the Greek's chin, and he went soft all over, as though his bones had turned to paste. Everton wrenched the gun from the idly clutching hand. The man beneath him sank hard fingers into his neck, and he rolled over and hit him on the head with the gun. The fingers slackened and Everton staggered up. The man on the floor was Ullmann, and he wore his glasses. Everton bent down, snatched the glasses, and broke the frame in two as he ran for the stairs. Ullmann reached forward and caught him by the ankle. He came down on his face and Ullmann was on top of him again. He braced himself on his hands and knees and heaved; Ullmann shot over his head and rolled half down the stairs.

Everton wavered, and then turned and ran foolishly to the flight of stairs above. He raced up, and on the top landing he wrenched open the first door on the right. There was a chair just inside the room. He snatched it, slammed the door shut, and put the back of the chair under the handle. Then he leant, panting wildly, against the door, and cursed himself for having come up instead of fighting his way down.

The window offered its meagre hope, but he had put another fifteen feet between himself and safety. He turned, and looked into the room for the first time.

There was a square of tired grey carpet on the floor, and there was blood on the carpet. He moved his eyes slowly forward until he saw the man. He lay face down, with his arms flung forward and his knees slightly bent and a knife sticking out of his back. There was nothing but the handle of the knife to be seen, a plain black handle of the clasp-knife type. Nothing but the handle. There was no blade to be seen at all, it must be all in the man's back.

Everton moved himself forward, slowly, over the grey carpet. He knew who the man was. The bright blue tweed coat was Cady's, the dirty grey flannel trousers were Cady's. It was Cady, Cady who had wanted to run, to go secretly and quickly, but who had been urged to stay.

Everton stood for a moment in misery, listening almost with detachment to the noise in the corridor. They were closing in on him, but the death even of Cady deserved a moment's calm. Listening to the shoulder against the door, he stared at the black handle of the knife. It might have been the knife that Cady had threatened him with in Mrs. Leonard's house, the knife with the blade hand-ground and pointed like a stiletto. Cady had prepared that knife. Perhaps he had earned its blade in his back, but at the moment death seemed too hard a fate for any man.

The crashing on the door grew louder. Everton, his eyes and most of his mind still on the body on the floor, moved back against the wall. The chair slid and fell, and Everton watched the door burst open. He looked at the gun in his hand and raised it slowly; his belligerence had ebbed away; he wanted nothing more to do with death.

A hand came round the corner of the door, and there was a gun in it. "They're drawing my fire," Everton thought, but he fired, knowing that he would miss. The bullet struck the wall, and the plaster was still falling when Ullmann leapt into the room. There was a shot, Everton felt a crashing blow on his fingers as though he had been hit by a hammer, and the gun flew out of his hand.

Ullmann sprang. Something crashed down on Everton's head, and he dropped slowly to the floor, clutching wildly at the space around Ullmann's head as he fell.

Light gradually receded, and he lay at peace in the darkness.

15

EVERTON LAY ON HIS BACK, LOOKING LANGUIDLY AT THE CEILing. It was grey, and time and dirt had filled in the cracks with a confused, reasonable pattern, like a map of the counties of England. He stared at the network idly, trying to find a path across it, and wondering who had crept into his bedroom and changed the ceiling. Soon he noticed that his bed had been changed too, and for the worse. He felt bruised from lying on it for so long. Then he looked at the threatening, dingy walls, and admitted for the first time that he was not in his hotel bedroom. The mind is evasive and alarmed when it awakens in the wrong place; the strange room may be part of the nightmare; he was less afraid when the memory of violence came bubbling back into his mind.

He made himself sit up and look across the room. He was ready to recoil from the sight of Cady's body.

The body was not there.

Shakily, he stood up. He had been lying on the floor, on the thin grey carpet. He looked at his watch. It said quarter past one. He had not been there for long, the sunshine was still luminous against the grimed window.

His head was aching, and his hair, when he touched it, felt thick and wet. That would be blood. His right hand was swollen and aching, but the bullet had done no more than raise the skin. A few other things had happened, on the whole he felt as though someone had pushed a brick wall on top of him. Experiment showed that he could walk. The best place to walk would be out of the house.

He looked again at the spots of blood on the carpet. They were dry now. He looked again at the broken chair in the corner, the chair with which he had tried to hold the door. He looked at the hole in the plaster by the door. He had done that himself, with the bullet that missed Ullmann. Illusion was not part of the case, and the body must have lain on the floor.

He went downstairs with the weary triumph of the cat who is halfway through his ninth life. There was no sound from anywhere in the house. The quietness would be a pleasant change for the neighbours, he thought, remembering the battle on the stairs. It might be a district that had been immunized against revolver shots and the crash of falling bodies, but when he went out in the street it looked respectable, although in a very small way.

He walked with some happiness in the sunshine, glancing appreciatively at the window boxes, and almost lovingly at an old woman in black who crept along the street, her bobbing head bent towards the pavement, her old shoulders weighed down by the shopping basket she carried. He hoped she lived to be a hundred and ten. He was in favour of life.

When he had turned the corner he found himself in a busy street, with the usual Woolworth's, the common chemists, the ubiquitous grocers, and the normal traffic jam. He saw a bus marked Railway Station, and he followed it up the street, dawdling so that it could stay ahead.

At the station he found that a train was leaving in a few minutes. He bought a third-class ticket to London. He walked along the corridor looking for a corner seat, and then he walked back looking for any sort of seat. The only one he found was in a carriage with four children and their defiant parents.

'Measles,' the mother said to him briefly, expecting him to go.

'I wish I had something simple like that,' he told her, and sat down.

The children turned their solid, critical gaze on him. He would have liked to like them, but he sensed that any overture on his part would be followed by the touch of little sticky hands. He looked at the newspaper he had bought, and tried to imagine himself concentrating on his own problems, but those of the family with measles seemed more engrossing. When the train started he went to the lavatory to examine his face in the small mirror. When he saw the blood, the dust, and the pallor, he admired the children for not throwing themselves, shrieking, out of the carriage.

He washed as well as he could with two drops of liquid soap, and dried himself with his handkerchief. Then he stood for a long time, swaying with the movement of the train, thinking of what he should do next.

He went back to the compartment, intending to prepare his story in detail, but he found himself involved in friendliness with the children, and soon the youngest of them was adding a film of melted chocolate to the dust and blood on his suit. The conversation was not exacting, but it murdered thought. He said good-bye to them all with regret at Victoria, and took a taxi to the section of the Foreign Office that concerned him.

The man at the desk greeted him with restrained surprise. Although he had made himself moderately clean, he still looked wild and pale, more like a character from an epic poem than a visitor to the Foreign Office. He asked for paper, and sat down at a desk and wrote:

"My dear Bluett-Jones:

Two days ago I sent you a photograph and a drawing, with my suggestions for their identification. I have a little more information to add to my earlier remarks. May I see you about this now?"

He signed his name, slipped the note in an envelope, and gave it to the messenger. A few minutes later he was taken upstairs.

Bluett-Jones, a weary man with an alert moustache and eyebrows, met him with a cordiality that covered his basic coldness like tissue paper.

'My dear Everton, I'm delighted to see you again. Now why,' he wondered aloud, 'didn't you get in touch with me before? We might have had lunch, yes?' He saw the bluntness of exhaustion in Everton's face; there was obviously the danger that Everton would say why they hadn't met. He hurried on. 'This business is fascinating, of course, quite fascinating. I've been in touch with a Scotland Yard man about it, and he is really very interested indeed. The trouble was to find the right man, the man who would be interested, but I think I've solved that little problem for you. Inspector Porthouse is very keen indeed. He'd like to meet you. Actually, I've taken the liberty of telephoning him and he'll be here any minute. I think you'll like him, I think you'll like him very much indeed. And what are you doing now, Everton? What's your occupation?'

'I'm rather busy,' Everton said, 'analysing the reactions of the British people,' he said with a vague largeness. 'And sometimes I analyse the reactions of aliens,' he added, with even less precision. 'And what have you been up to, Bluett-Jones?'

'Oh, you know how it is. In-files, out-files, sugar for the Minister's tea,' Bluett-Jones said with equal vagueness.

The buzzer rang. 'And here is Inspector Porthouse. I'll introduce you two, and move along. We must have a long chat, one day, Everton. We'll fix a day, and have lunch, perhaps.' He strolled out, long, lean, casual, untouched by any calamity, and probably untouchable.

Porthouse was a solid, savage man, with a pallor about him, like a torch with a weak battery.

'We'll jump straight into business,' he said, 'if you don't mind, Mr. Everton.' He laid the photograph and the drawing on the table. 'I can identify these men. Can you?'

'I can now. I wasn't sure two days ago. The short square man with the glasses is called Ullmann. German. In trouble with French workers during war. He was given twenty years' imprisonment for using slave labour and causing what was roughly estimated as more than a hundred deaths. He escaped about a year ago.'

The Inspector nodded. 'Our people were particularly opposed to his escape. One lot of German miners would have been glad to see him hanged, and some of the others would have liked to make a hero of him. Either way, he's likely to create trouble, and Europe needs German coal. I had that from Mr. Bluett-Jones. Our position is simply that he's an undesirable alien and must go back to Germany. Arrangements would have to be made, naturally, to see that he was met at the German frontier. The other man is probably a Greek. Arcanides. We have no business with him but to see that he goes back to Greece.'

'They may use him as an example of some sort, when he gets back,' Everton murmured.

'Not our business,' the Inspector said angrily. 'The F.O. has decided he can't be admitted as a political refugee. There are charges against him that wouldn't be called political, in this country. Politicians don't behave that way here. They shout "swine" and "beast" at each other in the House of Commons but the Speaker would never allow murder. And now that we've disposed of these two, let's talk about the others.'

'The others?' said Everton, pretending surprise.

'You expect a bit of flotsam for years after a war. You even let some of it drift in, without too many questions. But in recent years the flotsam hasn't floated in. It's been brought in as part of a cargo. Whenever there's an undesirable trying to get out of his own country to save his skin, so long as he has the money, he ends up here. And it's not one of those melodramatic plots with communists or fascists or christian democrats or even peasant socialists plotting to seize power. It's just anyone, from any country, paying his way here. We've caught a few of them, but they don't say how they came. We've had extradition orders from nearly every country in Europe. The F.O. doesn't like it, and the Minister doesn't like it, and the Home Secretary doesn't like it, and the Prime Minister doesn't like it. I'll go further than that. Even Scotland Yard doesn't like it. Someone's organized the traffic and they've organized it for gain. We've traced them through a few capital cities. The French Security know the hotel in Paris that's one of the hide-outs. They think there's an office in Toulouse and they know there's a place in Calais. The Italians are on to something in Milan, but they don't know much more. And up to now we've only caught a few strays. We don't know how they get to this country and where they start when they get here. But the organization is laid out across Europe like a golf course, and when they get here they're in the eighteenth hole. If they move on to the States that's the nineteenth, and their own business, in a way. Now you've turned up, and we hope you're going to tell us where the eighteenth hole is.'

Everton groped in his mind for the right beginning to his story. 'There's been a murder,' he said tentatively. 'An ex-judge called Bath.'

Inspector Porthouse nodded. 'I keep up with things, in my slipshod way. I know about it.'

'I met him the night of his death, in the bar of the hotel where I stay. The hotel was full of inept foreign waiters. I think you might call it the eighteenth hole. The judge knew about it, although I don't know how long he had known. He was bullying the barman about where he came from. The barman said Genoa. It was an obvious lie, and Bath was taking pleasure in exposing him, when in an inexcusable desire to frustrate the law I spilt my drink on the bar and created enough diversion to stop the examination. I went back to Bath's house with some other people. His wife, a man called Atkinson, and another called Cady. The judge made some remarks that seemed intended to show one or more of these people that he knew they were engaged in this—this criminal enterprise. I didn't understand at the time, but I saw it would take an ice-axe to cut through the atmosphere. The judge took me out of the room for a private conversation, and I think he was going to ask for my help and tell me his suspicions—or certainties—but he changed his mind. He said because I'd spilt my drink in the bar. I missed the point at the time, but I understood afterwards it was because I had protected the barman, which made it an even chance that I was in the racket. The murder you know about.' He stopped. He felt faint and light-headed, his thoughts might blow away like wood-ash. He would have liked a drink, and he wished that Bluett-Jones would come back and bring a bottle of whisky or even a thermos flask of tea out of a box-file.

Inspector Porthouse sat with his hands folded on his stomach and his eyes shut. His battery seemed very weak.

Everton told him about Zoe and what Cady had said of her. 'And now I'll go back to Atkinson,' he said.

'He doesn't seem to have played a very active part, so far,' Inspector Porthouse said, opening his eyes for a moment.

'He's been fighting and clawing his way to the background,' Everton agreed. 'But that's not his place. I think—I'm sure—that he's a man called Ronson.'

Porthouse opened his eyes, and sat up, shining a little. He looked like a man with a new battery.

'I haven't told anyone about this before, except Bath himself. At least—I think I made it plain in front of them all that I thought he looked like Ronson. I told Bath I was fairly sure, and that Ronson was the man who threw me into the Seine with the intention of drowning me. He had first of all made me a proposition about using an Embassy car to run refugees over the frontier. I refused, and woke up in the Seine. Then I went to prison for cashing a fraudulent cheque,' Everton added steadily.

'I heard about that,' Porthouse said, and Everton directed a pungent thought to the absent Bluett-Jones.

'But tell me,' Porthouse said, 'why you think this man Atkinson is Ronson.'

Everton yawned. He was almost stupefied by exhaustion. 'General resemblance. Everything superficial changed, even to the colour of his hair. But he hadn't dyed the hair on the back of his fingers. It's still ginger. Then, that first night, he practically offered me a thousand pounds. It was awkward, you see, if I recognized him as Ronson. I would remember the offer he'd made to get the refugees over the frontier, and I might tie that up with the queer foreign waiters. Now I'd better tell you about this morning.' He described, with as much brevity as he could contrive, the fight with Ullmann and the Greek, and how Cady's body had been there when he was knocked out, but not when he woke up again.

He had finished his story, and now he waited for comment. Inspector Porthouse was rumbling in a pleasant way.

'We know about Ronson,' he said. 'We've known about him for years, although it's true we thought he'd been dropped in the Seine himself, by now, or buried in some basement. He's been in the game for a long time. He started in a small way as a boy, smuggling watches from Switzerland. Now that I think of it, he had his own sailing boat even in those days. He brought them over himself. He probably began with half-a-dozen, and ended with anything up to a thousand a trip. He was caught in the end, and given a small sentence and an enormous fine. He surprised everyone by paying the fine. He'd brought over more than we thought, and put some of the money away for a rainy legal day. People like that really can put some away,' the Inspector said indignantly. 'They don't get it all taken off them as tax. So where you and I couldn't save much, he could. He met up with a few improved barrow boys in prison, and when he came out he had a cosy gang. Then he organized smuggling on a really sizable scale. Cameras, wine, nylons by the million, and, naturally, more watches. He had two or three little boats crossing the Channel, and he used some of the deep-sea trawlers. He even found a farmer, a real farmer,' Inspector Porthouse said incredulously, 'who kept some of the stuff for him in an imitation pig-sty. He had a good business head, Ronson. However, the farmer, who ought to have been one of the dour peasantry, was a celtic type, and he talked too much in the local. The whole thing came out through him. We got a lot of them, but not Ronson. Then he moved into a currency racket, with some simple little chorus girls in the big cabarets doing the money-changing and taking the risks. They got caught. He didn't. Oh, yes, we knew Ronson well. We'd like to have had him on this. And now we can't.' Inspector Porthouse grunted, and settled down again in what seemed to be repose.

'And why can't you?' Everton asked. He would have liked a little restorative sleep, too.

'Why?' the Inspector repeated. He sat up suddenly and scowled at Everton. 'Why? Because you've been interfering. Because you've been clever and made it impossible to achieve anything. Because you attacked the waiters. Because you let them see you send a photograph away and drove them out of the hotel. Because you got in a fight with them and forced them into real hiding. Because you've scared the manager into hiring English waiters who're no doubt as innocent as daffodils. Because they daren't use the hotel any more. Because you've even driven them out of their catering staff agency. Because that part of the business, the eighteenth hole, has been abandoned, and we can't catch them there. We were tracking them down, all right. About a year's solid police work has run out of the plug-hole, and all because you've been so clever. God spare me from amateurs.' He groaned, and closed his eyes again.

Everton sat shaking. He felt as though someone had been cutting through his nervous system with a blunt bread-knife. He had expected, at the worst, grudging congratulations for what he had done. He looked at the Inspector, his vision blurred by hatred.

'I'm tired of police bluff,' he said in a voice that was nearly a shout. 'You didn't know a damned thing about this hotel, or the foreign waiters, or Bath's suspicions, or Ronson acting Atkinson. You've always got to pretend that you know everything, or that you're just on the point of knowing everything. You've sat around knowing nothing for years, and then when you're told something you shout Why did you interfere, you blundering fool.' He sat back, still furious, but happy, because he had cast off his fear of policemen.

'Well,' said a voice of immense moderation from the door. 'So you two are still chatting away?' Bluett-Jones looked amiably from one to the other. 'I've told my secretary to tell the tea-lady we'd like two extra cups in here.'

'Sorry,' Inspector Porthouse rumbled. 'We can't stop. Mr. Everton and myself are going back down to this hotel of his, to have a word with the manager, and so on. We should go now. We ought to be hurrying along, in fact.' He rose, but Everton stubbornly sat still.

'There's not so much hurry,' he said. 'I'd like some tea.' He turned to Bluett-Jones. 'Will you tell your secretary to tell your tea-lady I'd like two or three cups?'

'I'll do my best, my dear Everton, but surely you know how it is. People don't normally have more than one cup. I'll tell you what, you must have mine,' he cried gaily.

Everton drank his own tea, then he drank Bluett-Jones' tea. He wanted to prove that he wasn't afraid of the Foreign Office any more. He felt a stronger and more assured man when he left with Inspector Porthouse.

The drive back to the seaside town and the hotel was un-conversational. Porthouse asked a few questions, and Everton answered them shortly. In between questions he relapsed into a state that was nearly sleep.

Porthouse had sent a man to the Coastal Universal Service, and he had also warned Inspector Leigh of their coming.

'We'll go to the hotel first,' he said. 'I've asked Leigh to meet us there, in the bar. Do you mind?'

'No,' Everton said, waking with a start. 'I don't mind.'

'You've been asleep. Did you hear what I said? Leigh will meet us at the hotel. Do you mind?'

'I don't mind,' Everton said. 'Do you mean to keep asking me until I break down and confess that Bath left his money to me? He didn't,' he added quickly, as Inspector Porthouse turned on him with a magnificent glare.

They were driving at an even fifty miles an hour. It was a dull road by daytime, the kind of road that confronts a man with his own thoughts. But now light was slipping away round the world, and England was shadowed by the darkness of the universe. The dull houses and the flat fields had turned into walls of blackness, the road was a puny, impermanent thread, and the scene was as magnificent and as commonplace as anything in the whole black world. There was encouragement for the kind of philosophical reflection that suffocates interest in ordinary human affairs. Everton felt a noble detachment from the sordid fact of murder, and it wasn't until he saw the lights of the town sparking in the valley that he descended to the other kind of reality.

It was late, and the sounder citizens were already putting their trousers in the press for the night. In the hotel all the lights shone subdued through the thick curtains, and Leigh waited for them in the entrance hall. He and Porthouse measured each other quickly, then shook hands with a great appearance of mutual respect.

'The manager's here still,' Leigh said. 'But he knows nothing. That's his story. He hired waiters from the agency, and I think it may be hard to prove he did anything else. Your man has phoned through from the agency. It's deserted, naturally, and he says if there were ever any documents there, they've gone. There's no written evidence of any sort. The two English waiters here now claim that though they came through the agency, they never went there in person. All arrangements by correspondence. They're simple enough; if they were in the racket it would show though. The daily women who clean the hotel have been seen. Two of them say they always knew there was something funny going on, the way foreign waiters came and went. They say Ullmann made them feel queer. The third says she never thought about it. I think that's probably true. So we are left with no one connected with the case at all, unless you count the manager.

'I think we'll count the manager,' Porthouse said ominously. 'But you see how it is.' He turned a mournful, reproving gaze on Everton. 'You've messed everything up.' The accusation was made now without particular rancour; Everton's activities had become part of the unalterable past.

Everton waited while the two Inspectors discussed esoteric matters in low voices in a corner. He was not anxious to hear their conversation, he felt that his part of the drama was over, he would like to spend the rest of the play in his own room.

'I suppose I'd better tell you, Everton,' Inspector Leigh said. 'You're an interested party, in a way. In fact, very interested, if we can judge by your actions. I believe you went swimming this morning?'

'Yes,' Everton said flatly, remembering with surprise the glittering morning, the sharp sea, and his fear that something would rise and float beside him as he swam. 'Yes, I went swimming.'

'You were lucky to leave the beach when you did,' Leigh said brutally. 'If you'd been an hour later, you might have had a shock. The body came in. Just floated in. She must have gone swimming, after all. Black Jantzen, red bathing cap, death from drowning. Why, with any luck, that's what the coroner will say.'

'How do you mean, any luck?' Everton said slowly.

'Any luck for the person who killed her,' Leigh said.

16

E VERTON HAD THOUGHT THAT, ONCE ON HIS BED, HE WOULD collapse into sleep, but over-exhaustion churned his mind into wakefulness. He tried to lie still, but his hotel headache was battering its way up from the back of his neck to his temples. He had finished with the case, he repeated again and again. He had said his piece, exposed himself; he had fought and nearly murdered in the interests of law and order, and as a result he was universally hated and despised. The night was around him, and he would be alone for ever. He knew that Lucy, whom he had loved, had planned his ruin; he knew that by loving Lucy he had planned his own ruin. He was a romantic who hated ordinary life so much that he had chosen to destroy himself rather than not escape at all. And Lucy was a romantic who chose to destroy others. The well-ordered terror of the common day was more than they could face: he had endured his escape, and now he must return. There was still Jan, who had once been the apostle of the ordered life and the organized day, the day that went on forever into death. But Jan was not entirely what she had been before; Lucy had made her hate, and hatred destroyed with the speed of a bonfire in a wooden house. He realized with astonishment that he himself hated no one. He had spent years overcoming his hatred, and now at last he had won. He had been afraid, but now he was not even that. He was almost a reasonable man again, he thought, and went to sleep.

In the morning he sat at breakfast and studied the railway time-table, while a sad and totally respectable English waiter served him with lukewarm coffee. There would be an inquest, naturally, there would in fact be two inquests, but as soon as they were over he would be a free man. He was appreciating the idea of freedom when he saw Leigh coming across the dining room. He abandoned freedom and happiness at once.

'I am afraid,' Leigh said in a peremptory voice, 'that we must ask you to come and see the body. Identification. You seem to be the only person apart from her father who knew her well.'

'I'd known her for about two days,' Everton said in agitation. 'Her father—'

'Her father has his heels in the ground and a nervous breakdown up his sleeve. He seems to have some legal tip-off that it would be compromising to see his daughter's body. He's very keen on the law,' Leigh said drearily.

'I know. But if he can get out of it, why can't I?' Everton pushed his breakfast away. His appetite was in revolt.

'He won't get out of it. We'll drag him along with his heels in the ground. But I don't think,' the Inspector said with disapproval, 'that he is a very steady type. He may collapse.'

'But this is nonsense,' Everton said. 'You know who it is. It can't be a coincidence. I'm not connected with the girl. And I may collapse, too,' he added, not in a joking tone.

'You were the last to see her,' Leigh said, in a voice of official monotony. 'And it might make you think a bit when you see some of the other people,' he added in a different tone.

'What? What do you mean?'

'I didn't say anything,' Leigh said. 'I might have said that your morals are slippery, but I didn't. I might have said you're preparing to clear out, but I didn't. I might have said you could have prevented this girl going on her blackmailing expedition, but I didn't say that either. All I said was that you are required to come along and identify the body.'

Everton, sick and pale, followed Leigh from the hotel into the waiting car. Leigh talked steadily.

'She was in a black Jantzen swimming suit when she was found. The old man at the sheds is one kind of fool; he takes a pride in the fact that he'd never have noticed a woman in a black Jantzen. He's a professional non-noticer. Her father, now, is another kind of fool. He doesn't know what kind of swimming suits she had. He keeps his head in a cloud composed of nineteenth-century legal books. He's a slow thinker. If he'd started work in his cradle he'd be up to about 1925 now, with the books, but he began late and he'll never reach the twenties. The woman next door is a bit brighter. She didn't know the girl to speak to, scarcely even to speak about, which is more remarkable, but she did very often look at the washing in the garden, usually done by Zoe on Sundays. Other days there wasn't much she could see, but in the summer there was very often a swimming costume drying in the back garden, and she noticed that Zoe had one of those two-piece costumes, in yellow, and she's seen a one-piece, blue with a white pattern. She hasn't ever noticed a black one-piece, and she seems a noticing type. If she'd been working in the swimming sheds we'd have been able to get somewhere. However, the assumption is that the girl didn't own a black Jantzen. We've had a man look at it, and his opinion is that it is not new.'

'So she borrowed it,' Everton said. The car had stopped now, and, looking at the building before him, which resembled a disused church hall, he was in misery.

'You might call it borrowing,' Leigh said, on a note of disagreement. 'I'll let you see the costume. Well, here we are.' He walked in the door, and Everton trailed behind him.

'Here,' the Inspector said, picking up a damp garment from a table. 'Here is the costume. And here is the swimming cap.'

Everton looked at them, although there was nothing to study but a black woollen costume with a red trade-mark of a diving girl in the corner; and a cap of plain rubber with a strap fastened by studs at each side. 'That's all, is it?' he asked foolishly.

'That's all. Except that I'm afraid I must ask you to do your job of identification,' Leigh said gently.

Everton went with him to another table, looked quickly at the object under the sheet, and turned away. He went outside the door and stood in the fresh air. He remembered that her condition had almost been his, and his disgust turned to anger.

'It's time the watery grave was closed,' he said over his shoulder to Leigh.

'It will be,' Leigh answered. 'This may be the last day of conjecture. Your friend Porthouse is stirring up some mud. Your two friends the waiters haven't come up for breath, but the Italianate barman is in the bag. He was found this morning shaking ice-cream sodas in a Margate milk bar. The life of crime. There's nothing to equal it. The two cleaning women at the hotel who claimed to have been full of suspicion seem to be quite innocent, but the third, who saw nothing and heard nothing, is married to a man who works as a deckhand. He helped Cady run the fugitives over from France, it seems. There's no charge against either of them, but they're being held for questioning. The trouble is that although all this business will stop the racket, none of it proves anything. Your friend Atkinson, or Ronson—. Now why didn't you tell me about that?' Leigh stopped speaking, and looked at Everton with the weariness that comes from too much amazement.

'I didn't tell anyone about that, at the time. No one, that is, except Bath, just before he was killed. I can't explain. I didn't want to talk about it. I don't even want to talk about it now, if you'd like to know. I've identified this girl for you. Now what do you want me to do?' Everton asked jerkily. He was trying to think of some way to wash the vision of the dead girl from his mind: if he could swim in the cold sea for an hour his memory might heal.

'I'll confide in you, Everton,' Leigh said, and Everton knew some piece of chicanery was coming. 'There's this black Jantzen. Someone might have bought one. Well, someone did.'

'What? Who?' There was only foreboding in Everton's mind now.

'Your friend, Miss Deverell,' Leigh said with some satisfaction.

'Jan? That's nonsense, complete nonsense. She's not the type,' Everton said with a savage conviction that surprised them both.

'She bought a black Jantzen. There aren't many shops here with a big line in swimming suits. It's late in the season. I've sent the men around. The only black Jantzen sold this week was sold to Miss Deverell, and she asked in two other shops that were out of stock. There's no doubt about it.'

'Then there's a trick in it somewhere,' Everton said flatly.

'There would be a trick,' Leigh agreed, 'but I don't know who's playing it. She bought it yesterday.'

'Yesterday? But Zoe was already drowned.' Everton looked curiously at the Inspector. 'We found the clothes the night before, you say her body was washed up yesterday morning. Why would Jan buy a black Jantzen? When?'

'She bought it in the early afternoon,' Leigh said comfortably. 'She had probably heard the body came ashore. It's all right. Just something to think about. You like thinking, don't you? And why don't you think about the clothes in the swimming shed, now? What was missing from the picture?' He put the car into gear, and Everton sat silently beside him until they had reached the hotel again. His mind was working over the box in the swimming shed where Zoe had changed her clothes for the last time. The blue-and-white cotton frock, the underclothes, the sandals, and the white handbag. The Inspector had emptied the handbag on the seat. Lipstick, rouge, powdercase, nailfile. A handkerchief, a comb, a small mirror. Some old bus tickets. No cigarettes, no matches, no lighter. A purse, with a few odd coins in it. No letters, no photographs, and, of course, no glasses. It was like the game of remembering objects that children play. Lipstick, rouge... he went over them all again. What was wrong? The frock had been hanging on a hook. It had been a blue-and-white frock, and what more could he add to it? The flimsy undergarments had been lying on the seat beside the sandals. And that had been all.

He opened the door of the car to get out.

'I can't think of anything wrong,' he said.

He stepped on the pavement and shut the door.

'Wouldn't she take a towel if she went swimming?' the Inspector asked. He started the car again and drove away.

Everton crossed the road to the promenade and held the rails as he looked at the sea. This morning it was grey: all the light had been emptied from it.

She would have taken a towel if she had gone swimming. There had been no towel on the beach. She would not have gone swimming without a towel. She might have swum from some lonely cove without a towel, and dried herself by the sun or with her underclothes, but from the swimming sheds, no. Everyone who went to the swimming sheds would have a towel, and Zoe was a criminal, but not an unconventional, type.

She had been drowned first, Everton thought, clutching the promenade rails, and her clothes had been taken to the sheds afterwards. Taken by a woman, of course, and that was why Leigh had been so anxious to question the three women, Jan, Lucy, and Mrs. Leonard. And before she had been drowned, someone had stripped the clothes from her and forced her into a swimsuit and a bathing cap. This was to have been a natural death. Her clothes would be found in the swimming sheds; later her body would be washed on shore. In a black Jantzen.

The natural death had gone wrong. Zoe, who never confided in her father and who appeared to have no friends, had told him, Everton, about the glasses and the blackmail. Cady had lost his nerve and talked about death and swimming. And the woman who went to the sheds to leave Zoe's clothes had forgotten to take a towel. Atkinson, or Ullmann, or the Greek, or even Cady, might have been the murderer. But a woman had taken her clothes to the swimming sheds, knowing already why the clothes must be there; thinking, perhaps, of the body in the black Jantzen. So he was back again at the black Jantzen, and why must he suppose that a man had murdered Zoe? The woman who left the clothes might be more than an accessory. Zoe had not said it was a man she was going to blackmail.

Everton turned slowly away from the rail. He would see Jan, and find out why she had gone shopping for a black swimming suit.

He walked slowly along the shore road towards the house. He was not in a hurry now. He would be there in an hour, or an hour and a half, and something might have happened by then. Someone, for instance, might confess. He let this foolish hope soothe his mind for a few minutes, and then abandoned it.

As he passed the cliff top he looked curiously around, but there was no sign of Mrs. Leonard. She might be writing indoor poetry, or eating her vegetarian sausage. He had a curious impulse to see her, to ask for her help. When he came to her gate, the white gate marked

Via, he stood for a minute outside it, then opened it and went slowly up the little shingled path.

At the door he wondered why he should see her, and the hand he had raised to ring the bell dropped again to his side. He stood motionless, and he thought he heard voices within the little square house. He rang the bell, and waited.

There was a long pause, then the door opened without warning.

'I didn't hear you come,' Everton said in confusion, for he had not prepared his speech or thought out his purpose. He looked dubiously at her feet. She was wearing white canvas shoes: they would have rubber soles, there was nothing mysterious about her silent arrival at the door.

'You came very quietly, too,' she said. 'I knew it was you. I sensed your suspicion through the door.'

'Suspicion!' Everton said sharply. 'But I came only to ask a question, Mrs. Leonard.' He thought she looked wild and harassed, but in her this was not unusual. Communion with nature, if carried out too deliberately, usually fails to produce serenity.

'For the last three days I have lived on questions,' she said. 'For the last three days I have had no other conversation. The wind on the cliff carries questions, and they are written across the sky at night.'

'That's the way I feel,' he said sympathetically. 'Only with me it's the police and not the wind and the stars. What I wanted to know was if you found that knife in the garden. The knife I threw out the night Cady attacked me.'

She looked at him, thinking. She held the door so tightly that her knuckles stood out: she must be afraid that he would push past her and into the house. She might have been writing a poem. Most poets don't like to be interrupted when they are writing.

'I found it,' she said finally. 'I threw it into the sea.'

'Oh,' Everton said in surprise. He had supposed that the knife he had seen sticking from Cady's back had been Cady's own. He repressed any comments. He regarded Cady's death vaguely as a secret.

'Well, that was all,' he said weakly, and turned away. She held the door and watched him until he was out of the garden and on the road again.

He was sure that he should have asked her something else, but she had not been friendly, perhaps because she already had a visitor in the house. She had never seemed to him the kind of woman who would have visitors; he had supposed that the wind and the stars would keep the neighbours out. A town this size, however, might well have someone who was interested in Yogi, or mermaids, or the dew on the morning grass, or murder. Most people had something in common with someone else.

Jan was gardening, or, at least, kneeling with a trowel in the garden.

'Burying something?' he asked as he approached her from behind. She stood up, and tried to move the hair from her eyes with her arm. He gave her a handkerchief, and she wiped the earth from her hands, and then pushed the disordered hair from her forehead.

'Your face is pinker and your lips are redder and your teeth whiter and your nose shorter than ever before,' he told her. He thought he would like to kiss her, but if he did it wouldn't be light-hearted enough. He would find himself supporting her, perhaps for ever, and he would lean on her for comfort. It was better for him to stand without props.

'I wasn't burying anything,' she said. 'People here use the sea when they want to get rid of the evidence.'

'And then the poor fisherman draws up his nets, keeps the humblest fish for his own supper, and breaks his teeth on the pearl-handled automatic that shot the gay baronet. Even the sea can't be trusted to keep quiet about murder.'

'It's doing fairly well at the moment,' Jan said. 'Hugh, do you know who shot my uncle—supposing I didn't?'

'I don't know who shot your uncle. And I know you didn't. You're not the type. I said that about you earlier to-day,' he added comfortably. 'Only not about your uncle.'

'And who was suggesting—'

'Only the police,' he said. 'Nothing to worry about. It's about Zoe. No, not about drowning her. Jan, why did you buy a black swimming costume yesterday?'

'I'm fond of swimming.'

'Jan, why did you go round the shops yesterday until you found a black swimming costume?'

'I look my best in black.'

'In a black Jantzen. Why did you need a black Jantzen yesterday? Tell me, Jan?'

'I can't tell you, and I won't.' She knelt down again, and began to prod the roots of a chrysanthemum with the trowel.

'That's one flower that will never bloom again,' he said. 'You've broken the stalk. Put down the trowel and spare the others. Jan, they had found her body before you bought the costume. Why did you have to buy it? You must answer me. Can't you understand? The police didn't say what she was wearing. You didn't see the body. How did you know she was wearing a black Jantzen. They're bound to think you knew before. Can't you see?' He put his hands to her shoulders and pulled her to her feet. He looked into her face. Her eyes were frightened, and he felt her tremble beneath his hands.

'Jan, you must understand. Whatever else they think, they think you knew what she was wearing, before. Did you, Jan?'

'Take your hands away,' she said, and he let her go. 'Hugh, you don't trust me, do you?'

'I trust you,' he said. 'Absolutely,' he added with too much fervour, and she laughed.

'No, you don't, Hugh. But you should have a mark, for trying. I didn't kill that girl, and I didn't have anything to do with killing that girl. Is that enough?'

'Of course it's enough,' he said, trying to hear the undertones in her voice, looking into her face with too much intensity. 'It's enough. Now we'll talk about gardening. Why do the petals of those flowers look like sieves?'

'Insects have been eating them.'

'Can't you import some other insects that will eat the insects? Or a repair gang of ants, that will fill up the holes in the flowers again? Jan, why did you buy that costume?'

'Go away, Hugh,' she said.

He knelt down beside her. She was crying.

'You should buy a watering-can,' he told her. 'It's going to take a long time to reach all those flowers with your tears. And salt may be bad for them. You must tell me, Jan. I can't help you unless you tell me. And don't say it. I know I haven't been a wonderful helper until now. I haven't found who killed your uncle, I haven't found who killed Zoe. And I haven't even found who killed Cady. There will be no Sherlock Holmes gold medals for me.'

'Cady? Cady dead?' She still knelt on the grass, staring at the earth.

'I tracked down the villainous waiters, they tried to kill me, I found Cady's body in a room, then they hit me on the head and when I woke up the body had gone. I'll tell you all about it, sometime. I'm trying to be modest, you know. The police have congratulated me. At least, they've almost congratulated me,' he said doubtfully, remembering Detective-Inspector Porthouse's anger and disgust. 'They've come as near congratulating me as they're ever likely to get. There was an organization for importing unpopular characters with money from their own countries, or their own countries' jails, over here, and starting them off as waiters until they'd built up a past. Your uncle had found out about it, of course, and that's why he was being unpleasant in a dramatic way the night I was here, the night he was murdered.'

'I knew about the waiters, in a vague kind of way, without knowing very much or being sure it was criminal. I mean, I supposed it was criminal, but I didn't know if it was criminal enough to matter.'

'Criminal enough to matter,' Everton repeated hopelessly. 'What very queer morals women have. Your uncle would be sure. You know, I think he was sure. He was probably going to expose them. I'm not quite certain whom I mean by them. Anyway, if they knew he was going to expose them, that would be a very sound reason for murdering him.'

'Sounder than Lucy's reasons? Sounder than getting rid of a husband you didn't want, inheriting his money, collecting his insurance—and perhaps saving yourself from exposure too? Do you think Lucy isn't concerned with the waiters?'

'Oh, we're back to Lucy,' Everton said in disgust. 'And you accused me of always talking about Lucy. You're the one who can't keep off the subject. Whatever happens, it has to be twisted round to be Lucy's fault.'

'Don't say it,' Jan said furiously. 'I'm sure I make you tired. I keep saying that a woman who is vile and beastly and unscrupulous is perhaps not very nice, and you accuse me at once of being eaten up by hatred.'

'What are we going to quarrel about when Lucy goes away?'
Everton asked. 'We'll have to think of something. You look delicious
when you're angry.' He leant forward and very carefully smoothed
back the hair that was falling over her eyes again. 'She will go away,
Jan. She's not part of us. She's just something to quarrel about. She'll
go, but you'll stay, won't you?'

Jan ignored the question. 'Perhaps I'll tell you about the swimming costume,' she said. 'I'll tell you why I had to buy it. And I swear
beforehand I didn't know what—what she would be wearing. But
there was all that talk about swimming, with the police-inspector.
The night you found her clothes in the swimming sheds. And when
I thought about it, I was quite sure he hadn't said what he meant.
Because it was nonsense to suppose she could have been forced into
the sheds against her will and made to change and taken out to sea
and drowned. But I didn't think it was nonsense she might have been
drowned. And afterwards, I was looking at my things, clothes and
things.' She stopped.

'Yes,' Everton said, and waited very quietly for over a minute. He
knew Jan would go on with the story.

'I've always had a black Jantzen,' Jan said in a burst of words, then
was silent again. 'I've always had one, but when I looked that night I
didn't have it any more. I didn't lose it. Someone took it.'

'Well.'

'I had an idea,' she said hesitantly, 'I know it sounds queer, but I
had an idea why they might have taken it. And I thought, suppose
they find the girl and she's wearing a black costume and then they
find mine is missing—Mrs. Simmons would know, she would tell
them—then I'll have to explain. So I thought if I bought one, then
no one would notice mine was missing. So that's why,' her voice
died away.

Everton let his glance wander to the sky. 'Have you told anyone you bought this swimming suit? No, of course not. The police know. I know. Well, hide it.'

'Why?'

'It might be safer,' Everton said vaguely. 'Promise to hide it?'

'Very well.'

'Promise not to mention to anyone that she was wearing a black Jantzen when she was found?'

'Yes.'

'Promise to live with me and be my love?' he said in a very different tone.

'No,' she said in a small, frozen voice. 'Never, never, never,' her voice diminished until the last "never" was less than a whisper.

'I'll go to work in the packing department of a cup-and-saucer factory and work up to be the leading manufacturer of plastic Ming vases. There's a future in it. There's a future in all sorts of things. I'm a man with ideas. Come live with me and share the profits.'

'No.'

'I have an uncle who lives in an Ivory Tower near Fleet Street, publishing rather delicate editions of the foreign classics. He wants to branch out into the moderns. He wants someone like myself who knows so many languages that they can exchange quips with Hungarians and write Limericks in Basque. He offered me a job a long time ago. I was shy about taking it. I'm not shy now. Come and be a publisher's wife. You can wear clinging gowns and entertain tiny French authors with cod cooked in a new way.'

'Hugh,' she said pathetically, 'why have you changed? Why do you ask me to marry you now? There were so many other times you might have asked, when I might have said yes. But why now? Is it because you're being chivalrous? Because I may be in trouble—over that swimming suit? There's no limit to the things you'll do for a woman in trouble, is there? Stealing or marrying.'

'You're tempting me to violence,' he said. 'I'm not going to be dragged into another row about Lucy.'

'But it's true, isn't it? You're asking me to marry you because I'm in trouble. And then for ever and ever you'll think "I'd never have married her if she hadn't got mixed up with the police." And I'll think "I needn't have married him after all." And we'll sit around wallowing in deeper and deeper swamps of regret until the only solid thing to clutch at will be hatred.'

'Be quiet,' he said furiously. 'I'm asking you to marry me because it's the first time for years I've been sure of myself. I've been a coward. I've been frightened of violence—and a lot of other things. I've made myself face a few things I couldn't face before. For the first time since I parted from you I know what I am. I feel a little happy and confident at last. And you begin talking about chivalry and regrets. I was afraid of you, too, you know, because you were always in the right. Now that you have managed to do something thoroughly stupid I feel you wouldn't be totally insufferable as a wife.'

'Totally insufferable!' she repeated, in a voice weakened by rage. 'You—oh, I wish I was strong enough to knock you down! You're the most unpleasant man I've ever met.' She turned and began to walk away very quickly. He followed her, caught her by the shoulders and swung her round.

'You have mud on your face,' he said. 'You'll have to give up gardening. It makes you look very untidy.'

She tried to push him away, but he leant forward and kissed her. He held her close to him, and felt immensely peaceful. He could feel her happiness against him. He thought that it would always be like that when they were together. He let her go.

'Now we're engaged,' he said. 'Right?'

'Yes,' she said softly. She looked up at the vicious sky. 'It's raining.'

'Let it rain,' he said, and kissed her again, while the rain beat against their faces.

'I like a little water down the back of my neck when I'm arranging to be married,' he said.

17

'THIS IS THE FIRST PIECE OF LUCK I'VE HAD IN FOURTEEN years,' the sadder of the English waiters said to Everton.

'Do you mean you've been trying to get rid of this macaroni cheese for fourteen years?' Everton said incredulously. He touched the pale yellow mountain on his plate experimentally. It did not yield easily to the fork. 'I don't think I'll eat this. I'll keep it for sticking wild flowers in my album.'

'It's never happened to me before,' the waiter said, hovering. 'Fourteen years, and I've never seen anything better than a divorce or two. And now! sir, did you know there's murder been going on here!'

'I know,' Everton said heavily. 'Is there anything else I could have to eat?'

'There's one of those French dishes. Tinned meat and garlic. With fried potatoes. There's plenty people,' the waiter said truculently, 'would be glad of the macaroni cheese. Whole families starving.'

Everton lifted the plate and held it out. 'If there is anyone who would like this, take it away and give it to him. But you won't, you know. You wouldn't carry it a hundred yards to give it to a dying man. Your philanthropy consists of trying to make other people uncomfortable, my dear friend. Now bring me the quaint French dish you speak of.'

The waiter shambled off, mumbling to himself, but before he had reached the service door he turned and shambled back again.

'I should've told you,' he said, in a voice that indicated resignation to the almost unendurable fatigue of living, 'that there's a phone call for you. They're waiting. I'd have told you before,' he said, triumphantly meek, 'but you wouldn't let me get a word in.'

'You're not very persistent,' Everton said bitterly, and hurried to the telephone.

'Hugh,' Lucy's voice said, 'Hugh. What have you been doing? I've been waiting for hours. Didn't you want to speak to me? Oh, Hugh, I do want to see you. Could I come to the hotel? In the bar? In half an hour? No, don't say anything, Hugh, just expect me.'

'All right. But where do you buy the honey?'

'What honey?' she asked in bewilderment.

'To spread on your voice.'

'In the grocer's,' she snapped. 'Where you get the vinegar for your cheap jokes. I'll see you in half-an-hour. Good-bye.'

He turned away from the telephone, grinning. Lucy sometimes used the wrong fly for the time of year and the state of the river, but it didn't matter much, now; he knew all her tricks, and he would stay in his safe place under the bank.

She was wearing opulent black when she swept into the bar, and her hair sparkled as though it had been brushed by sunlight. Her face was eager, pathetic, appealing. She looked like a film wife trying to win her husband back.

'Perhaps I shouldn't come to meet you like this,' she said. 'I'm so obviously in mourning.'

'You look enchanting,' he assured her. 'As though some master confectioner had made some magnificent icing for a piece of cake-shaped rock. I mean it,' he protested, 'the illusion is only just resistible.'

'You're objective, to-night, aren't you?' she said, letting the rock show through.

'I am,' he said. 'To-night and for ever. I know you've come here carrying a supply of fire and water under your arm. If you want me to go through them for your sake, don't waste time disguising them. Just tell me quickly why you think I should burn myself.'

'You sound so bitter, Hugh,' she said sadly. 'But you never trusted me, did you?' She looked at him, and her eyes sparkled like sunshine on rippling water. 'But please, please, don't pretend to hate me. Everything is so much against me, now. And I don't want any more hatred. I may be hard. Perhaps I am. But I'm not hard enough to bear any more.'

'What's wrong, Lucy?' he asked gently. 'No, don't tell me,' he said quickly. 'I don't want to know.'

'He suspects me of something,' she said, shuddering. 'That policeman. Ladders, balconies, dogs, shots. No, I won't have a drink, Hugh. Yes, buy me one, for the appearance. It must seem terrible, my coming to see you here. But, Hugh, whom can I trust?'

'Your grammar's too good, Lucy,' he said. 'You rehearsed that speech. I know the way you talk.'

'What's wrong with my grammar?' she said suspiciously.

'It's splendid. It's like a stage dialogue. You had plenty of time to think it out. Whom can you trust, indeed!'

'Well, who can I trust?' she said angrily. 'Not you, it seems. I come here in desperation, and you talk about grammar. I'm desperate, Hugh. He's driving me mad. And I didn't kill Gregory. I didn't. I didn't.' She opened her handbag and felt in it without looking.

'Don't produce a handkerchief,' he said. 'I know you don't cry real tears in emergencies. Your character is too strong for that.'

'What has changed you?' she asked. 'You sound so hard, now.'

'I am so hard, now,' he said grimly. 'You didn't kill your husband. And the others? Cady and Atkinson? Are you so sure of them?'

'I am,' she said. 'But that inspector—he's after them too.'

'If he thinks all three of you are in it, isn't it lucky I was there that night. Was that why you asked me?' he said slowly. 'Because all three of you were in it, or at least that all three of you had reason to be in it? If you could be suspected of conspiracy it was wise to have a stranger there. Any old stranger might have done, but I turned up, and I was easy to ask. I was the wrong stranger, of course. Do you know why? Because, although I've never admitted it before, I've wanted to destroy Ronson ever since he tried to destroy me. And I'll destroy him just as gladly under the name of Atkinson.'

'And me? Do you want to destroy me, Hugh?' she asked in a voice that seemed to glitter.

'You look pale and radiant,' he said, 'as though you were flood-lit. You're so beautiful, Lucy, I don't want to destroy you. It would make me feel like a vandal in a museum.'

'Hugh,' she said. 'Oh, I like to hear you talk as you used to. We were so happy, once, weren't we? Won't you help me now, Hugh? No, I don't even want you to help me. I just want you to stop trying to hurt me. You see, when you met me again you—you hated me. You know that's true. It is, isn't it?' She hesitated for a moment, with her eyes cast down. 'I don't like being hated. You hated me so much you wanted to turn things against me. Oh, I think it was quite unconscious. But you said, at least you suggested, to that policeman that I was upstairs a long time when I found Gregory. I think you made it longer than it really was, didn't you, Hugh?' She looked at him in glorious appeal.

'And that's the help you want,' he said. 'You want me to lie, to say you came downstairs at once. I won't do it,' he said deliberately. 'I won't do it—unless you tell me the truth. What did you do upstairs, Lucy? Why were you so long?'

'I was shocked. It's the truth, Hugh. I was so shocked I couldn't move.'

'And what shocked you?' he asked harshly. 'You were expecting his death, weren't you? He'd found out about the business you were running with Atkinson and Cady, bringing the vilest criminals in Europe to this country to hide in hotels until they'd acquired some kind of English identity. Murderers and torturers, the executioners of the last war and the assassins of the epilogue: these were the people you were smuggling here. Your husband, in his pompous way, was quite incorruptible. He meant to expose you and your gang, Lucy, so he had to die. And now you tell me you were shocked.'

'It's not true,' she said wildly. 'It's half-true. That's why it's not true. I did help, in a way. Political refugees—why shouldn't I have helped to save them? And it was something—I'm not the kind of person who could stay in a place like this darning my husband's socks until my blood congealed.'

'And one of your innocent refugees tampered with that balcony and then brought the dog along, so that your husband would step on the balcony and fall to his death. He was shot—and you stayed in that room a long time, working out how to get the balcony made safe again. You talked to Atkinson, then you came down and had hysterics to keep me in the room while he fixed the balcony screws again. Was that the only reason you tried to keep me in the room? Or were you holding me there while he moved the body down into his car? He took it, didn't he, when he went to fetch the police instead of telephoning? Simple, but very, very risky, because he might have been seen. He dropped it in the harbour before he went to the police. It's true, isn't it?' he said in a bullying tone. 'It's true because it must be true. The body could only have been moved by car. It had gone by the time the police came. The only car that left the house was Atkinson's. It's true, because nothing else can be true. And the glasses—the glasses fell from the body that was bundled in the back of the car, and Zoe found them when Atkinson picked her up later on. That's how it happened, isn't it?'

'You're guessing,' she said contemptuously. 'You can't prove any part of it.'

'It can be proved, because it's the only thing that could have happened.'

'I know enough about the law to know that isn't proof. A good lawyer would think of a dozen different things that could have happened.'

'I see why Zoe was important,' he said despairingly, 'she had the proof that was needed. The glasses in the car and the girl who found them would have ruined your good lawyer's case.'

'But there isn't going to be any lawyer, Hugh, is there?'

'Not now.'

'And if there isn't going to be a lawyer, need you make things so much more unpleasant for me by insisting I was out of the room for so long?'

'You're trying to make me sound spiteful, instead of honest. And you don't understand the depths of honesty I've reached since I left you.'

'It must be the influence of a good woman, although she is not an honest one. She came to blackmail me, the other day. Did you hear? I think you did. Has she offered you the money already? And now you're going to marry her—for so little.' Her eyebrows arched into a purer curve of incredulity.

'If I were a butterfly my wings would be bruised by those steel-tipped words. But I'm not a butterfly. I'm an armoured car. I've changed, Lucy, and you don't understand me any more. I have occasional patches of transparency, but they're bulletproof.' He stood up. 'If we both put our shoulders to this interview, we may be able to push it shut.'

Lucy sat still, looking with mild approval at her own reflection in the bar mirror. 'If you marry her, you'll end by having a share of Gregory's money—and his very substantial insurance. So you won't be so entirely without motive as you seemed. And the imaginary lawyer we were discussing may remember you were the last person to speak to my husband, that you were out of the room and in the garden a long time by yourself, that it's possible you moved the body out of the house and through the garden to a waiting car—driven, perhaps by Zoe, who was there, and perhaps by Jan, who can't prove that she wasn't.' She smiled at her reflection. 'It may not be true, but at least it's spiteful.'

He went to the bar and asked for two whiskies and soda. He wanted to think without being watched by Lucy. The story wouldn't hold enough water to moisten a juryman's lips, but he didn't want another cloud of notoriety to trail behind him. He brought the drinks back to the table and smiled at her. 'And what do you suggest?' he asked pleasantly.

'If you repress your honesty, I'll repress my spite. And, Hugh,' she leant towards him, soft, luscious, perhaps ripe enough to fall, 'don't pretend to hate me.'

He tried to grope his way to some defence. 'I don't understand everything,' he said dreamily. He let his mind drift back to the night he had seen Bath, lying on the floor with the hole in his head. He had looked in the dead man's face. He had not had time to look at Cady's face, and when he woke up the body had gone. Both bodies had gone. They were fond of moving bodies. The waiters must have put Cady in the green van, but Atkinson had taken a dreadful risk, carrying a corpse downstairs, depending on Lucy and her talk and her hysteria. He had driven the body to the harbour. A face might have looked from a yacht; a fisherman might have crouched among the mooncast shadows; a boy and a girl making plans by the sea might have seen the bundle slip over the harbour wall. He had been lucky in everything, except that the glasses had fallen from the body in the car, and Zoe had found them. He had been lucky, but what could have made him risk so much?

'Why did the body have to be moved, Lucy?' he asked absently. 'He was dead. You had your alibi. You were rid of him. You would get your legacy—and, in the end, the insurance. What was there about the body that mustn't be seen?'

She shook her head and smiled at him. She looked gracious and remote, like a stage duchess, but alarm was sparking in her eyes. They looked at each other and sipped their drinks, silent as a couple whose conversation died with marriage, and seeming as bored as two horses on a hot day.

It was common enough, possibly, to move a weapon. If Sir Ethelred Someone had shot Bath with his elephant gun, he might have dropped it in the lake and hoped that suspicion would centre on the man with a Colt under his arm. The police might have noticed the size of the wound. Had they got rid of the body with the idea of hiding the wound? But they had let him, Everton, see it, and the body had been found. What had they done with the weapon? He let his mind wander around the room again. There had been no weapon. The murderer had moved it, or they had taken it away before they let him come up. No weapon. If the gun had been lying in sight, he would have wondered about suicide. But there had been no gun by the dead man's hand, and the room had been in disorder. No weapon, no suicide. And the murderer had moved the body. Atkinson had moved the body, but he wasn't the murderer.

He sat with his eyes on Lucy, amazed by her composure, almost offended by her beauty. The light in his mind was growing stronger: the flicker raged into flame; there were no longer any shadows where doubts could hide.

'Did I hear you say to Jan that the insurance company didn't pay on suicide?' he asked, and was rewarded by only the slightest paling of her lips. 'And of course they don't,' he went on. 'A man can't insure himself for forty thousand pounds and then provide for his wife's future by shooting himself. It would have been odd, wouldn't it, if your husband had killed himself when you had planned that he should die by accident? What would you have done, Lucy, if that had happened? You might have taken the gun from his hand, stirred the room up a little, to suggest that a stranger had entered and looked for something. You would still be afraid that the body would tell its story to the experts. The body was dangerous, in that way, but that wasn't the real reason for moving it. Who could suspect suicide when the murderers went to the trouble of putting the body in the sea? When the body vanished, the suspicion of suicide went with it. No wonder you were shocked when you went upstairs. You saw him lying with the gun in his hand, and your forty thousand pounds back in the bush. You had to plan quickly, but surely you could have done better than that.'

Her eyes had darkened while he spoke, and now she closed them for a moment. When she opened them again they looked cold and dimmed. 'If this nonsense was true,' she said in a low voice, 'would there have been much harm in it? To move a body already dead— would that have been wicked? Would you hate me for that, Hugh?' Her eyes grew warmer, begging for sympathy and love.

'The insurance people would call it fraud.' He stopped, resenting again the lovely line of her face. She was the most beautiful woman he had ever known; she was lovely in composure and radiant in action, with rather less morality than the war-head of a rocket.

'It's not much of a crime, Hugh, to get money from an insurance company. Why, it's what they're for, isn't it, to pay money when someone is dead? And Gregory couldn't have died any more thoroughly if he'd done it in bed.' She spoke with the idle earnestness of a woman discussing her hairdresser. 'You have come on a lot since I used to know you, Hugh. I'd never have believed that you'd be clever enough to work it all out.' She looked at him with a glint of admiration. 'If I don't collect the money you won't feel bound to say something to the police, will you? It has all been a waste of time, hasn't it?' She glanced at her watch. 'It's half-past nine,' she said, rising. 'I have an appointment with that Inspector. I shan't tell him it was suicide.'

'Don't,' he said, 'because it was murder.'

He thought that was a good exit line, so he nodded to her quickly and left the bar.

He went upstairs slowly; he felt as though he had been battered by heavy surf. He must be careful not to see Lucy again: even the memory of the dead was insubstantial in her presence. They were supposed to cry out for justice; but how feeble were those noises from the grave! Already they seemed hardly strong enough to make their case against Lucy heard.

He opened the door and went into his room. Two hands came out of the dark and gripped him by the throat. He fell back against the wall, his mind blacked out by fear. He struggled weakly, feeling death's explosion in his lungs. Then the hands slackened, and he was flung across the room and on to the bed. The door shut gently and the key turned in the lock, the light was switched on, and heavy footsteps approached the bed. Everton, scarcely conscious, looked up into Cady's face.

'You're dead,' he said, and shuddered as Cady put a knife to his throat.

'No,' Cady said. 'They saved me. To kill you.' He smiled, his old, stupid smile. His cold, religious eyes watched Everton's throat. 'I could have killed you then, in the dark, but I thought I'd like to have a look at you first. They said they'd be caught if they killed you now.'

Everton moved a little, tentatively, and the point of the knife pricked eagerly at his throat.

'You'll be caught, anyway,' he said in a hoarse whisper. He hoped that his own voice would sound more loudly from the grave.

'I won't be caught,' Cady said, 'because I'm going away to-night. And they won't be looking for me. As you say, I'm dead. You were the one to see my body. They arranged that. You're not the only clever one. So I'm dead, and when you're dead too they certainly won't think of me. And the others are taking good care not to be alone to-night.'

It was true, Everton thought. He had announced Cady's death and armed him with the innocence of the grave. After all their bungling, they had planned the ironically perfect murder. Ullmann and the Greek would be far away by now, and Lucy, he thought with pain, Lucy had known she should be with the police. The circle of innocence would be complete unless he, at the centre, should break loose.

'Where's Atkinson?' he asked, still gasping.

'He's at a meeting of the yacht club,' Cady said, the knife in his hands quivering hungrily.

'No, he's not,' Everton said, shrinking. 'He's there!' He looked in horror past Cady to the door, and Cady's eyes wavered for a moment from the knife. Everton swung upwards with his right hand against Cady's wrist. The knife slipped, plunged downwards, pierced the flesh, cut, and glanced sideways into the blankets. Cady, paralysed by the sight of the blood at Everton's throat, leant for a moment on the knife, his pale eyes staring. Everton brought his knee up against Cady's chin and he fell forward on the bed. Everton, fumbling wildly with his left hand, found the square glass ashtray that stood on the bedside table. He lifted it and brought it down weakly on the back of Cady's neck. Cady grunted, and Everton swayed off the bed and towards the door, clutching his throat with one hand. His fingers, slippery with his own blood, would not close on the door handle, and before he remembered that the door was locked he heard Cady lurching across the room behind him. He turned the key and pulled again at the handle. The door opened and he fell into the corridor, almost at the feet of the dreary English waiter. Cady came through the doorway with the knife in his hand, and the waiter hit him hard on the chin.

There were other men running along the corridor, and the waiter turned to them.

'This is what I call an hotel!' he said, looking with the terrible pride of the meek at the hand that had knocked out Cady.

18

'NOW, THAT'S A FASCINATING LITTLE STORY,' INSPECTOR LEIGH said, folding his hands on his stomach. 'How's your throat, after all that talking?'

Everton made a weary gesture with one hand. The bandage round his neck made him look sinister and unreliable; he felt as though all emotion had been sieved out of him; he had not even enough energy to hate the police.

'I believe most of what you've told me,' Leigh said, 'but let's see how it will look in court. They tried to murder a man and make it look like accident. They failed, and he committed suicide, so they moved the body to make it look like murder. They did this so that Mrs. Bath could collect the very heavy insurance that would not be paid in the event of suicide, but that she would collect if he were murdered by someone other than herself without her connivance. The only evidence that they moved the body died with the girl Zoe Stokes. It would be more reasonable to start a whist drive in court than to use it for that kind of story. Cady is the only one we can keep, and he'll certainly be convicted on a charge of attempting to murder you. For the rest, all I can suggest is that you stand around until another of them tries to kill you. It seems to be the most useful part you play. I'll telephone Scotland Yard and see if I can get you a job as murderers' provocateur.' He pushed his chair away from the desk, then stood up and walked angrily to the window. 'Cady may talk. I think he'll have to. There's another point.' He swung round and confronted Everton. 'We have only your word the girl had Bath's glasses in her bag—and your word has been the most unreliable in Southern England, so far. You assume she took the glasses with her when she went to meet her murderer. Now, that's a most unusual way for a blackmailer to behave. Surely she wouldn't take them with her. She'd hide them somewhere.' He smiled dimly. 'I haven't your acquaintance with the criminal classes—I'm only a policeman. Would you have expected a blackmailer to have carried the evidence around in that way?'

Everton let his mind travel back to the morning in the hat shop, the last time he had seen Zoe. 'Girls don't have many pockets,' he said. 'They feel their handbags are safe. But that morning I snatched her bag and looked inside. She wasn't stupid. If I could do it she must have thought a murderer could do it. Do you think she posted them to herself?'

Leigh shook his head. 'We've looked over the house, since.'

'There's the hat shop,' Everton suggested.

The Inspector grunted. 'I had a look at the high-class head under that hat in the window. I thought she might have slipped a pair of glasses on its nose. But she hadn't. We've had a man go over the shop. Now we'll go back to the hotel and pick up a coat and scarf for you. I don't want people staring at your neck.'

'That's kind of you. Why?' Everton asked. 'Do you think it would spoil their aim, if they happen to be firing at my eyes?' He stood up, trying to keep his exploring fingers away from his throat. He had another memory now, to lay beside the river. He should have been exuberant in escape: instead, he felt as worn-out as a post-office pen.

Leigh dropped a heavy hand of spurious affection on his shoulder. 'We're going to see them all, my boy,' he said. 'We are going unravelling. We will confront them.'

'What with?' Everton asked sourly. 'Lack of evidence?' He followed Leigh out of the room and into the car.

They stopped for a minute at the hotel, and when they left Everton's throat was hidden under a scarf.

The harbour was sullen beneath the oppressive sky. The small sailing boats, like summer birds, had begun to migrate; the season of tents and sails had ended. As they drove along the coast road to the house they saw a figure on the cliff top; Mrs. Leonard was no migrant.

'She looks less like a herring-gull every day,' Everton said with a sigh. 'Are you asking her to your party, or throwing out a few scraps for her afterwards?'

'The party is a very private affair,' the Inspector said. 'Atkinson, Mrs. Bath, her niece, her husband's niece, that is, you, me, and the sergeant here, who has a university degree in shorthand. That's right, isn't it, Firth? I'll be the only uneducated man present.'

Lucy, gracefully relaxed, welcomed them with too much ease. Jan sat stiff and quiet, like a doll that has been bent and propped up in a chair. Atkinson was as carefully neutral as ever.

'I'm sorry if I appeared to stare at your servant,' Leigh said to Lucy. 'It may be my last chance for years to meet a butler.'

'Do you mean you're not going to call on us again?' Lucy asked with lazy interest.

'Not here,' Leigh said amiably, and Lucy stiffened impatiently like a photographer's model who has held a pose too long.

'To business, then,' Leigh said. 'I'll begin with my story. And I don't think it's necessary to repeat what I've already told you about the balcony. But I should say that Scotland Yard has tracked down your foreign friend Ullmann. Actually, he's so blind without his glasses, he bumped into them. That is going to lead them to a few other people. We haven't so far decided if it is essential to deport Ullmann. He's been very useful to us. He is prepared to swear that Cady gave him the dog to hide for a day, with instructions that it should be brought back here, beneath the late Mr. Bath's window, at about eleven-thirty on the night that turned out to be the night of the murder. He was told to make sure that the dog howled beneath the window. Being the kind of man he is, he overdid it and broke the dog's leg. We have no reason to doubt his statement. Mr. Everton detected the smell of dog in this man's room—it's rather a large, smelly dog—the dead girl Zoe Stokes saw a man lead a dog in the garden and told Everton she thought the man was Ullmann, and Mrs. Leonard also saw the man with the dog. It was of no obvious personal advantage to Ullmann to lure the late Mr. Bath to his death on a balcony that had been tampered with. We think he is speaking the truth when he says he acted on Cady's instructions. And that leaves us wondering what the personal advantage to Cady was.'

'He must have had some connection with my husband that I never suspected,' Lucy said magnificently.

'I disagree,' the Inspector said quietly. 'But he had a connection with you that is more than suspicion. A large part of the organization for passing undesirable fugitives through Europe was already known, before this murder occurred. A few of the people concerned have already been arrested. Flattering reference has been made to a beautiful woman with golden hair.'

'It's lucky I'm not the only woman who is beautiful and blonde,' Lucy said smiling.

'Modesty would be a safer policy,' Jan said in a marble voice.

'But you are the only woman who has been writing references wholesale, to get these men the quiet jobs and the easy start they needed if they were to be assimilated gently into England. It is difficult for a foreigner to drop from the sky without attracting attention.

But for a foreigner to go to an hotel looking for a job, armed with a fulsome reference from a woman married to a man of eminence—a judge, perhaps—is moderately easy. And it is not so difficult, then, to leave the hotel, and move to the other prepared jobs. The background can exist. Or there may be a short spell as a visitor at another hotel. "I come from Bournemouth, or Cheltenham, or Huddersfield," the man can say. "I used to live at the George, or the Swan Inn, or what the name might be." The organization was very good. The stone entered the pond with the smallest ripple. And the organizers didn't concern themselves for five minutes with what the stone did on the bottom of the pond. Shall I give you an example? One of the fugitives bought up a small business in the chemical trade. It suffered like its competitors from a shortage of raw materials, but it didn't suffer for long. The man was an expert at corruption, and he found his corruptibles, even in the British Civil Service. You must remember the case. It was only a few months ago. Didn't you read in the papers of the clerk who allowed this man, Baron, to pay off the mortgage on his house? And how, when his wife discovered the transaction, she sold the house and all its furniture and offered the proceeds with all the family savings to this man Baron. What she wanted for the money was Baron's promise to leave her husband alone, to let him stop his fraudulent dealings with the importers in Baron's favour. Baron refused. The clerk was too useful to be dropped. The wife committed suicide. The clerk broke down then, and confessed. Baron vanished. Did you run him out of the country, as you ran him in?'

'I haven't run anyone anywhere,' Lucy said, and although she had not moved, she gave the impression that her back was arching.

'I was speaking to your friend Atkinson as well as to you,' Inspector Leigh said.

'Good lord, I've never had anything to do with that sort of thing,' Atkinson said in horror.

'But you own the hotel where so many of your immigrants started. You have a sailing boat, like Cady—and we know that one of Cady's jobs was to sail the men over quietly from France. And I think we can prove that your real name is Ronson. You have been in the smuggling racket, and one of your consistencies is that you like to work with small boats. I don't think you ever used an aeroplane when you were importing your cameras and watches. Sailing boats are small and quiet. You used them before and you've been using them now. I have a warrant here for your arrest, Mr. Ronson, on the charge of securing the illegal entry of aliens to this country.'

'My name is not Ronson,' Atkinson said harshly. His eyes flickered towards Lucy, and then back to his own hands.

'Everton here will say you are Ronson, and that when he knew you before you were already engaged in running fugitives to the French frontier. In any case, I think, I might almost be sure, that your finger prints are already in the files.' The Inspector sounded apologetic: it was true that he resented dependence on the central organization.

Atkinson looked rapidly round the room. His glance rested wistfully on the french windows, then he smiled, and shook his head. Leigh, who had looked alert, as though listening to a far-off voice, sank back into placidity.

'Securing the illegal entry of aliens,' Atkinson murmured. 'Is that the only charge against me?'

'It's the charge written on this warrant,' Leigh agreed. 'The only reason for taking you into custody.'

Atkinson wore the concentrated expression of the chess-player. They waited for him to speak, and the moment of silence expanded until it grew too big for them all.

'Don't,' Lucy cried, 'they can't prove anything!'

'The only charge!' Jan said. 'Oh, it's not fair that people should escape so easily.'

'If it's the only charge,' Atkinson said in a coarse, mocking tone that abandoned military stiffness, 'then I will yield gracefully to your impertinence. And ask your permission to get in touch with my lawyers.'

Lucy wore an expression of desperate coldness Everton had not seen before. She stood up and turned her back on them all. She crossed to the window and looked out at the hostile sea, then she turned abruptly and went to the mantelpiece. She opened the silver box that stood there, looked at it blankly, shut it again.

'No cigarettes,' she said. 'I have some in my handbag. I think I left it in the hall. Would you get it, please?'

She looked at Atkinson, but Leigh started up like a sheepdog that has noticed dissidence in the flock. Atkinson, who had begun to rise, sat down again. Everton went into the hall for the bag, gave it to Lucy, and sat down on the arm of her chair. He watched her strong, clumsy hands grope in the bag for the cigarette case. He lit her cigarette and waited, watching her.

'There are other questions we might ask now,' Leigh said heavily. 'There is this business of the late Mr. Bath's body being moved. Mr. Everton, now, has a theory that you moved it.' He looked directly at Atkinson, who listened with the impatient interest he might have given to a weather forecast. 'It would be an understatement to say I agree with the theory. I formed it before he did. On the very simple grounds that you drove the only car known to have left this house in the relevant interval—in the time that elapsed from eleven-forty, when Mr. Everton saw the body, to twelve ten, when we discovered it to be missing.'

'I didn't kill Bath,' Atkinson said harshly. 'And as I didn't kill him there was no reason in the world why I should have moved his body.'

'I've had a talk with the insurance company,' Leigh said placidly. 'It's a fact they don't pay on suicide. You didn't kill him, you say, but if you'd found him with the gun in his hand, when he should have had an accident with the balcony like a reasonable creature, you might have felt yourself forced to a quick decision. Up with the ladder and undo the balcony trap, instruct Mrs. Bath to hold Everton in the room downstairs with any kind of histrionics she could rake up, while you carried the body downstairs and out through the french windows in the dining room and into your car in the drive outside. Then you went off to fetch us, the police. But you stopped for perhaps two minutes, on the way, by the harbour, and dropped the body in the sea. It's all hypothesis, naturally,' he added smoothly. 'And it would certainly presuppose a very chivalrous attitude, on your part, taking all that risk, just to help Mrs. Bath to the money. But if you'd moved the gun, before Everton saw the body, so that he thought it was murder and not suicide, and then you moved the body, to imply that some murderer had something to hide, and the room had been disturbed a little, so that Everton assumed someone had searched it quickly, then the coroner would scarcely think of suicide. Everton, in fact, is such a valuable witness I'm surprised anyone ever behaved maliciously towards him. The weakness, you know,' Leigh said reprovingly to Atkinson, 'was the greed for getting another bird with the stone. You wanted Bath out of the way because he was going to destroy your black refugee traffic, but instead of being happy and contented when you thought he'd killed himself, you began to regret the insurance at once.'

'Thought he'd killed himself?' Atkinson repeated involuntarily.

'"Thought" was the word I used,' Leigh agreed. 'Just in the way of friendly discussion, I'd like to say that if you or anyone else moved the body for the reasons I've given, you, or someone else, acted on a stupid impulse. Bath didn't commit suicide. He was killed. The sea is a great destroyer,' Leigh said moodily, 'but it is slow. Quicker than the earth, much quicker than the air, but very, very slow compared to fire. We've had the post mortem, and there's no doubt at all that he was shot at a range of several feet.' He stopped, and Everton realized that his mind was fascinated by death. The Inspector, in his own way, was an unbalanced man. The professional contemplation of death had twisted him from his natural course.

Lucy had been staring at Everton. 'You knew about the post mortem,' she said, 'when you told me last night he'd been murdered?'

Leigh snapped into briskness again. 'He didn't know, because he hadn't been told. If he said your husband had been murdered, he was guessing.'

'I was guessing,' Everton agreed wearily. 'But I'm not guessing when I say that Zoe was murdered. What about her?' He looked at Lucy, at Jan, at Leigh, and finally turned, almost in appeal, to Atkinson. 'What about her? Was she knocked in the head, and thrown in, as I once was? No. This was worse. I threatened to expose the traffic in fugitives, and automatically I invited my own death. I'm the voice from the grave,' he said to Atkinson, 'but I am the only one that can be heard. Was this girl drugged, or beaten, or smothered before she was slipped in the sea? She could swim. What was done to her first so that she would drown? And what kind of mind have you,' he said in loathing, 'that could think of putting her in a swimming suit before you drowned her?'

'Come now,' Leigh said in tepid reproof, 'you mustn't make charges you can't substantiate.'

'What nonsense, Hugh,' Lucy said impatiently. 'If she came to blackmail someone, she certainly wouldn't bring her swimming clothes with her. Don't be so impetuous, Hugh. I know you believe she went to blackmail—someone. Perhaps she did. But don't you think it's likely she had her interview, then went swimming in the perfectly normal way? People do go swimming, you know, without being thrown secretly into the water. I don't do it myself. I'm frightened of the sea. But Jan goes swimming a lot. I don't for a moment think that anyone drowned this girl. She went swimming of her own free will in her own black Jantzen swimming costume and swam out too far and was drowned. It's stupid to look for a morbid explanation. No one put her in a swimming suit because no one had a swimming suit to put her into.' She paused, and her eyes flashed like glass in the sun. 'Jan is the only one round here with a swimming costume, and you still have your swimming costume, haven't you, Jan? The black one, I mean.'

In the dark silence that followed, Jan seemed to diminish.

'I've said something wrong, have I?' Lucy looked from one face to another. 'Or have I said something right at last?' she added in a whisper. 'Jan, do you still have your black bathing suit?' She waited. No one spoke. Atkinson made a gesture, but it was too late. 'I know you haven't,' Lucy said, almost screaming. 'I know you haven't, because I've looked.'

'Well,' Leigh said peacefully, 'you people do like to fire charges at each other. You've made a very interesting suggestion, Mrs. Bath, but it leads to another idea,' he said, still in a lazy voice. Then his tone changed suddenly. 'Where did you get this idea she was wearing a black suit? She was in one of those green two-piece elastic affairs.'

'That's a lie,' Lucy snapped. 'She was in black like the missing suit.' Then she stopped, and the light left her face, so that her skin looked suddenly like snow under a faded sky.

'You couldn't have known she was in black,' the Inspector said softly, 'you couldn't have known, unless you'd seen her.'

'I was guessing,' Lucy said harshly.

'You guess in a confident manner. The more so, that you think Miss Deverell has lost a black swimming suit.'

'I still have it,' Jan said in a whisper.

'That's a lie,' Lucy said venomously.

'We did think, Mrs. Bath, that whoever took the swimming suit from Miss Deverell would draw attention to its absence,' the Inspector said apologetically. 'You keep on accusing yourself, Mrs. Bath. Perhaps it's time I warned you that anything you say may be taken down and used in evidence.'

Lucy opened her handbag again and snatched at her cigarette case.

'You have nothing against me,' she said, trembling. 'Nothing.'

Everton leant forward and struck a match. 'But we have, Lucy,' he said, and took the handbag from her. 'I've been looking into your handbag,' he said. 'It's true you weren't in the habit of going swimming. But you did go once to the swimming sheds. The old man gave you a little brass tag to fasten to your swimming costume. But you didn't put on a swimming costume. You put the brass tag in your handbag, and you went along the concrete corridor—perhaps you were wearing a green dress, for the occasion, but that doesn't matter. You carried Zoe's clothes. They wouldn't make a big bundle. You left them on the seat of a box and then you came out again. But you forgot the brass tag. If Zoe had swum from the sheds she would have worn it on the strap of her swimming costume, because everyone who entered the sheds had either to pay, or show by the brass tags that they had paid already. She didn't have it on her costume, but I see you still have it in your handbag.' He held the bag out silently to the Inspector. Leigh took it, and drew out a round numbered piece of brass, like a coin with a hole in it and a loop of elastic secured to the hole.

The Inspector held it in his hand almost reverently. 'You've saved us a lot of trouble, Mrs. Bath,' he said with approbation. 'I suppose you didn't realize the brass coin was important. If you'd never been in a swimming shed before, you wouldn't. So one half of the nation really doesn't know how—'

'Be quiet!' Lucy interrupted him. 'You can't charge me with murder. I didn't do it. I didn't. Damn you,' she shouted to Atkinson. 'Why don't you say something.'

'I've nothing to say,' Atkinson replied smoothly. 'I'll wait to see my lawyer. I advise you to do the same.'

'I think Mrs. Bath will easily be convinced that her best plan is to plead guilty to being an accessory,' Leigh said threateningly. 'But you are both within your rights in demanding legal advice.' His face had lost its lazy humanity, and now he droned in an official voice: 'I must ask you both to accompany me to the police station.'

Everton watched Lucy with pity and despair. He had never seen her look so beautiful as now, when her face was frost-pale with fear, and her eyes alight with the fires of rage. In the dark hostility of the room his compassion could be felt as human warmth, and she turned to him.

'Hugh, they can't take me away. I've done nothing. I was told, I was ordered, to leave some clothes, and I left them. He told me she wanted to prove she had been somewhere else when she was doing something for him. I'd never even seen the girl. Why should I want to kill her?'

'So you're going to turn on me,' Atkinson said, in coarse contempt. 'Why should I want to kill her? She was standing in the way of the insurance money, and you were the one who wanted to collect it, weren't you?'

'You knew she was wearing a black Jantzen, and you stole mine, so that if any questions were asked, they would be asked of me,' Jan said, and every word was delivered wrapped in hatred. 'Perhaps—perhaps it was even my swimsuit that she wore.'

'I think we'd better finish this discussion at the station,' Leigh said in his official voice, but Everton sensed his satisfaction and relief. Lucy and Atkinson were turning against each other. Lucy was bewildered and betrayed, like a child who has been told a hundred times not to light matches in the house, and finally, when the house is burning, is forced to blame some other child. She hadn't the mind that is capable of assessing consequences, and now, when the end had come, she could understand nothing except that she had been betrayed.

She rose, with a magnificent semblance of composure. 'You'll speak to me when I come out of prison, Hugh?' she said. 'I spoke to you when I saw you again, although I see now that it would have been better if I hadn't.'

There was nothing he could say in consolation. She had planned to destroy her husband; she had been saved from the guilt of murder only because she had been forestalled. She had helped to destroy Zoe, and if the major guilt was Atkinson's, it was still true that she had played a monstrous part. He nodded dumbly, and watched her go.

He and Jan sat in silence, for the moment disunited by their thoughts of Lucy. In their lives there would always be this wall. Two people could never be as one. They would remain alone, with their different frailties, but there would be some comfort, some love, some loyalty. Jan would never be all softness for him; she would always carry within her the sharp-edged, relentless hatred.

'Hugh,' Jan said miserably, 'I think she'll go to prison anyway, for trying to defraud the insurance company.'

'Yes,' he said dully.

'I—I couldn't say it. But—I was in the garden when you asked me to marry you. Do you know what I was doing? Burying the evidence, you said. And it was true. Zoe was at this house, Hugh. I was leaving the house, that afternoon. The Simmons were out. It was their day off. I was leaving. Something was thrown from the window and landed at my feet. I looked back. I thought I saw a face at the window. It might have been Lucy's. I don't know. But without knowing why, I was frightened. I didn't look down at what had fallen. I kicked the little parcel into the side, into the weeds and flowers, and walked on as though I'd seen nothing. I was a coward, you see. I knew that something was wrong. Then, the day that you came, I went into the garden to look. I found the packet among the weeds. It was the glasses, of course. She must have thrown them out of the window when she found she was in danger. If I'd had the courage to look at the time I would have known she was in the house. I might have saved her. I was thinking of that, when you came. Then I put some earth over them and left them. Now—Hugh, I don't want to prove she was in the house. Lucy will suffer enough.'

He looked at her with infinite love and tenderness.

'There's Zoe,' he said, thinking of the small, shrill voice that would never be heard again.

'I know. But Hugh,' she said desperately. 'I can't speak. I can't join the hunters.'

'There's Zoe,' he said again. 'I don't want to join the hunters, but someone must speak for the hunted.'

He rose slowly and walked out into the garden, back to the leafy border where he had found Jan digging. He bent down and parted the leaves, thinking of Lucy and how her radiance would be dimmed behind high walls. Her lust for action had driven her too far: nothing could save her, and nothing she could say or do now would make her worthy of salvation. And Jan, after all, did not want to join the hunters, he remembered with a torrent of gratitude. But the secret, the secret of such magnitude, would bite into their lives, and he had no right to sacrifice Jan again for Lucy.

He found the little pile of fresh earth and stirred it with his foot. It would be easy enough to let it lie. He bent down and felt with his fingers until they touched the soft wet paper. He picked up the little bundle and shook the earth from it, then he walked back to the house. He stopped in the hall by the telephone, and rang the police station.

'I've been looking in the garden,' he said, when he heard Leigh's voice. He put the packet on the table and unwrapped it with one hand. 'It occurred to me she might have had a chance to drop something on her way to or from the house. I found a packet underneath a window. It's wrapped in paper just as it was when I saw it in her handbag. The paper's a bit earthy, but it's scrawled with lipstick, it's a bit hard to read, but I think it says something like "Atkinson—got me." Perhaps that's what I want it to say, still, I think I'm right.' He sighed heavily and put the telephone down, then he went to tell Jan that she was not, and never need be, one of the hunters.

That left only one thing to be done.

19

EVERTON WALKED ALONG THE TOP OF THE CLIFF, WITH THE soft mist from the sea clinging to his hair and touching his skin with a thousand gentle fingers. At the foot of the cliff the slate-grey, surly ocean muttered. If he could rest on the sea he might drift to the dead frozen water at the end of the world, or float on the monstrous ruffled Pacific.

Mrs. Leonard sat on the edge of the cliff, as watchful as a bird on its nest, an old, mad bird, on a desolate nest. He sat down beside her on the wet cushioned turf.

'There have been events,' he said cautiously. 'Trivial, in relation to eternity, but events. An event is something that happens and it is no less real if it happens to a grain of dust instead of to a star a thousand times greater than our sun. The dust blows in the wind, and something has happened: the star explodes in outer space and flies through a million miles of emptiness, and something else has happened. What you suffer from, Mrs. Leonard, is too great a sense of proportion. Do you think you could write a poem about that?' He was conscious of something hard in his pocket. 'I still have the book of poems you gave me. When I've had time to read them all I may find you have written the poem already.' He took the book from his pocket and laid it on his knee.

'We love the things that are bigger than our lives,' she said. 'The sea is greater and the dust is less, and against the magnitude of the stars our sea is a drop of water.'

'And how much is a life?' he asked, 'when it has been pinpointed in eternity?' She looked at him wildly, but she did not answer. 'I think,' he said, 'it is as much as seventy years, or seventy million years. It is as much as eternity, if you like, because it happens only once, and against eternity each man can put the statement, Never Again. Eternity is a mild idea, compared to its opposite. And now,' he said in a different voice, 'Bath is dead, his widow has been arrested, Atkinson has been arrested, and so has Cady.'

She took the book from his hand, and her lined, eager face was no longer ridiculous, but crushed into the terrible importance of the destroyed. 'So, after all, that is the end of it,' she said. 'All for nothing— and nothing is a word that equals infinity, if I believe what you say.'

'What was Cady to you?' he asked. He thought he knew the answer. She opened the book of her own poems that she had taken from him, and turned to the title page. 'To my enemy, my son Gerald,' he read, and abused himself for his stupidity. He had carried the book in his pocket for days, and on any one of these days he could have read the secret.

'So we have come to the reason at last,' he said. He looked at her worn face, that was capable of ecstasy. In her strange way she was nearer to life than the women who sit indoors on rainy days, polishing the silver, or talking to other women about the rain. She was also nearer to death.

'May I talk to you about the night Bath died?' he asked. 'I was the last person to speak to him, you know. Meeting these people again was a shock to me. It drove me back to the thoughts I'd stamped down for three years. Bath took me out of the room to look at the sea in the dark, and he demanded the truth about me. For reasons of my own, I told him. I told him what I had never told anyone else, what I didn't even tell the police that night. I told him that Atkinson

was a man called Ronson, and that Ronson had thrown me into the
Seine and left me to drown, that I was rescued and put in jail. Some
of these things no one knew but Ronson and myself, and possibly
Lucy. They would certainly not talk about them. They had no reason
to talk about them, because I existed only in the past. The meeting
that night was an accident. I told Bath these things, and half-an-hour
later he was dead. If he spoke to anyone after me, it was to his murderer. But the next day, Mrs. Leonard, when I went to your house,
you told me what Atkinson had done to me, as I had told Bath. He
told you what I had said. You used almost the same words to me that
I used to Bath—"He's a dangerous man. I suppose it seemed clever
to know him." You were alone in that room with him, then you shot
him. You left the gun in his own hand, didn't you?' He looked at her
sadly. 'Why did you kill him?'

'He was going to put my son in prison,' she said. 'My son hated
me, but he only hated me a little, until he met that man.'

'Atkinson?' Everton asked, handling the poisoned name gently.

'Yes. I don't think you know what hatred is,' she said. 'Your mind
isn't deep enough to contain it. Gerald was everything to me once. I
loved him so much there was no other reality. His father was brutal.
He hit Gerald, and I turned him out of the house. Until he was sixteen, he grew closer to me every day of his life. I taught him to read,
I played with him, we read aloud to each other every night. He didn't
even want to go to school, but when he was fourteen I let him go. It
was torture for him to be separated from me. Once, when he was a
little boy, a dog bit him.' She paused, her face twisted with anger at
the memory. 'I killed the dog,' she said. 'One of the only two living
creatures I have ever killed.' She looked at Everton wildly. 'I was wrong
to kill the dog. He was a gentle boy; he cried for hours when he found
I'd killed it. Then when he was sixteen, he learnt something, from

another boy. He blamed me for driving his father away, and his hatred began. I tried to save him from the war. I put him on a farm, but they came and took him away. He hadn't the kind of mind for war. People tried to kill him. How could he stand it? He turned away from me. Do you know, he burned some of my poems. But I needn't go on. He denied me, absolutely. Then he met that man and turned to crime. I came to live here to be near him. Then I found that cold man, who worshipped the law and hated justice, had discovered that Gerald and Atkinson and his own wife were trading in the vilest human beings for their own profit. He might not have cared, but they were also breaking the law. He wanted them all to be tried in court and sent to prison. It was his duty. Duty was another of his ugly idols. He would have put Gerald in prison.' As she spoke she bent forward and looked over the edge of the cliff. On this wet day the sea had only surface. It was hard to believe in its depths.

Everton tried to imagine things as they had been. Bath, intent on exposure; the other three, planning his death. The situation had arisen slowly. What had given the final impulse?

'And then?' he asked. 'There must have been something else?'

'They thought they were private,' she said. 'But I watched the balcony. I saw the man go and another come and take his place. I knew what was done, and I knew I must save him. And I thought that when I had saved his life I could make him promise to do nothing against Gerald. While you talked to him that night, I went in the house and up to his room. I promised to take Gerald away, if only he would spare him. I told him how weak Gerald was—far, far too weak to bear a prison cell. He told me that justice was absolute, above weakness and above strength. When he saw that I condemned him for his brutal-ity, he told me that Gerald was as criminal as Atkinson, and that he had just learnt Atkinson was capable even of murder—that you had told him how Atkinson, under another name, had thrown you into a river to drown. "Where Atkinson leads, your son will follow," he said. "And now Atkinson can lead him to his punishment." So then I told him what they had planned to do to him. He tried the balcony, and when he found that what I said was true, that his own wife had planned to murder him, he took his gun from the drawer. He meant to kill himself.'

He would never have killed himself, Everton thought. The dead man on the floor with the gun in his hand had made even Lucy suppose it to be suicide, but he, who had known the old man for only a few hours, knew it was not. Bath had been willing to sacrifice his wife and his self-respect for the sake of his principles, he would not have spared himself. It was true that he was a man who couldn't live with crime, who would always be driven on to expose and punish, to search for the ideal world where every action was accounted for, where every man harvested the fruits of his guilt. When he found that his wife had plotted his murder, what would he do? Have her arrested and made to stand trial, or kill himself and put an end to all the needs of his soul? He thought that even in his age and weakness, Bath had been too strong a man for that last evasion.

'He didn't kill himself,' he said. 'Even if the police hadn't proved it, I would still know that he didn't kill himself.'

'No. He tried, but he couldn't kill himself. He put the gun down, and asked me to go. He said he had a letter to write to the police. I asked him again to spare my son. He refused. I took the gun and shot him. He was dead so quickly. A flash, a bullet too quick to see, and his life was over. That's all, really,' she said in a hopeless voice. 'The dog howled, and when I looked out of the window I saw the man creep away in the moonlight. I remembered no one knew I was there. I put the gun in his hand and ran out of the house. I meant to kill myself, but then I knew I must wait, to look after Gerald.'

'You can't do anything for him now,' Everton said harshly. 'He's going to be in jail for a very long time.'

'There's nothing I can do for him,' she agreed. 'Nothing.' She looked at him, and the decision, the decision that cannot be put in words, was in her eyes.

'I don't want to escape,' she said. 'I believe in justice, not in the law.' She peered down again at the sea. 'Will you go now?'

'Yes,' he said in real helplessness, 'I'll go.'

He walked away slowly, looking at the gulls beating through the damp air, flinging themselves into the wind, falling in beautiful control towards the sea. When he came to the road he turned inland, leaving Mrs. Leonard alone for ever with the birds and the sea.

THE END